Catch of the Day

Stories By William J. Cook

ISBN 13: 978-1983418204
ISBN 10: 198341820X

Cover: "Catch of the Day," original watercolor by Sharon Cook. Used by permission.

The Paleographer was first published in the 2016 NIWA Anthology *Artifact: A collection of short stories by members of the Northwest Independent Writers Association,* edited by Pam Bainbridge-Cowan.

The Affect Bridge was first published in the 2017 NIWA Anthology *Bridges: A Collection of Short Fiction by members of the Northwest Independent Writers Association,* edited by Lee French.

Biblical quotations are from the *New American Standard Bible*, copyright 1960, 1962, 1963, 1968, 1971, 1972, 1973, 1975, 1977, 1995 by the Lockman Foundation. Used by permission.

Other books by William J. Cook:

Songs for the Journey Home, a novel
The Pieta in Ordinary Time and Other Stories
Seal of Secrets: A Novel of Mystery and Suspense

Dedication

To Sharon, my wife and inspiration on this long journey home. And to my children and grandchildren, my village, who have kept me young and full of joy on the quest.

Acknowledgments

This is my fourth book and I have yet to acknowledge all the people who have supported me in this adventure. Let me correct that oversight now. My wife Sharon has been tireless in her support and in her generous criticism of my work. Of course, I love her artwork for this book's cover. Tom has been my spiritual mentor along the way. The Salem branch of *Willamette Writers* and the *Northwest Independent Writers Association* have provided invaluable insights into the craft and have pushed me to hone my skills. At *NIWA*, Jennifer, James, and Emily have been especially helpful. My critique group—Ginger, Cris, and Ron—have been most kind and instructive, as has the Salem Library group, *Writers Yesterday, Today, and Tomorrow*. I am indebted to my friends at *Goodreads*, especially Michael and David, who have written reviews of my work that would make any writer blush (and then order a bottle of champagne). Of course, my Thursday afternoon wine-tasting partners, Devon and Dallas, have been most helpful as well. Lord willing, I will carry on.

Table of Contents

My short stories are like soft shadows I have set out in the world, faint footprints I have left. I remember exactly where I set them down each and every one of them, and how I felt when I did. Short stories are like guideposts to my heart.
                    -Haruki Murakami

A short story is like a kiss in the dark from a stranger.
                    -Stephen King

The Affect Bridge

A name you will never remember...
A name you will always forget...

Lily Barrington leaped up from sleep, heart pounding, breathing in short ragged gasps. It had happened again. Shadow images of the murder of her mother from decades ago. And the voice. Sing-song. Hypnotic. Repeating itself over and over again. Whose voice? What name?

She took several slow deep breaths to calm down, and then used her *anchor to the present*, a tool she had instructed so many patients to use when the past began to overwhelm them. She stroked the diamond ring on her finger, the only remnant of a five-year marriage. "This is today," she said aloud. "November 30, 2017. It's not April 24, 1997. I'm not back there. I'm not in danger. I'm here in my own bedroom and I'm safe." She turned on the light and threw back the covers. "Therapist, heal thyself," she muttered as she slipped into a plush white robe.

The clock on the wall showed 5:30 as she walked out into the kitchen. Standard wake-up time. She charged the coffee pot and turned on the laptop to review her schedule for the day. Three patients before lunch and then five afterward. It would be a busy day. Since she had begun to specialize in treating women who were trauma survivors, she had no dearth of clients, and several psychiatrists and psychologists in town had begun to use her as their primary referral for such patients. Her personal history made her particularly empathetic, but she had to remain aware of the risk of being re-traumatized by the stories her patients told her. *Is that what's happening to me?* she thought. *Do I need to go back and see my own shrink again after all these years?*

As she sat sipping coffee at the kitchen table, Lily looked

up at the picture on the bookshelf. "Hi, Ma," she said. She and her mother were baking bread. She must have been...eight years old? Her mother had set the camera on the counter top to snap their picture. Bread-making was how they coped with the loss of her father to cancer the previous year.

"No prospects in the love department yet. My last two dates were real bummers. Are all the good guys taken? Anyway, I know I gotta get serious if I want to have a kid of my own. You don't have to tell me I'm not getting any younger." She got up and put a slice of bread in the toaster.

"I dreamt about it again last night, Ma. That's twice this week. Do you think I should go see Dr. Ingersoll again? If he's still in practice?" She grimaced and shook her head. "It's not clear, like a bad connection on a cell phone. I was there, right under the bed where it happened all those years ago, but I can't put all the memories together. I don't know why. It doesn't make sense. I'm missing big chunks of it." She took another sip of coffee. "Most of all, I miss you." She raised her cup to the image. "But it's made me a pretty decent therapist. My patients seem to like me, and I think I'm really helping some of them. At least they keep coming back and paying their bills."

She poured another cup of coffee as she munched her toast. With the boost of the caffeine, her morning ritual kicked into high gear, and within two hours she was at her office, reviewing case notes on her computer. As she read the file of a young woman who had seen her mother killed in a motor vehicle accident, she found herself thinking about her dream. "That does it," she said aloud. "It's distracting me too much." She pulled up a telephone directory and found a listing for Hugh Ingersoll, M.D. She tapped it into her cell phone.

"Dr. Ingersoll's office. How may I help you?" came the receptionist's voice.

"I'm Dr. Lily Barrington. I was a patient of Dr. Ingersoll's about twenty years ago. Something's come up and I wondered if I might schedule a brief consultation with him."

"Of course, Dr. Barrington. He's booked out for a couple

of months, but he always reserves two appointments a week for emergencies. He has an opening Friday at 9:00 AM."

"I'll be there. Thank you so much." She gave the secretary her new contact information and concluded the call.

Friday was typically a light day for her and she had no trouble rescheduling her nine o'clock patient so she could keep her appointment with Dr. Ingersoll. After reading a couple of journal articles while she finished her coffee, Lily showered and dressed. This would be a good day to try out the new boots, and she smiled as she slid into them. She looked in the mirror and made a final adjustment to her hair. She had always been very frugal with makeup, and she eschewed fragrances altogether on work days. Too many patients had too many allergies. She called it good and headed toward the garage, where her *indulgence* was parked. The low-end Bimmer had been the one treat to herself after the divorce. She got into the car and pulled out of the driveway. The weather was what she called *Portland Twilight*—cold anonymous gray that would last from dawn to dusk, punctuated by an occasional shower. Minutes later, Lily parked in the garage nearest the psychiatrist's office and walked the block to the front door.

The office was very much as she remembered it, though the carpeting and furniture had been updated. The art work was the same. Dr. Ingersoll was proud of his collection—a Matisse, a Monet, and a Van Gogh. Several small sculptures decorated the end tables by the leather sofa. In one corner, a play area had been arranged, complete with small table and chairs, coloring books, and a collection of toys and puppets. Twenty years ago, this had been her port-in-the-storm, a safe harbor from the horror her life had become. She gave her name to the pretty receptionist behind the desk and took a seat.

Twenty minutes later, the door to the inner office opened, and the doctor strode into the waiting area. Lily saw that he had retained his full head of hair, but that it had turned a distinguished gray. In keeping with her recollections, he was impeccably dressed in what she now decided must be a bespoke suit from Savile Row.

"Lily...Dr. Barrington! You're all grown up! Look at you!" He extended his hand in greeting as Lily stood up.

"Hello, Dr. Ingersoll. It's been a long time." She shook his hand firmly as he ushered her into his office and closed the door.

"Please sit. Bring me up to date. I understand you're a therapist now yourself."

"I am, Dr. Ingersoll. A psychologist specializing in treating women who've survived some kind of trauma—domestic violence, sexual abuse. I believe my past makes me ideally suited for it."

"Indeed. And family?"

"Divorced. No children. Dating, but not very successfully."

"And may I ask what brings you back today? Has it been twenty years?"

"Closer to twenty-one now. Do you remember when I first came to you? That scared ten-year-old girl?"

"Yes, I do. And I reviewed my old case notes before you arrived. Horrible what you had been through. And you wouldn't talk about it. You suppressed it."

"I was mute for several months afterward. You used hypnosis to relax me enough to begin to talk again. But the memories never completely came back. Important pieces were missing."

"Yes, yes. I remember. The police were stymied. They never found who did it, and you couldn't recall enough to really help them."

"Well, I've been dreaming about it—the murder. I'm under the bed, hearing and feeling parts of it, but it's like through a veil or something. It's beginning to distract me when I'm treating my patients. My mind will drift off. My heart will start racing. I'm not there for them like I need to be."

Ingersoll smiled at her. His was the voice of a loving

father comforting his anxious daughter. "Ah, Lily. You specialize in treating trauma survivors? How long has it been since you've had a vacation?"

"Probably eight months. Do you really think that's what it is?"

"I'm sure you've read the articles about vicarious trauma—secondary traumatic stress. I prefer the term 'compassion fatigue' myself. It's real. I've seen it many times. Listening to the stories you hear all day long takes its toll. Give yourself some time away. Get out from under this Portland rain. If you want a little something to help you sleep better, I can prescribe a medicine for you."

They chatted for another fifteen minutes. Lily had not been aware how clenched her body had been until the muscles began to relax. As she stood to leave, she said, "Thank you so much for seeing me today, Dr. Ingersoll."

"My pleasure, Lily. Come back and check with me in a month. If you're still having trouble, we can try something else. For now, here's a small prescription that should help."

Three weeks later, Lily found herself smiling at the airline tickets on her kitchen table. In two short weeks, she would be lying poolside in Cabo San Lucas, sipping a Margarita, soaking up the sun. As she drove the few short blocks to her office, she remembered needing more coffee and tea for the waiting room. She liked to offer patients something warm to hold on to when they visited her, telling her stories that were anything but warm. She pulled into the lot of the small convenience mart where she often shopped.

"Hi, Theresa," Lily said to the proprietor as she entered. "It's almost the weekend."

The middle-aged woman in the long beige sweater smiled at her. "Not soon enough, Dr. Barrington. But at least my son Joey will be covering for me Saturday, so I'll have a little time away."

"How's he doing at school?"

"Still doesn't know what he wants to major in, but his grades are good. He's a pretty sweet kid. Not the hellion my daughter was at his age."

Lily walked down the right-hand aisle, looking for a new tea to catch her fancy. The smells of the coffees and teas were pleasant in the morning. She paid no attention to the ringing of the bell that announced another customer. Then a gravelly voice riveted her to the spot.

"Open the cash register, bitch! Now!"

Lily froze, eyes wide with fear. At the roar of the gun going off, she sprinted for the bathroom in the back corner of the store. She closed the door and turned the bolt. She left the light off.

"Hey! Is there somebody else back there?"

"Leave it, Tony. Let's just get the money and get outta here."

"I don't want no witnesses, man. You get the money and I'll check it out."

Lily huddled on the floor by the toilet bowl. She felt for the phone inside her purse and dialed 911.

"What is the nature of your emergency?" said the emotionless voice.

"Robbery. Quick Mart on Holiday. He's got a gun," she whispered.

A sudden bang high up on the door made her drop the phone.

"Who's in there?" came the reptilian snarl. More pounding on the door. "Open up!"

Lily felt around in the dark for the phone, which had fallen screen side down. She felt abandoned, helpless. She was going to die. Her heart felt as though it would burst through her chest. She couldn't catch her breath. In a flash, she was ten years old, hiding under the bed, listening to the men brutalizing her mother. She saw everything, heard everything. The memories that had been only fragments before were now whole and terrifying.

The gunshot made her shriek. She saw the tiny hole about four feet up the wooden door. She put her hand over her mouth as another bullet ripped through the tiny bathroom. She realized that if she kept making noises, the robber would keep shooting. She bit down hard on her hand and curled into fetal position, willing herself into the smallest possible space.

"Jesus, Tony! Come on! The whole neighborhood can hear you blastin'. Let's get the hell outta here."

Silence. Lily didn't move. She heard the bell above the front door. Was it a trick? Were they waiting for her just outside? Minutes passed. She heard sirens. Then the bell again.

"Call an ambulance, Jake. She's still alive. I'll put pressure on the wound till they get here. You check out back."

Footsteps outside the door.

"Police! Drop your weapon and come out of the restroom now!"

"Don't shoot! Don't shoot! I'm the caller." Lily unlocked the door and slowly opened it, squinting at the sudden light. Tears stained her face.

The young officer holstered his weapon and took her hand. "You're gonna be all right," he said. "Come with me."

"Theresa? The owner?"

"An ambulance is on the way. Now tell me what you know."

Lily had her answering service cancel all appointments for that day and the next and went home. She couldn't stop her body from shaking. It was as though the temperature had fallen ten degrees and she were shivering in the cold, unable to get warm. She was still reeling from the enormity of what had happened. She had survived yet another confrontation with death.

She put the tea kettle on to boil and took out a bag of Earl Grey, her long-time favorite. She let the tea steep for several minutes, relishing the fragrance of the bergamot. Outside, Stellar's jays and crows were arguing over possession of the peanuts in the bird feeder. "I'm OK," she told herself. "I'm OK."

Lily thought a hot bath would be perfect, but first she called the hospital. Theresa was out of surgery and in satisfactory condition. Before anything else, Lily would visit her.

"It'll take a lot more than a bullet to keep an old bird like me down," Theresa announced.

"Glad to hear it. You sure gave me a scare."

"You and me both, Dr. Barrington." All bravado left the woman's voice. "Worm food. You know what I mean? I thought I'd bought the farm."

"I know. I'm glad you didn't. But there have to be easier ways to get you to take a vacation."

"That's what Joey told me."

Lily sat in the bedside chair, holding Theresa's hand for the better part of an hour. As she was getting up to leave, Theresa pulled her close.

"How are you doing, Dr. Barrington? Did they hurt you? How did you get away?"

Lily told her about what had happened in the restroom. "I thought I was going to die. I really did. And it brought back all that crap from my past."

"You mean, about your mother?"

Lily nodded.

"Oh, you poor girl." Theresa shook her head back and forth. "Go home now. Get some rest. Don't worry about me."

"I'll come in and see you tomorrow. I've taken the day off."

"Good for you. Now get out of here."

After her visit, Lily went home and drew a hot bath. She carefully folded her clothes and watched the mirror fog over. Then she eased herself into the steaming water, letting it drain the cold and the tension from her tired, nervous muscles. She closed her eyes in relief.

While she lay in the water, she reflected on the day. In the bizarre way the mind sometimes worked, she was psychically whole again. She recalled all that had happened the day her mother was killed. All that was said. All that was done. She felt the rug burn a little girl's cheek as she scrambled under the bed. Felt the sudden warmth as her bladder emptied. Heard her mother begging for release.

The tears came again. Lily drew her knees to her chin and embraced her legs, rocking in the tub to soothe herself. Her sobs echoed off the hard tile floor and walls. She cried until her body felt empty.

As she stood to get out of the tub, another thought struck her. *I know the name and the voice!* Lily caught her breath under the impact of that, staggered by the implications. The name and the voice. She gritted her teeth as she felt her heart break within her. "No!" she wailed.

Lily checked in early for her follow-up appointment with Dr. Ingersoll a week later. As she sat in the waiting area, she could not fend off the sorrow that had been haunting her since the robbery. It possessed her now like a malicious spirit, and her body trembled. She dug her nails into her palms and clenched her teeth to prevent herself from crying.

"Hello, Lily." The gray-haired psychiatrist emerged from his office. "Please come in and sit down." His charming smile and warm manner made it easy to follow him. "I can see from your expression that something isn't right. How are you feeling today? Sleeping any better?"

"I had been, Doctor, but it's changed again." Her voice was matter-of-fact, a further defense against collapsing into tears. Before she could stop herself, she blurted out, "The memories have come back to me."

Lily saw the psychiatrist's eyes go wide and his posture stiffen.

"The memories of your mother's murder? That seems unlikely after all this time."

"I can see and hear everything that happened."

"Oh, dear," he said. "Would you like to talk about that with me today?"

"That's why I'm here. To review it all, organize it, make sense out of it."

"Shall we use hypnosis again? To make sure you stay relaxed and don't get overwhelmed?"

"If you think that's best, Doctor."

"I do. Why don't you switch over to that recliner chair and push it back to make yourself comfortable?"

Lily positioned herself on the red leather chair and closed her eyes. Just then her phone rang. She removed it from her purse. "I'm sorry. I forgot to silence it." She fiddled with the screen, then put the phone in her lap.

"Now follow my voice, Lily. Imagine you're walking down an ornate circular staircase, and with each step I count off, feel yourself getting more and more deeply relaxed."

Lily tuned in to the psychiatrist's voice, allowing him to paint word pictures that helped her body relinquish all its tension.

"When you are as thoroughly relaxed as you would like to be for our work together, signal me by briefly raising the index finger of your right hand."

Lily's finger went up.

"Excellent. You're doing very well. If you feel yourself becoming too anxious, signal me with that same finger, and I will draw you back to the present, away from what's upsetting you." He cleared his throat and continued. "Now you're going back to that day, twenty years ago. Without disturbing your relaxation at all, tell me what you see and hear."

Lily's voice sounded pinched, younger, a ten-year-old trying to explain things to a grown-up.

"I'm in Mommy's bedroom. I didn't go to school today. Mommy thinks I'm coming down with a cold, so she's letting me stay home. I pull the blanket off her bed to make a tent for me and my dollies. Now the doorbell's ringing."

"Who is at the door?"

"I can't see, but Mommy sounds scared. They ask if anybody else is in the house, and she lies and says I'm in school. I crawl under the bed as far as I can go. I drag the blanket with me to hide behind. That way they can't see me if they look underneath."

Lily heard the doctor rise from his chair and begin to walk about the office.

"How many voices do you hear, Lily?"

"Three besides Mommy's. They bring her upstairs and throw her on the bed. She's right above me. I hear her crying. I hear them rip her clothes. The bed is bouncing up and down. I'm peeing. I can't help it."

Lily's face contorted with shame and grief. Tears were streaming from her eyes. Her body was trembling violently. She raised her index finger. Instead of drawing her back to the present, the psychiatrist pushed her further.

"What happens next, Lily?" His voice was calm but cold. He stood directly behind her chair.

"'Finish her, Brad,' one of them says. 'C'mon, Ingersoll. Do it. It's your turn.'"

Lily heard the psychiatrist inhale sharply, then slowly expel his breath. Then in a deep and melodious voice he said, "That's a name you will never remember. A name you will always forget." He began to repeat the phrases over and over—a mantra designed for a terrified child.

Lily shook her head back and forth, as if fighting off the spell of the seductive words. "No! Please!" Her fingers clawed at the arms of the chair as she began to hyperventilate. She struggled to open her eyes, feeling as though the lids had been glued shut. "I will not forget!"

Lily's eyes popped open as she gasped for breath. She straightened the recliner as tears continued to pour down her face. "How could you, Dr. Ingersoll? I trusted you."

The psychiatrist appeared flustered. He quickly composed himself. "What do you mean, Lily?" She heard an unfamiliar edge in his voice.

Lily looked around the office at the shelves of books, the paintings on the walls, the massive oak desk. She smelled leather and polished wood. "This was my safe place—my fortress." She shook her head, still reluctant to say what she had come to say. "You abused me by fracturing the memories of my mother's murder. You obstructed justice. Withheld evidence."

The psychiatrist looked as though he had been jolted by an electric shock. "I did no such thing! How dare you make such absurd accusations! I restored your ability to speak. I healed you." He came around the chair and faced her, brushing at his sleeves as though she had soiled him with her words.

She recoiled from his wrath, pushing herself back deeper into the chair. With a grim act of will, she said, "That was your son and his cronies who killed my mother. Brad Ingersoll. I heard that sonofabitch say his name. But you couldn't let your son go to prison, could you?" She pointed her finger at him, indicting him for his crimes.

The man turned his head, visibly shaken. "Family trumps all, Lily. He had his whole life ahead of him. How could I let him throw it away for one terrible mistake?"

"Mistake? Is that what you call rape and murder?"

"He's a changed man now," Ingersoll protested. "He has a wife and two children. A good job."

"He killed my mother!" Lily's voice was fingernails down a blackboard.

The psychiatrist leaned toward her, his jaw taut, his eyes splinters of ice. "How were your so-called memories restored?"

"The affect bridge, Doctor." She knit her brows and returned his gaze. "A week ago I was trapped in a convenience store robbery. I was locked in a restroom. Convinced I was going to be killed. And my mind went back to the other time I felt the same way—*listening to your son kill my mother!* Those feelings —that affect—was the bridge that took me back there, before your *therapy* messed with my mind."

"My dear girl, you're delusional. The affect bridge is

merely a regression technique we psychiatrists sometimes use in hypnotherapy. You've allowed your hysteria to completely distort reality." His tone was arrogant, condescending.

She saw him reach for his phone. "If you're thinking of calling your son, I'm afraid you're a little late. The police have already picked him up." She shuddered in fear as she watched the psychiatrist's face turn purple with rage. He raised his fist.

"It will be my word against yours!" he shouted at her. "A respected psychiatrist versus a psychotic female patient. Before this is over I'll have you committed. You'll be so full of medication all you can do is drool!"

With trembling fingers, Lily picked up the phone that was still in her lap. Summoning her remaining courage, she said, "Did you hear all that, Attorney Madison?" She turned to Ingersoll and said, "The District Attorney called at the beginning of our session and I left the phone on speaker."

"I sure did, Lily," came the voice from the phone. "I've dispatched several policemen. They should be there momentarily."

"Thank you, sir." Lily ended the call and looked at the man she had once regarded as a father, now her vanquished adversary. She didn't feel vindication so much as a bitter mixture of sadness and anger. Her betrayer had collapsed into his chair. The rage that had suffused his face moments before had been replaced by what looked to her to be utter defeat. Just then the intercom on his desk buzzed.

"Doctor, there are three policemen here to see you. They told me to interrupt whatever you were doing."

Lily stood, unsteady at first, and walked toward the door. Just as she grasped the knob, she turned back to the psychiatrist.

"My name is Lily Barrington, Doctor Ingersoll." Her lips curled in a rueful smile. "It's a name you'll always remember. A name you'll never forget."

Winter's Walk

Good morning, Pop! Or I guess it's good afternoon to you." It was my regular Saturday phone call to him, but I still couldn't get used to the three-hour time difference. If I wasn't careful, my morning call would hit him just as he was sitting down to lunch. Afternoons were even worse. I'd lost count of the times I'd interrupted his supper. "How's the weather in Orlando?"

"Lovely today. Eighty degrees. Sun shining." I could hear him struggling to clear his throat. That had become an increasing problem over the last few months. "But they're expecting a front to move in tomorrow. Thunderstorms. Maybe some tornado action." He cleared his throat again. "I hate it when that happens. They'll break into every TV show every ten minutes for three hours, telling us to watch out for high winds. I'll sit on the couch and yell back at 'em, 'All right already! I heard you the first dozen times!' But they don't listen. I mean, how many different ways are there to say, 'Watch out for high winds?'"

"I remember that happened the last time I visited you. The weathermen were tripping over themselves to tell us the sky was falling. Never did get to see a whole television show that night."

My father harrumphed in affirmation, then became quiet. He didn't usually talk about the weather, so I figured he was stalling for time, reluctant to tell me something he knew would get a rise out of me.

"I lost another tooth last night." He said it as though he were ashamed of himself, as though he had disappointed me. His teeth had been breaking off at the gum line, one by one, over the past year and a half. Six months ago he stopped going to church because he was embarrassed by his smile.

"No steak for you tonight," I said. Although I made light of it, it was no joke to me. I worried about what would happen to his already impaired eating habits. A few months ago, when I offered again to pay for implants, he blew up at me. It injured his pride to even think of accepting a gift like that from his grown son. And it only made matters worse when I told him to think about it as payback for the private school tuition he had funded in my high school years.

"You don't think I could afford new teeth if I wanted 'em? It's too damn much hassle. Besides, I can handle ground beef OK. And chicken and fish if I cut 'em up small enough. And soups are always good."

"Dad..."

"What? It's a good week. No damn doctors' appointments." I could sense his building up a head of steam. "Hell, they're not even *appointments* anymore. The doctor just sits there, looking at the computer screen instead of you, tap-tapping away on the keyboard until he prints you out an after visit summary and pushes you out to the pharmacy. What kind of doctoring is that anyway?"

"Yeah, but those appointments are the only thing that get you out of the house anymore." My dad had been a snowbird until two years ago, when he simply became too frail to manage the grueling ordeal of modern air travel. He finally sold his northern home in Connecticut and moved to Florida full-time. Now just getting out of the house became an accomplishment.

"I told you I'm doing OK."

"I know you're OK, Dad, but you sound a little out of breath."

"Of course I'm out of breath. I've been making my damn bed. With these bum knees it takes me a bit longer to walk back and forth around the bed to tuck the sheets in."

I happened to know that it took him upwards of two hours to make his bed. He couldn't extend either arm its full length, nor could he raise them above the level of his shoulders. With most of the cartilage gone in his knees, they creaked like old barn doors when he stood up and walked. And he needed a walker to get around safely—something he called his *Green Hornet*. I could see him now, back and shoulders hunched over, fists clenching the handles of the walker, taking one small step at a time, the walker

22

zig-zagging ever so slightly as he shuffled forward. And his brother Bill had been in the exact same shape until his death three years ago. I prayed I hadn't inherited those awful genes.

"How about reconsidering the idea of a home health aide, Pop? You know, just a couple of hours a day. Help you with your bed. With your shower. Getting dressed."

"I don't need a damn health aide! I don't need a stranger in my house. I suppose she'd hold my pecker while I peed, for Chrissakes. I told you I'm doing fine. I cook my own meals. I do my own laundry. I get myself to my appointments."

I winced. He still wouldn't give up driving. He'd never had an accident, except when that dumb kid on a cell phone backed into him in the Save-On Groceries parking lot. Still, what was his reaction time? With his knees the way they were, could he lift his foot onto the brake pedal fast enough in an emergency, when split-seconds mattered? And could he ever forgive himself if he hit somebody? I shuddered. I had promised him I wouldn't bring it up again after our last go-round three months ago. He had really let me have it.

"I'm a good driver! Better than you! Never an accident in my whole life. Can you say that about your driving? Can you?"

"But Dad..."

"But nothing. Mind your own damn business. When I want your opinion on my driving skills, I'll ask for it. Until then, shut up about it."

And so it went. There was no arguing with him, but I always tried. "You think it would be any better if you came out here to Oregon and lived with me and Jenny? Your nephew and his family are out here, too. It'd be fun to be all together." I knew it was another dead end, but I had to try again.

"I'm not moving to Oregon. Too damn cold." He paused for a breath. "Besides, she doesn't like me very much," he added quietly.

"That's not true, Dad. You know you can be pretty stubborn sometimes."

"There's a right way to load the dishwasher. A right way to

fold clothes."

"I know, Dad. I get it. She was just trying to be helpful when we visited you last fall."

"Like I've been saying. I don't need any damn help. I can manage on my own."

"Right. So how's the cough?" Decades of sparring with him had taught me that changing the subject, like discretion, was often the better part of valor.

He coughed in response. "Still hanging on."

We chatted for another fifteen minutes, carefully avoiding anything that smacked of his needing something from me. I said goodbye with that characteristic tension in my gut. Was there a word for the sad, angry, frustrated feeling that was always the residue of our conversations?

I slipped the phone into my pocket and looked again at the eight-by-ten photograph on my desk. Dad, the bombardier, and his crew in their flight suits, posing in front of the *Malfunction Junction*, the B-24 Liberator with the pin-up girls painted on the nose. The B-24 that flew him on 42 missions over Austria, his eyes glued to the Norden Bombsight. The B-24 that treacherously deposited him behind enemy lines when it was shot from the sky. I looked at that cocky 19-year-old face, marveling at how the 92-year-old man I knew could have been younger than my sons, full of sex and swagger—what he described as "piss and vinegar."

After refusing to talk about his war-time experiences for most of my life, he had relented a few years ago and began dropping little anecdotes out of the blue. I hadn't known about his getting shot down over Austria—that it had been a month-long walk in winter snows to the safe haven of a British base. That little trek had cost him two toes—his payment for frostbite. It also answered my longstanding doubts about those missing toes. When I was a kid, he told me a German Shepherd bit them off when he and his buddies climbed over old man Derringer's fence to swim in his pond. It was a great story and I shared it with all my friends at school. It was also a good way to keep me out of forbidden waters. I wondered if Mom had known all along.

I looked at the photograph of Mom and Dad on their last cruise together, before Alzheimer's ravished her. She had always been such a beauty, and the two of them looked so happy. Not long afterward, the disease began to eat her from the inside out, the way those wasp larvae consume their host caterpillar. It was an awful way to die. How many times had I called Florida or Connecticut and just allowed Dad to vent his frustrations at being her caregiver?

"She keeps saying she wants to go home and she's sitting in our living room! Yesterday, she called me her brother's name and said I would go to hell for divorcing my wife. Last week, she worked herself into a frenzy. Said there was a dog in the house, pooping all over everything."

"Don't you think she needs to be in a care facility, Dad? A home where professionals deal with dementia?"

"No!" he shouted. "She stays home. I'll take care of her here. I've seen those places—people tied in wheelchairs. Pissing their diapers."

"We could find a nice one, Dad. Not like that. They'd take good care of her."

I had never heard my father swear before, but he dropped a string of f-bombs on me that made me blanch. OK, Dad. Do it your way. The right way.

I stood and walked into the kitchen for another cup of coffee. Jenny saw the frown on my face.

"Talking to your dad again?"

"Yep. I guess you could say he's pretty set in his ways."

"You could say that if you were a master of understatement," she quipped with a smile. "It's probably just as well he refuses to come and live with us. He'd have us crazy inside of a week."

I smiled back. "I know you're right, honey, but it doesn't stop me from worrying about him."

"That's because you're a good son." She rested her hand on my shoulder. "Suppose we'll be like that someday?"

"Probably." I nodded. "Our daughter-in-law already thinks we are."

Jenny chuckled. "And we thought we were the ones who invented sex, drugs, and rock and roll."

"It creeps up on you, for sure—so gradually, you don't see it coming. They should give it a disease name. Like *Who's-That-Old-Guy-in-the-Mirror Syndrome*."

"That's the old guy I love."

"But I'm not gonna be like my father. I'm not gonna be stubborn like that. I'll accept help when I need it."

Jenny laughed. "Oh, yeah? Well, who was that guy up on the ladder last night trying to install that new smoke alarm? You know, the one fussing and fuming and getting himself shocked even though his son told him he'd do it for him next weekend?"

"That was different."

"It always is, Steve. It always is. Think that young dude in the picture ever imagined being a 92-year-old curmudgeon?"

I took another sip of coffee. Curmudgeon? My dad wasn't a curmudgeon.

But Jenny had hit a nerve. My seventieth birthday was barreling down on me like a semi on I-5. Seventy? How did that happen? And what about that bizarre separation of mind and body, the one that gets worse with every passing year? In my mind, I still felt young and stupid, still liked a flash of skin on a Netflix movie. But my body was another story. It was definitely old and stupid. It was harder to get in and out of cars, harder to drop to my knees with our grandkids. My fingers ached with arthritis. And moles and skin tags were sprouting like mushrooms all over my body. What's with that?

"I'm out to run some errands," I told Jenny. I needed some space.

"Well, I'll be painting. I want to finish that hummingbird."

I was so proud of her. She had begun painting when she retired and had just sold her first piece at a gallery in Newport.

"I may go to a film."

"OK. See you later."

In fifteen minutes I was walking up and down the aisles in Rauley's Hardwarehouse, shopping for nothing in particular, but needing to move and be alone with my thoughts. I could hear my father's voice again. It was last July and the temperature outside was ninety-four, but his story still chilled me. He told me about his winter's walk.

"You never really hear anti-aircraft fire unless it's really close. The planes are too damn noisy. You just see the black smudges in the air around you and say a quick prayer. This time the prayers didn't work. Flak shredded us. In a heartbeat, we were going down, smoke like razor blades in my nose and throat. We all knew we had to bail out. Problem was, the only parachute practice any of us had had was inside an airplane hangar back home. We were making it up as we went along.

"I got to the ground OK. How, I'll never know. Scared out of my mind. I was alone for three days before I found the rest of my crew. Our pilot was pretty banged up, so we had to take turns carrying him. We never did find our tail gunner.

"It was winter in Austria and the place was crawling with German sympathizers. We were miles behind enemy lines, short on food and water. We packed snow into sacks we wore against our chests, hoping to melt it into drinking water. But it wouldn't melt. Some days we ate only a few shriveled apples left behind on spindly trees. It snowed every day.

"Halfway into our trek, God smiled on us. We found a band of partisans who took us in. Got food and water from them and help getting out. Finally, after twenty-nine days of marching through Austria and Yugoslavia, we walked out into the port town of Zadar on the Adriatic. A British gunship got us back to our airbase in Italy."

At this point in his story, I remember my father grabbing me by the shoulders and staring straight into my eyes.

"I couldn't give up. I couldn't let down my guard for a minute. I knew that if I stopped, I'd be dead."

The memory shook me. *Of course*, I thought.

I decided to go to a little sports tavern I sometimes frequented with my sons. I nursed a beer at a corner table and thought about my father and me. I wondered, not for the first time, if he resented my not fighting in Vietnam. I had never known what he thought about having a son who was a conscientious objector. I resolved to ask him during our next phone call.

Thirty minutes later, as I set my empty glass down and left a tip on the table, my phone rang.

"Your sister just called," Jenny said. "Your dad's been in an accident. T-boned at an intersection. He's in the hospital, in surgery. I think you should go."

"I'll come home and pack."

I'm not a big guy by any stretch, but I still find it hard to fit into an airplane seat. Even that reminded me of my dad, describing to me what it was like to cram your way into a B-24. *"And it was cold! First time anybody pissed into the funnel, it froze and jammed our little makeshift latrine for the rest of the mission."* At least I didn't have to worry about that.

The trip across country was luxurious by my father's standards, nothing like the accommodations on his "tinfoil and duct tape" Liberator. How had he done it? And where did he find the courage to fly again after being shot down? I looked out the window at the empty sky and counted my blessings.

My sister met me at the airport.

"He seems to be stable for now, but his pelvis is broken. He looks pretty beat up." She pushed a lock of red hair out of her eyes. "You know it's not my fault he's been living alone. I've offered a hundred times to have him come live with me and Marty, but he refuses. He won't even let me come to cook a meal for him or do his laundry once a week. Drives me crazy."

"Believe me, Sandy, I understand. What happens now?"

"He'll have to go into a rehab facility when the hospital's through with him."

"He'll love that."

"Tell me about it. And the police are telling him he has to take his Driver's License test again."

"Can they do that?"

"It was that or they'd take his license on the spot."

"Whew! Talk about poking a sleeping bear. Does he know?"

"Sure does. He'll give you an earful about it."

I wasn't looking forward to that conversation.

We arrived at the hospital a half an hour later. My sister smiled at me.

"I'll be in the cafeteria when you're done. I've already put in my time for today. He's in 437."

I found my way to the elevator and rode it to the fourth floor. Then I navigated the fluorescent-lit hallways, past stainless steel carts full of medical supplies, past empty gurneys parked along the walls, until I finally reached room 437. The smells of disinfectants were particularly strong, and I shuddered as I recalled a frightening statistic: healthcare-associated infections killed more people every year than car accidents, breast cancer, and AIDS. We'd have to get Dad out of here as soon as possible.

I wished Sandy had prepared me for what to expect. Dad looked like he had gone ten rounds with Rocky. Both eyes were blackened and swollen almost shut. I large gash on his forehead sported a zipper of stitches. I hated to imagine what he looked like under the sheets.

"They pretty much bolted me back together," Dad announced. "I got more metal in me than your Terminator friend Arnold."

"Hi, Pop," I responded.

"I told your sister you didn't have to come."

"I know. How are you feeling?"

"Like shit, of course. How do you think I feel?"

"What do the doctors say?"

"They want me out of here as soon as I can move a little bit. Supposed to go to that new rehab place by the house." He sighed. "That'll be the end of me."

"Don't say that, Dad. It'll only be temporary. You'll be back in your own house in no time."

"They're taking my damn license!"

"Sandy said they're just making you take the test again."

"Do you honestly think I'll be able to pass it now? Wise up, Stevie. They don't want me driving anymore. Say I'm too old. That's the long and the short of it."

"C'mon, Pop. There's all kinds of services that can take you to your appointments and to the market and the library. You'll be fine." Why was I trying to minimize what was obviously so important to him? Why couldn't I simply accept what he had to say?

He turned his head and frowned. "I didn't think you'd understand."

I sat in the bedside chair. The TV hanging in the corner was on, but the volume had been muted. For several long silent minutes, I stared at the moving images.

"Did it bug you that I never fought in Vietnam?" My old change-the-subject strategy.

"Hell, no," he said, as he turned back to face me. "My war was different. Clearer. We knew who the enemy was. Yours was a mish-mash. I'm glad you objected to it. I did, too."

A wave of relief washed over me. "You know, I've been thinking about the stories you've told me. About your crew. About the *Malfunction Junction*. Especially about your walk out of Austria."

"Can you raise my bed a little so I can see you better without having to lift my head so much?"

I picked up the control device and pushed the button.

"Thanks. Hand me that water, will you?"

I helped him position the straw in his mouth.

"Sorry I lied to you about my toes. I just didn't want to talk about it back then. You were too young. It was a pretty good story though, wasn't it?" His cracked lips formed a smile. "And I never had to worry about you drowning in Derringer's pond."

"My fourth grade friends sure liked that story." I laughed and he began to laugh with me. It felt good. "So about your walk."

He frowned. "What about it? Everything I told you is true. That's the way it was."

"I know, Dad. I know. But it just occurred to me the other day." I extended my arm and rested my hand on the back of his, careful of the IV needle taped there. "Your winter's walk didn't really end when you got to Zadar, did it?"

It's hard to describe the look that came over his face then. It was affirmation and relief and the purest love for me I had ever seen shine through his eyes.

"No it didn't, son. No, it didn't."

"You've been on your winter's walk your whole life, haven't you?"

Tears had begun to stream down his face. It looked as though he were trying to form words but couldn't. I leaned over him and hugged him as tightly as I could between all the IV tubing and catheters and electrodes.

I stayed for another twenty minutes, sitting beside him, holding his hand. We said little else. He talked briefly about the book he was reading, about which teams might make it into the Super Bowl this year, about the new hearing aids he had ordered from the VA.

When the doctor called my sister and me the next morning, she said it was a pulmonary embolism that took him, apparently a common risk for this kind of surgery.

I knew that my father finally had a chance to rest after his long, long walk.

The Paleographer

He barely felt the needle's prick in his neck, but he collapsed instantly. When he awoke later, he had a black cloth sack over his head, and he felt the bite of a plastic zip tie around his wrists. He bounced to the motion of the car.

"Hey!" he said. His tongue felt thick from the drug, and his head was still spinning. The last thing he remembered was standing before the urinal in the restroom outside the lecture hall. "Where are you taking me?" He struggled not to slur his words.

"Please be still, Mr. Bergman," said a deep masculine voice with a distinctly British accent. "We mean you no harm. The effects will wear off soon, and you will be perfectly sound. It was necessary to meet in this...unusual way." The voice paused as if in regret. "We apologize for the inconvenience."

"Kidnapping is pretty damn inconvenient. If you know who I am, you know I don't have any money to pay a ransom. But you're welcome to the stipend I just got for my address."

"We don't want your money, Mr. Bergman. We want what you do. You are a prominent paleographer from the United States. You authenticate ancient documents. We need your authority."

"You could have asked me. I respond pretty well to verbal communication."

"Indeed. We have an offer you may like to consider. We will discuss it when you are fully awake."

"Any chance you can take this bag off my head?"

"When we reach our destination. And lest I forget, we know about your gambling problem, Mr. Bergman. In fact, your debts far exceed your income." The voice assumed a paternal tone. "That is not a judgment, just a statement of fact. You have certainly had your share of woes to justify your indiscretions. But rest now. We will talk later."

Minutes or hours later, the car came to a stop. The passenger door was opened, the seat belt was unfastened, and Bergman was pulled unceremoniously from the car. He could feel one person on either side of him, each holding him firmly by his upper arms.

"Mind the steps," the voice ahead of him said. "There are three of them. Once inside, I will remove the sack from your head."

The world had stopped spinning, but it was difficult to walk without being able to see in front of him. "I'm really thirsty. Can I have some water?"

"Of course. Let us get you situated in my office first."

Bergman heard a door being opened and then another voice.

"Welcome back, sir. I see your mission was successful."

"Indeed. Please bring Mr. Bergman to my office."

A strong hand grasped his, and Bergman was led inside. He sensed he was walking down a hallway. Several long paces inside, he was pulled to the left. He heard a door being unlocked, and he was ushered in. He heard three sets of footsteps leaving him, followed by the closing of a door. *That's four people so far*, he thought.

"We are here at last, Mr. Bergman. Allow me to remove your hood."

Bergman was momentarily blinded by the light. As his eyes recovered, he looked at his captor.

"You seem surprised by my dark skin, Mr. Bergman. It is a common prejudice among you Americans. You hear a cultured British accent, and you expect a Caucasian face. In fact, my mother was Pakistani and my father, Saudi. The university at which you spoke is my alma mater." He was about to extend his hand in greeting, when he saw the restraint still on Bergman's wrists. "Excuse me for my rudeness." In a flash, he had withdrawn a butterfly knife from his pocket and fanned it open with a flick of his wrist. "Click-clack, Mr. Bergman," he said, mimicking the sound of the knife opening.

Bergman was unnerved by the lightning fast motion of the

six-inch blade. In an instant, the razor-sharp knife had parted the zip tie binding him. "Was that standard issue with your degree from Oxford?" he said, hoping his bravado would still his pounding heart.

"My balisong? Hardly. Knives like these came originally from the Philippines." With another quick flip of his wrist, he closed the knife and returned it to his pocket. "Do you know how long it takes for a man with a severed artery to die, Mr. Bergman?"

"Not long at all, I'm sure. Don't cut yourself." Anger was beginning to dilute his fear for his life. "Your knife makes quite a fashion statement, Mr...."

The man frowned as he extended his hand. "Abd al samad." He was a foot taller than Bergman and impeccably dressed in a black suit and tie. His face was hard and angular, with dark hair and a neatly trimmed mustache. His gray eyes were merciless. "Now please have a seat, Mr. Bergman." He pointed to a dark leather armchair, while he walked around his enormous desk and deposited the black sack in one of its side drawers.

The desktop was empty except for a closed laptop computer. Behind the desk, Bergman saw a curtained window from floor to ceiling, its draperies open to reveal a view of palatial gardens. The surrounding walls were bookshelves of dark mahogany. He smelled oiled wood, old paper, and traces of tobacco.

His kidnapper drew a pitcher of water from a small refrigerator behind the desk and filled a crystal glass to the brim. "Here, Mr. Bergman. We are blessed with good spring water on the estate."

Bergman emptied the glass in moments. "You said you had an offer?"

"We do. Should you choose not to accept it, however, we are prepared to pay you $10,000 for your trouble today. That will not solve your gambling problems, but it will satisfy your creditors temporarily."

Bergman's eyes went wide with surprise. "You would pay me to walk away?"

The man nodded gravely. "Of course, we hope you will accept our proposition. We are businessmen after all, Mr. Bergman, not criminals."

"You have my undivided attention."

"We would like you to devote the next two weeks of your life to authenticating a document of ours. We will pay you $500,000 for your efforts."

Bergman whistled. "Mr. Abd al samad, you know I study ancient manuscripts. I don't write bestsellers. I don't forge checks. I've been at this job for 20 years, and even with my teaching and occasional speaking engagements, there is no money like that in old books."

"Which is why we had to bring you here against your will, Mr. Bergman. You would not have believed a letter, a phone call, even a face-to-face meeting at your hotel. You would have dismissed it as a scam."

Bergman watched his kidnapper's eyes and the set of his jaw. *Is he lying?* He looked and listened intently as the man opened his laptop and turned it on. *Was that 9 or 10 keystrokes for the password?*

"Ah, here it is. It was your last publication that finally convinced us to hire you, Mr. Bergman. It was really quite good."

"It was pretty esoteric, as I recall. You have strange tastes in reading. I write for a very limited audience."

"Please use your prodigious imagination," the man said. "That audience could be much wider, even global. The right ancient document could be worth millions on the world market. We happen to possess one worth billions."

Now Bergman began to laugh. "And what might that be?"

"I am afraid I cannot tell you that, not until you agree to a binding contract with us."

"So here comes the catch." Bergman turned his head and took a deep breath. "If you're looking for me to sacrifice my firstborn, you're too late." His eyes misted over and his voice caught briefly in his throat. "A drunk driver took care of that two years ago."

"My condolences for your loss, Mr. Bergman, but may we return to the matter at hand? Our contract with you is quite simple. If you agree to work on the project, you will be sequestered here on the estate for two weeks. You may have no contact with the outside world for the duration of the project except for the computer work directly related to your research. Any attempt to circumvent our firewalls will immediately invalidate your contract, and you will be summarily dismissed. Also, we will be obliged to file complaints against you for criminal trespass and breaking and entering. Have I made myself clear?"

"Crystal. But I do have a life, such as it is. You must know I teach at BU. I chair a faculty committee that meets every Wednesday. I have a meeting with my attorney next Friday."

"That would be for your pending bankruptcy, would it not?"

Bergman grimaced. "I admire your thoroughness," he managed to say between his clenched teeth.

"We will allow you to make phone calls before you start the project, so all necessary parties are assured of your well-being, all scheduled meetings and classes are canceled, and your time is free. We will confiscate your phone until the completion of your task."

"So I'll have to wear the same undies for two weeks?"

The man huffed impatiently. "Your attempts at humor when you are nervous are tiresome." He stood and came around the desk. "Of course, we would address all your needs here, including food, clothing, and sleeping facilities. We have a gourmet chef and a wine cellar that rivals the finest in England. Please consider our offer seriously."

As the man walked toward the door, Bergman took the moment to scan the office once more. He saw no camera, no visible alarm system, no keypad by the door. It looked like an ordinary room.

"Dinner will be served at 7:00. You will be escorted to your room to refresh yourself." He opened the door and a liveried servant with Middle Eastern features entered.

"Would you please accompany me, Mr. Bergman?" the servant said.

"Auditioning for a part in Downton Abbey?" Bergman quipped.

The man made no response, but led him down the hallway to the left and up a broad flight of stairs. Midway down another hallway, he opened a door and gestured for Bergman to enter. Bergman had seen no cameras in either hallway, heard no dogs. "I will return for you in 30 minutes," the servant said, as he closed and locked the door.

Bergman was in a suite that would have surpassed a Four Seasons Hotel, all done in understated elegance. The centerpiece of the large sitting room was a splendid glass table, spread with portfolio-sized volumes of fine art. The sumptuous furniture was of the finest leather. The walls held a priceless collection of paintings from the Old Masters.

Walking down the short hall, he came to the open doorway of a bedroom that looked to be larger than his apartment in Boston. Farther down, he glimpsed an enormous bathroom, done in white marble, with a glass shower stall big enough to hold the entire faculty of his department. He spied no visible cameras or other monitoring devices.

What have I gotten myself into? he thought. He had accepted the speaking engagement at Oxford on a lark, flattered to have been asked and happy for the honorarium. More importantly, he was eager to see Papyrus 90, that fragment of John's Gospel known as Oxyrhynchus, in the Sackler Library. His parents had brought him to see it first when he was 12 years old. That experience had launched him on the path to becoming a paleographer, triggered that yearning to immerse himself in ancient manuscripts, to compare grammar and style, word choice and syntax. As a later adolescent, he imagined authors taking pen to papyrus, scratching out *messages in bottles* that floated down the seas of time, finally to be opened and appreciated by him.

But now this. Kidnapped after giving his address at Oxford. Taken who knows where in the English countryside. Made an offer that sounded absolutely preposterous.

But what if...?

What if Abd al samad actually had such a document, one worth billions? Would Bergman's name forever be associated with it, as the one who first translated and authenticated it? Would he be the one whose seminal articles on the manuscript would garner him world-wide acclaim? Would he actually get a half-million dollars off the top, followed by speaking tours that would discharge his gambling debts once and for all? Or was he falling again into the old delusion that had fueled his gambling addiction —that he could win a world in which his son wasn't dead and his wife hadn't left him?

"To hell with it," he said aloud to the empty room. "In for a penny, in for a pound."

Dinner was superb. Filet Mignon Oscar, asparagus tips, and baked potato, accompanied by a decade-old Cabernet Sauvignon. For dessert, crème brulée and Chateau d'Yquem. As Bergman took a final sip of the sweet white wine, he turned to his host and raised his glass. "I accept your offer, Mr. Abd al samad."

"Excellent, Mr. Bergman. You may now call me *Boss*. My secretary will draw up the necessary paperwork. While he is doing so, please make your necessary phone calls." He withdrew Bergman's phone from his pocket, where he had stowed it during the abduction. "Asad, please." He handed the phone to the waiter at his side, who carried it to Bergman at his end of the long dining table. "I hope you harbor no ill will about the manner in which we brought you here," he said. What Bergman heard was, *Do not attempt to call the police. Click-clack.*

Within a half-hour, Bergman had canceled his plane ticket, left messages at his university in Massachusetts, and canceled the meeting with his bankruptcy attorney. He was free for two weeks. He quickly read over the contract which had been placed before him, and noticed it was printed on letterhead for the Shalam Corporation. "I recognize that name. *Shalam* is a transliteration of the Hebrew. The verb for returning a thing lost or stolen. Your group made quite a business for itself after the War, tracking down arts and antiquities looted by the Nazis."

"Very observant, Mr. Bergman. Yes, we were quite successful at restoring important pieces to their rightful owners, who were more than happy to pay handsome fees for our services."

Just then, a man in a black suit hurried into the dining room and whispered something into Abd al samad's ear. The host stood and swiftly back-handed the man, who cowered subserviently. "Forgive this unpleasantness, Mr. Bergman." He turned back to the other man and offered him a napkin for his bleeding nose. "I am sorry, Behzad. You are only the messenger."

"Yes, sir," the man said, as he scurried from the room.

"Just a minor business matter, Mr. Bergman. No need to be concerned. I must tend to my email. Asad, please stay with our guest while I am gone."

Bergman sat silently for several minutes, acutely uncomfortable at what he had witnessed. The waiter stood by quietly, arms folded, watching him. Finally, Bergman signed the contract and stood up. He wondered if he might get more information out of the waiter in an unguarded moment. "I guess you don't kidnap many people, Asad."

Asad tilted his head and frowned. "What is your point, sir?"

"Well, I haven't noticed any fancy cameras or motion sensors or anything like that. So this isn't the villain's fortress out of a James Bond movie." He was fishing for some response, some subtle telltale clue that would confirm or deny his hypothesis. "This place seems to be just...*an ordinary mansion*." There was no blink, no change in facial expression or posture to signal that Asad did not accept his conclusion.

Then Asad smiled. "If a mansion such at this can be called ordinary."

"Certainly. It must take at least a dozen people to run an estate as large and exquisite as this."

"Hardly."

So not a lot of security and less than twelve men.

At that moment, Abd al samad walked back into the room. "Did I give you leave to speak with our guest, Asad?" The voice had an edge to it that sent a chill through Bergman. "Go now, Asad. We will decide on your punishment later." He turned his attention to Bergman, who handed him the signed contract and his cell phone. "Excellent. Now come with me, my friend."

They left the dining room and walked down a long hallway hung with photographs of dour-faced old men wearing *keffiyeh*. "From the family album?" said Bergman.

"Indeed," was the terse response.

They came to a small elevator. His new boss inserted a key into the switch and turned it, and the stainless steel doors opened. They entered and descended to the sub-basement.

When the elevator doors opened again, Bergman felt the chill in the air. He heard the whir of air conditioners maintaining a constant temperature and humidity. They walked straight ahead through a doorway that opened into a large room. It was a document research laboratory, dominated by a large empty glass table and surrounded by computer work stations, each supplied with all the paraphernalia of a modern office. To the rear, Bergman recognized the equipment for multi-spectral imaging, used to make hard-to-read manuscripts more legible in differently filtered light. Perched overhead was the watchful eye of a camera. Conspicuously absent was any sign of a staircase. *Curious,* he thought. *Elevator access only.*

Then Bergman did a double-take. He realized the table was not empty at all. It was a display case that held pages of papyrus sandwiched between dual plates of glass.

His boss extended his arm toward it. "Please observe, Mr.

Bergman."

As Bergman approached the table, he felt the same stirrings he had felt as a 12-year-old drawing near to antiquity in the Oxford library. The hollowness in the pit of his stomach. The tingling of the skin along his back and his neck. The pounding of the blood in his temples. He leaned over the glass, squinting at the pale Greek letters adorning the cracked brown papyrus. He began to translate.

"Paul, an apostle of Christ Jesus by the will of God, to the church which is at Laodicea: Grace to you and peace from God our Father and the Lord Jesus Christ."

"This isn't possible. This document doesn't exist. There have been forgeries over the centuries, but no evidence of a Greek text." Bergman's mouth had gone dry. He shook his head in disbelief.

"Yet here it is before you. We have had it radiocarbon dated—little snippets analyzed with Accelerated Mass Spectrometry. Circa 50 to 100 C.E. by their science, but we know it is the original document, in Paul's or his scribe's own hand. That puts it to 55 or thereabouts. You will be the first to translate it and subject it to paleographic study. You will officially authenticate it for us."

"Original? Did you say *original document?"* Bergman's knees buckled and he sat heavily on the floor. "There are no original documents in the whole Bible. All we have are copies. The oldest is the Rylands fragment, and that can't be any older than about 117 to 138. Five verses of John's Gospel. The earliest copies of Paul's letters come from around 200. What are you saying? Where did this come from?"

His boss cleared his throat. "What I am saying, Mr. Bergman, is that you have the opportunity of a lifetime. To be the first to translate, authenticate, and write about the most important archeological find of the 21st century. The only original manuscript in the entire Jewish and Christian canon."

Bergman was in a daze, mumbling. "Where? How?"

"It has been in our family since an Arab brigand first relieved Paul's courier of it in 55. We did lose it briefly to the Nazis during the war, but we retrieved it soon enough and discovered a lucrative enterprise in the process."

"But if you've had it all this time, why didn't you come forward with it sooner? Why now? And why all the secrecy? Why not just release it to the world? Plaster it over the internet and get other institutions working with you on it?"

"Let us just say that at this moment in history, we have a pressing need for the capital this document will generate." He assumed the tone of a parent addressing a child. "Do you know how many Christians there are in the world, Mr. Bergman? If even one-half of them were willing to pay one dollar to read *Paul's Lost Letter,* that would generate more than a billion dollars. And I can assure you, we will not be selling it for one dollar." A self-satisfied smile curled his lips. "There will be leather-bound coffee table copies of the codex, complete with high resolution photographs. There will be publication of *The Complete New Testament* and *The Definitive Pauline Corpus.* There will be documentaries on BBC and Public Television, National Geographic and the History Channel. Museums will compete with each other for the privilege of putting the pages on display. It will be a financial juggernaut."

"So it's all about the money?"

"And what the money can buy, my American friend. Does that offend your religious sensibilities?"

"I have no religious sensibilities."

"Pity. You've dedicated your life to the study of ancient Scriptures, and you do not believe in God, do you, Mr. Bergman?"

"I'm a scientist. Religious belief has nothing to do with it."

"Indeed. Be that as it may, we are poised to amass the largest fortune in the world. Once we make the simultaneous announcement to the world news media, the flood of capital will begin. And you, Mr. Bergman, will share in our success."

Bergman had a sour taste in his mouth. He frowned at the man before him.

"You may wear that frown all the way to the bank, Mr. Bergman. We will see then how your scruples withstand the wealth that erases your debt once and for all. You will start life anew as a world-renowned scholar of the first order, sought by every university on the planet."

Bergman harrumphed. "I need a drink."

"Of course. I have a superb Pinot Noir that I had specially imported from your country. Allow me."

That night as he lay in bed, locked in his suite, Bergman grumbled to himself. He wished his son Ethan were alive to advise him. In the year before Ethan's death, Bergman had grown accustomed to consulting with the 25-year-old, who had such a keen grasp of the world. *Son, what would you do? None of this feels right. This guy is buying me. He's convinced the money and the fame will prevent me from accusing him of kidnapping. Or does he just plan on killing me when he's gotten what wants? That would be simpler.* He trembled as that possible scenario sunk in. *And what is he not telling me?* His last thoughts as he drifted off to an uneasy sleep were, *That kind of money can buy governments.*

Or topple them.

He was awakened at 5:00 the next morning, given 30 minutes to shower and dress, and then was escorted downstairs to the dining room.

"I trust you slept well?" his host said. "We will dine on eggs Benedict, and then you can get right to work. Asad, please serve our guest some coffee."

"Did you have an accident last night, Asad? Your face looks pretty beat up." Bergman looked at his boss, who was glowering at him. Asad glanced briefly toward the other end of the table and said nothing.

In an hour, Bergman was peering over the glass in the sub-basement. The display case was designed like a large picture frame, anchored by two stout legs on either side, with axles to rotate the table and reveal the reverse side of the pages. He guessed the glass was reinforced, impossible to shatter.

With notebook and pen in hand, he began to translate the codex. He decided to do a rapid translation first, then go back over the pages in a more painstaking fashion, sifting through vocabulary and word choice, grammar and syntax, comparing them with other known Pauline letters. The pages were surprisingly legible, so he could forgo the process of multi-spectral imaging.

At mid-morning, he took a coffee break and used the intercom on the wall to call the kitchen. In moments, the same man who had accompanied him back and forth from his bedroom stepped off the elevator, with a carafe of coffee and a tray of pastries. "Anything else, sir?" the man said, as he set his charges down on a small serving table.

"That will be fine, Downton, thank you."

The man looked puzzled at the nomenclature, then returned to the elevator and was gone in an instant.

It sure sounds like Paul so far, Bergman mused, as he sipped his coffee. *No new doctrine. Encouraging a church that's grown lukewarm in his absence. Inspiring them to put on a new self. Pretty standard stuff.*

He took a bite of Danish pastry and raised his cup to salute the camera. He expected to have a first fast read-through done by evening. Then he would start a word-by-word analysis tomorrow. If he could stick to his timetable, he would have a good translation by the end of the week and the beginning of a rough draft of his piece, *Translating and Authenticating the Lost Letter of Paul to the Laodiceans.* He smiled as the realized he would have no trouble getting it accepted for publication. Journals would be clamoring for his attention. *I really am going to be rich.*

Then his frown returned. *But what am I contributing to?*

Where will all those truckloads of money be going?

At 6:00 his boss announced over the intercom, "Dinner will be at 7:00, Mr. Bergman. Please conclude your work for the day and freshen up. My man will be down shortly to escort you to your room."

Bergman did as he was told. He waited at the elevator door, staring at the key-operated switch. It appeared to be a simple lock, no more than five pins. Maybe less.

Then it struck him like a thunderbolt.

"You locked us out of the house, Dad. I can see your key on the kitchen table." Ethan was looking through the window.

"What are we going to do, son? Your mother can't leave work early and your cake will melt before she gets here." He was holding an ice cream cake for his son's 19th birthday.

"No sweat, Padre. I've been practicing this for weeks, ever since I found it on the internet." He withdrew two paperclips from his pocket, and in a matter of minutes, he had the front door open.

Bergman was dumbfounded. "How did you do that? Teach me."

Suddenly, the elevator doors opened and Bergman was yanked from his reverie.

"Good evening, sir. Please come with me."

That night he lay in bed trying to formulate a plan. *OK. So I remember how to pick a lock with two paperclips. What do I do if I get out of my room? Find my phone and call 911? No, this is Europe. 999? Should I just run for my life, or would I be running away from a fortune? Not to mention the chance to start my life over.* He scratched his head, resigned to the fact that sleep would be a long time coming. *I already think this codex is the real thing. And if it is, it's the Holy Grail of paleography. I'll never see anything like this again in my entire lifetime. People would kill for this opportunity.* That thought sobered him. He pursed his lips. *I need to find out what's really going on.*

The next day, he fired up one of the computers to type in his rough translation. Then he returned to the codex and began his analysis. In a few minutes, he started another computer and dedicated it to researching the finer points of Pauline grammar and style. He pulled up his 2004 article from the *Journal of Biblical Literature* to refresh his memory of a particular verb usage. Along the way, he surreptitiously pocketed several paperclips.

The voice on the intercom startled him. "Would you like some lunch, Mr. Bergman? It is getting late."

Caught up in the thrill of his work, five hours had flown by. "Sure. Just a sandwich and black coffee."

He bolted down his lunch and was back examining the codex. *It is you, Paul,* he thought. *It is you.* He laid his hand on the glass over the tenth page, overwhelmed by the sensation of being centimeters away from a document that Paul himself had written. He, David Bergman, was the first to read this living, breathing time capsule. It was the pinnacle of his career.

The entire day passed that way, in the giddy flight through millennia. What might be tedium for another, researching minute variations of vocabulary and syntax, was high adventure for him. He was Christopher Columbus and Vasco da Gama and Sir Edmund Hillary, the first to gain this hallowed ground.

It wasn't until later that night, as the heady glow of his enthusiasm faded, that his doubts returned.

Had he fallen asleep? He sat bolt upright in bed, the words *Remember Matthew* echoing in his sleepy brain. It was one of the very first projects he had worked on all those years ago, authenticating an early fragment of Matthew's Gospel. He had been struck by one of the verses.

What will it profit a man if he gains the whole world and forfeits his soul?

That clinched it. He threw back the blankets and stood up. The clock by his bedside read 3:00. He dressed quickly but remained barefoot. He reached into the pocket of his pants and withdrew two paperclips.

With swift motions, he straightened one of the clips to make his lock pick. The other he opened so one end stuck out at a 90 degree angle from the remainder, creating his tension wrench. He inserted the wrench clip into the lower part of the lock on his bedroom door and gently tried to turn it. He kept a steady pressure on it, while he inserted the straightened clip above it and raked it along the pins of the lock. One by one, he raised each of the pins above the shear line. The wrench clip turned and the bolt slid open. *Thank you, Ethan,* he thought, as he stepped out into the darkened hallway.

He stopped to listen, hoping his boss had not posted any guards. He also hoped there were no motion sensors or alarms he had not spotted during his earlier reconnoitering. His bid for freedom would be very short-lived otherwise.

Five minutes passed and no alarms were sounding. He padded down the darkened stairs to the office. He remembered seeing his boss's laptop there and thought he might find his phone as well. He listened at the threshold, then held his breath as he slowly turned the knob. As he had expected, it was locked. He pulled out his paperclips, and within a few minutes, he had the door open.

He exhaled deeply and entered, quietly shutting the door behind him. Streaming through the window was the light of a full moon, bathing everything in an eerie silver glow. The laptop was still there. He walked behind the desk and sat in the chair. One more lock obstructed him, the one on the main drawer, which also locked the side drawers. It was no match for his newly found skill.

The main drawer held correspondence from several

different banks, some written in Arabic. Although he knew ancient Hebrew for his work, he had never studied modern Arabic, so it was indecipherable to him.

Next he explored the side drawers. The upper one held only pens and pencils. The middle one held a stack of 3x5 index cards, on which were written titles of applications and accounts, followed by single words made up of a combination of letters and numbers. *Passwords*, he thought. He pulled them out and put them on the desktop. The bottom drawer held the treasure he sought. Underneath the black hood were his cell phone and a set of keys. *A gun would have been nice, Boss, but I'll take the keys.* He set all three items on the desktop.

Then he turned his attention to the laptop. He opened it and turned it on. When prompted for a password, he remembered his boss on the first day he was here. Nine or ten keystrokes. He impulsively typed *Laodiceans* and entered it. He was in. He first clicked on the document file and scrolled through pages of schematics, with an index itemizing thousands of parts with 20-digit serial numbers. *What is this?* he wondered. He felt no closer to knowing what was going on, and he was becoming more anxious the longer he stayed in the office. Finally, he turned to his boss's email file. He looked through the cards of passwords until he found what he needed. He opened one sent yesterday.

My Dear Brother-in-Arms,

We are very close. The authentication of the codex is proceeding apace and we will be able to make our official news release next Sunday as planned. The financial impact will raise our company's credit score to the highest rating, and money will never again be a concern for us.

Have your assembly team ready. We will start shipping the parts to you within the week. We anticipate enough for two devices. With those and the huge influx of capital for arms and munitions, our armies will be victorious on all fronts.

Are you a student of irony, my friend? Is it not wonderful that the single greatest artifact in Christian history will destroy Israel and its western allies? Alhamdulillah!
Please keep me apprised of your situation.

Bergman sat back heavily in his chair. *Two devices? As in nuclear devices? Biological or chemical devices? And what armies?* His heart was pounding. His breath came in shallow gasps. His throat was dry.

Here was the smoking gun.

He closed the email file and turned off the computer. Gone were his dreams of wealth and fame. In their place, a desperate sense that he had to do something to stop what his boss had called the financial juggernaut, the funding for armies that would turn the tide forever in the Middle East and the world.

But what could he do? How? Calling 999 might get himself rescued, but could he convince the police to investigate his boss, police who were probably on his payroll? And his boss already had enough material from Bergman to proceed with the authentication announcement as planned.

He became painfully aware of the ticking of the clock on the far wall. As the minutes slipped away, he felt more and more desperate. *Think! Think!* And a moment of clarity. He knew exactly what he had to do.

He grabbed the keys, stuffed the hood and his phone into his pocket, and left the office. He had to find the laundry room.

How soon before the kitchen help would be up to begin meal prep? Would there be any guards about? He crept quietly down the stairs, lit just enough by moonlight through windows to keep himself from stumbling. His heart pounded in his chest so loudly that he imagined its awakening his captors. Down he went, guessing that a laundry room must be in the basement.

Suddenly, he froze. Voices at the next landing. Were they climbing the staircase? He rushed back up and turned into the darkened hallway. He went as far as he could into the darkness, then lay down on the floor next to the wall. He held his breath and waited. The minutes passed in agonizing slowness. When no one appeared at the landing, he retraced his steps to the stairwell.

Back down he went, stopping after every few steps to listen for danger. At the final landing, he was plunged into total blackness. No moonlight penetrated here. Dare he use the flashlight on his phone? Again, he listened. When he heard no sound, he withdrew his phone from his pocket and turned on its light. The corridor extended to the right, and he felt as though he were entering an underground cavern. Other hallways intersected his own in a bewildering maze of shadows. Just as he was giving up hope, his light illumined a room on his left that held a long line of washers and dryers.

It was a large utility room with laundry materials on the right side and rows of workbenches on the left. With the aid of the small cone of light from his phone, he quickly scoured the workbenches for tools he might be able to use. He found two screwdrivers and a pair of pliers, which he put into his back pocket. More searching revealed a hammer, and he tucked it under his belt.

Now he turned and began to rifle through the cabinets over the washing machines, until he found a gallon jug of bleach. He grabbed the jug from the shelf and hurried back into the hallway.

In moments, he was back at the staircase and ascending as quickly and silently as he could. He heard no other sounds but his ragged respirations. At the level of the dining room, he turned and walked down the hallway toward the elevator. *I can do this*, he told himself, but he wasn't sure if he believed it. Soon he was at the elevator to the laboratory, keys in one hand and jug in the other. His thoughts were racing. *Once I engage the elevator, I'm on the clock. Somebody will hear it and they'll come looking for me. I'll only have a few minutes.* He inserted the elevator key into the switch, but hesitated to turn it.

I'm going to die today, he thought. *No half-million. No publications. No chair at Oxford or Cambridge.*

He wept.

And he turned the key.

The doors opened immediately and he dashed inside. He hit the button for the sub-basement. The motors whined and the elevator descended. When he reached his destination, he inserted the key into the switch on the control panel inside and locked the elevator with its doors open. Then he ran into the laboratory. He threw the black hood over the camera. Next he pulled the hammer from his belt and struck the display case with it as hard as he could. With a report like a gunshot, the hammer bounced harmlessly off the specially hardened glass.

"Mr. Bergman! What are you doing? What was that sound?" came the alarmed voice over the intercom. "The camera seems to be malfunctioning. I cannot see you. You were not in your room, so I presumed it was you on the elevator. Why are you in the laboratory at his hour?"

"Just finishing some work, Boss. I'm almost done." He hastily withdrew the screwdrivers and pliers from his pocket.

"Please come upstairs immediately."

"Will do, Boss. Just give me a minute." He worked furiously at the screws that held the frame around the dual panes of glass.

"Why is the elevator not working, Mr. Bergman?" Then the voice changed tactics. "Have we not offered you enough money, my friend? Please come up now and we can renegotiate your contract. Would two million be fair? We want you to be happy, Mr. Bergman. Please."

"Two million sounds about right, Boss," he said, stalling for time. "I'll come right up." *How long will it be before he comes down the elevator shaft after me?* he thought.

One last screw and the weight of the glass popped open its frame. The plates crashed to the laboratory floor.

"Mr. Bergman, what are you doing?" The voice sounded desperate.

"I'm invalidating my contract, Boss. I'm almost done."

"I am coming for you, Mr. Bergman!" The voice was a

feral snarl. "That codex is everything. Click-clack!"

Bergman slid the heavy top plate away and scooped up the pages of the codex in his arms. Overwhelmed by the enormity of what he was about to do, he stood for a moment, his whole body trembling. There was no other way. He embraced the pages as a lover and wet them with his tears. Then he laid them down and poured bleach all over them. He watched in despair as the 2000-year-old writing faded away, lost forever. Then he picked up the sopping pages and tore them to shreds. It felt like murder. He sobbed in grief.

Still weeping, he pulled his phone from his pocket and dialed 999.

"What is the nature of your emergency?" came the voice.

"My name is David Bergman. I've been kidnapped by a terrorist. His name is Abd al samad and he has at least three accomplices. Maybe more, but less than 12. He's holding me at his estate outside Oxford, but I don't know where it is. I'll leave my phone on so you can find me. He's equipping an army. Something terrible will be happening soon. Please hurry."

With that, he laid the phone down out of the way. He found a coffee cup the servant had missed and filled it with the remainder of the bleach. Then he picked up the hammer.

I'm no martial artist, he thought. *But I'll fight for my life. My only chance is for this to go quickly. If I can't end it in a few seconds, I'm dead. I'll be no match for him in hand-to-hand combat.*

He resigned himself to the confrontation, and his fear left him. He walked to the open elevator and waited, bleach in one hand and hammer in the other. Soon he heard sounds in the elevator shaft. His nemesis was coming. He stood at the doorway and watched the hatch in the ceiling of the elevator car. His enemy would drop through there. *And he'll expect me to be cowering in the laboratory.*

He heard the hatch being opened. In an instant, his boss leaped down into the elevator. Bergman hurled the bleach into his eyes. The man fell backward screaming, dropping his knife and wiping desperately at his burning eyes. Bergman lunged and struck him in the head with the hammer. The man's hands came up reflexively to ward off the blows, but to no avail. The hammer struck again and again, gore splashing the walls, until the man lay twitching convulsively on the floor.

Bergman staggered from the elevator and fell to his knees, retching violently. Great sobs welled up from deep within him. As he regained his feet and stumbled back into the laboratory, he heard the sounds of sirens over the intercom.

When the police finally climbed down the elevator shaft, they found him sitting on the laboratory floor, weeping, staring sightlessly ahead.

It took them several minutes to pry his fingers from the bloody hammer.

Holding Pattern

OCTOBER 18, 2016 and FEBRUARY 28, 2017. The sun had set and an intermittent rain tapped its Morse Code on the skylight overhead. A pot of beef stew was simmering on the stove, filling the small house with the spicy fragrances of comfort for a cold wet night.

"You know Hillary is going to win, don't you?" Tess poured herself another glass of Cabernet and resumed her seat on the couch next to Benjamin. The evening news on CBS was just about to start.

"What are you talking about, sweetie?"

"The election, Benny, the election. Who are you going to vote for anyway?"

Benjamin shook his head. "If this is your attempt at humor, it's falling on deaf ears, darling. I'm coming to terms with the outcome, but it'll take me a while. Please just give me some time."

"Now what are *you* talking about?" She put her glass down on the coffee table and frowned at her husband.

Benjamin could hear an edge of impatience in her voice. He sat back in the soft chair and sighed. He hated to argue politics with his wife. They might have to declare a four-year moratorium on such conversations. "It's over. Hillary lost. Trump won. End of story. I just hope it's not the end of our country as we know it."

"Have you been smoking dope again? And how many glasses of wine have you had, for Chrissakes?" Tess shook her head back and forth. "You drink too much." It sounded to him as though it were as indisputable as the sum of two plus two.

"I do not, goddamn it! I've had exactly one glass of wine tonight, for your information."

"Then why aren't you making any sense?"

He wanted to scream in frustration. If he weren't already

bald, he'd be pulling out his hair by the roots. The voice from the television interrupted him.

"This is Tuesday, October 18th, 2016, and this is our western edition. With only three weeks until the election, both parties are doubling down on their campaign strategies..."

Benjamin jumped up from his chair, pointing his right index finger at the flat screen perched above their mantle. "What did he just say?"

"Honestly, Benny, just listen to yourself."

"I mean it. He said it was October 18th and you know damn well it's Tuesday, February 28th."

"Now I know you're either drunk or stoned." Tess arose from the couch in a huff. "I can't do this anymore, Benny. You're making me crazy."

"But it's February 28th! Look at your phone if you don't believe me."

Tess stomped out into the kitchen. She retrieved her purse from the table and removed her phone. "There! Are you happy now? Tuesday, October 18th." She shoved the screen up into his face.

"I...I don't understand," he stammered. He took his own phone from his pocket and saw the same date. "But I know it's February. Trump won. I heard his acceptance speech. His inaugural address."

"Did you stop taking your medication again? Because if you did, I swear to God I'm calling my lawyer. I'm done with this roller coaster."

"Listen to me, Tess. I'm not manic. I'm not having one of my episodes. I'm not hearing any voices. I just know it's February 28th."

"And how, pray tell, do you know that, Einstein? When the whole rest of the country thinks it's October, how do you know it's February?" When he didn't respond, she said, "Do I have to remind you? Two and a half years ago you went off your medication. And what happened? The police caught you walking south on I-5, wearing nothing but a pair of boxer shorts in a winter rainstorm, for God's sake. You were hospitalized for two weeks after that escapade, mister, one of which you spent in a medical ward, recovering from pneumonia. And earlier this year..." She lowered her eyes and whispered, "Deirdre—sweet, sweet Deirdre... I almost left you during those first few months, but I couldn't move. I've got the strength to do it now."

"Trust me, Tess. I'm begging you." And it hit him like a thunderbolt. They had already had this argument. Everything had happened before. She was going to call the police and her lawyer and his psychiatrist. He was going back into the hospital and this time she would not be waiting for him when he got out.

MARCH 16, 2016 and APRIL 3, 2017. "You'll be late for your evening shift if you don't hurry up, honey." Tess busied herself making Benjamin a ham and cheese sandwich to bring to work.

"You're here? But you left. You filed for divorce."

"I haven't filed for divorce. What makes you say that? I love you even though you push me to the limit."

Benjamin sat down hard on a kitchen chair. "I don't get it," he muttered. Through the patio door, he saw the tulips and crocuses Tess had planted, blooming in a brilliant palette of colors.

"I've got a sandwich for your break tonight and a thermos of coffee to keep you awake."

"Ouch, Tess, you don't have to rub it in. I'm out of work, but I'm trying hard to find a new job. I'm online looking every day."

"What's the matter with your job at Journey Print?"

"You know Billy let me go after my hospitalization last October. I couldn't fight him on it. I missed too much, couldn't keep up with the work. But I'll get back on my feet."

"What are you talking about, Benny? You weren't in the hospital last year. It's been more than two years. And your boss sings your praises. Always on time, never stretching a break, nose to the grindstone. He loves a workaholic like you."

"That was after..." His voice trailed off. He shook his head. "That's how I coped with losing Deirdre. Threw myself into work so I wouldn't have to think."

"Losing Deirdre? She's out in the driveway right now riding her bicycle. She's almost ready to have you take the training wheels off." Tess pursed her lips. "Sometimes I don't know about you, Benny. You talk crazy even when you're being good with your medicine."

Tears had filled Benjamin's eyes. "I still can't think about her without crying. Is that normal?"

"Normal? Jesus, Benny! Go outside and talk to her before you go to work."

"She's not outside, Tess! Don't do this to me."

"Do what, for Chrissakes? Go talk to her."

"I killed her over a year ago! March 16th. It's my fault. I deserve all the blame."

Tess slapped him hard across the face. "Today is March 16th! Don't you talk that kind of bullshit to me! Our daughter is just fine. She's riding the two-wheeler we got her for Christmas. Maybe you've been out of the hospital too long. Do we have to send you back in?"

The afternoon sun was slanting through the kitchen windows. Benjamin saw the sandwich and the thermos on the counter. "Today is April 3rd, 2017," he said, in as calm a voice as he could manage. "I was hospitalized from October 19th to October 30th last year. I lost my job and I'm looking for another." He spoke with exaggerated slowness, trying to keep his growing rage in check. "My going back into the looney bin was the last straw for you. You served me with divorce papers even before I got out of the ward." He took a deep breath and exhaled slowly. "Our daughter has been dead for over a year." His body recoiled at the sound of the words, collapsing on itself like a styrofoam cup in a campfire.

"Goddamn you, Benjamin!" She was crying now, gouging her cheeks with her fingers. "You're crazy! Why the hell did I marry you? You mess up everything you touch."

"Something is happening to me, Tess. I can't explain it. It's like this is all a recording. It's like I'm replaying the worst days of my life."

She threw his sandwich at him. "You ruin everything! How am I supposed to keep loving you when I don't even know if we're on the same planet?"

"I'm trying my best. Why won't you listen to me? Something is terribly, terribly wrong." He couldn't hide the exasperation in his tone.

"The only thing that's wrong is that bipolar brain of yours!" she shrieked, as she poked him in the forehead with her index finger.

He swatted her hand away. "I'm going out," he said through clenched teeth.

She followed him to the garage door and was still shouting at him when he started the car and shoved it into reverse, backing up much too quickly. He felt and heard a sickening thump under the rear tire and Tess began screaming.

FEBRUARY 4, 2014 and MAY 26, 2017. The light blinded him as though he had just walked out of a darkened movie theater into a bright afternoon. His mouth was so dry he couldn't swallow. He rolled over to get out of bed and banged into a raised guard rail. The prick in his hand alerted him to the IV taped there. "Crap," he whispered to himself. "Back in the hospital." Then another thought frightened him. *But what year is it?*

A pretty Asian woman in a white lab coat walked in, a stethoscope draped like a badge of office around her neck. She logged on to the computer that hung on a hinged arm from a tall metal frame attached to the wall.

"I'm Doctor Li, Mr. Stone. How are you feeling today? We're almost done with your IV antibiotics. Then we'll move you over to our psychiatric ward for a few days. Are you all right with that?"

"What's today's date?" he said, reaching for a cup of water

he saw on the dinner tray.

"It's February 4th. You've been here almost a week. You were feverish when we admitted you. That may account for a little disorientation you could be feeling."

"I mean the year, Doctor. What year is it?"

"2014."

Benjamin's shoulders slumped.

"Do you remember how you got here, Mr. Stone?"

"I confess I'm a little foggy about that. I heard I was walking down I-5 in my underwear."

"Indeed. Any recollection how that happened?"

"I stopped taking my meds. I felt so good for so long I didn't think I needed them anymore."

Dr. Li scrolled through several more screens on the computer. "I see you were diagnosed bipolar as a late adolescent." She clicked on a menu item. "You were under the care of Dr. Jeanne Warwick. Fine psychiatrist. Looks like she tried you on quite a few medications before the two of you found the right combination." She looked up from the screen and into his eyes. "So how are you feeling today?"

"I'm fine, Doctor. Ready to go home."

"You looked a little...unsettled when I told you it was 2014."

"Doctor Li, I'm trying very hard to figure out what's happening to me." He assumed a soft conspiratorial tone. "I know it's really 2017, but no one else does. Would you believe Donald Trump is President?"

The psychiatrist chuckled. "Really? Donald Trump?" She stopped typing progress notes and pushed her designer glasses back up on the bridge of her nose.

"Have you ever had a lucid dream?" Benjamin asked.

"You mean the kind where you know you're dreaming and can even alter the flow of the dream from within it?"

"Yes, yes! I think it's like that, except I don't have any control over it. I can't change anything. It's as if I'm living a recording of my life. Events that have already happened. And no one else is aware of it."

"Are you enjoying it?"

"It's hell, Doctor. I don't get to live over any of the good stuff. The fabulous sex when my wife and I were young and dating. The time I won at Bingo and paid for our whole Caribbean cruise. The meal I had at a Michelin three-star restaurant in France. It's a recording of just the bad stuff—the worst days of my life."

"How long has it been going on?"

"I can't tell. I just know I can't take much more of it..." His voice trailed off. He turned his face away.

"Are you thinking about committing suicide?" the psychiatrist persisted.

"N-no. Nothing like that."

Li resumed typing her notes. As her fingers flew over the keys, she spoke without looking up. "Mr. Stone, I'm going to have my intern, Dr. Summers, look in on you. She'll do a complete evaluation to prep you for coming over to our ward."

She logged off the computer and walked to the bedside. "If you're living a recorded version of your life, is it possible someone else is playing the recording? If you found that person, could you somehow stop it?"

Benjamin's eyes widened. A broad smile lit up his face. "Thank you, Doctor! Thank you. That's exactly what I need to do."

The psychiatrist turned toward the door. "Dr. Summers will be in later today. Please be completely honest with her."

As she left the room, she encountered Dr. Summers at the nursing station. "Heads up, Deanna. You're scheduled to assess Benjamin Stone later today. I've taken a bit of a therapeutic gamble with him just now—entering his delusional system. I hope I've introduced some doubt into his elaborate scheme so he can begin to challenge it himself."

MEMORIAL DAY, MAY 29, 2017. It was an office like no other he had ever seen. The near walls from floor to ceiling were made up of banks of electronic equipment. In the center sat an immense wooden desk with half a dozen laptop computers on it. On the far side of the desk, aisles and aisles of electronics extended back as far as he could see. Behind the desk, a tall Caucasian man in an impeccable black suit, white shirt, and tie arose and extended his hand. "Welcome, Benny. May I call you that? My name is Lucius. Please have a seat."

Benjamin shook his hand, hoping the man couldn't feel his body trembling or hear his heart pounding. He lowered himself into the black leather chair in front of the desk. "Are you the one responsible for what's happening to me?"

Lucius had returned to his seat. He rested his elbows on the desk and tented his fingers. "I'm afraid you're the one guilty of that, Benny. I'm just re-watching some of my favorite parts. You're my catch of the day. My soup *du jour.* You're so entertaining!"

Benjamin cleared his throat and tried to speak in a normal voice. "Am I like in a holding pattern or something? Living the worst days of my life over and over again?"

"Good metaphor, Benny. I like it. You're one of those planes circling San Francisco or JFK or O'Hare, waiting for the weather to clear and a gate to open up."

"And when do I land?"

"At the End of All Things, of course."

"I knew it! I knew it!" Benjamin bounced in excitement. "My whole life I've never believed in God. And then, when I backed over my daughter, I knew that if God—you—existed at all, you couldn't possibly be both all-powerful and all-loving. Or else you could have or would have prevented Deirdre's death."

Lucius chuckled. "God, did you say? God? Oh, I met him once. A long, long time ago by your standards. I wasn't impressed."

Benjamin grimaced. He stood up and began pacing back and forth. "I've had another psychotic break, haven't I? Bonkers. Off my rocker. I'm really in a hospital bed somewhere. Tied down. Shot full of Haldol. Hallucinating like a banshee."

"Benny, Benny, please stop!" Lucius was guffawing. As he wiped the tears of laughter from his face, he grinned. "Let me catch my breath. You're too much!"

"I want out. Land the friggin' plane. I'm done with this."

"Patience, Benny. It's not the End yet. We've still got a ways to go, you and I." His face grew hard. His voice dropped several octaves. "Let's replay your suicide, shall we?" he said. "I don't think I've laughed so hard since Kennedy was killed."

"Stop! I've had enough! You're God. You don't have to do this to me."

"You're not listening," Lucius hissed, loud and monstrous. "I told you there is a God, but he isn't here. It's just you and I." As he stood, his massive presence seemed to fill the office space. He strode around the desk and towered over Benjamin.

"Wait! Wait! I don't understand." Benjamin cringed backward, throwing up his arms, a look of abject horror on his face.

"Of course you don't. You lack imagination as well as faith. Alas, that can't be helped now, Benny." He extended his hand and grasped Benjamin's left forearm. "Come. I've invited some of my...fellows to watch. You're quite the show. Four out of five stars."

His laughter echoed forever.

Dangerous Christmas

Long ago and far, far away, little boys risked their lives every December 25th. We often received Christmas gifts that could maim or kill us, and we were positively delirious with excitement and anticipation. Christmas in 1952, when I was six years old, was no exception. For the entire month of December, I was a wild child.

It had been a rather memorable year for grownups. I didn't read the newspaper or watch the news on television, but I heard snippets of my parents' conversations that often left me bewildered.

Last summer I remember Dad's telling my mother about UFOs buzzing Washington, D.C. He sounded worried. "They tracked them on radar. They scrambled jets but the saucers got away."

How cool is that! I thought. *Maybe one will land in our backyard!*

But last month, before Thanksgiving, he sounded more than a little worried. "They blew up the first hydrogen bomb, honey. Codename *Ivy Mike*. On that little island in the South Pacific. It was almost 700 times more powerful than *Little Boy*, the bomb they dropped on Hiroshima." He shook his head. "Maybe we should think about building ourselves a fallout shelter."

I found myself thinking how cute the names of our atomic bombs were.

In those days, there was always a cigarette burning in our house. On this particular Saturday morning, my father got up from the breakfast table and reached for my mother's cigarette, which lay smoldering in the ashtray by the stove, where she was cooking pancakes. He lit his own cigarette with the glowing ember of hers. Then he did what he always did when he lit a cigarette. He held it between his lips and inhaled and exhaled deeply several times in rapid succession, until fully one-half of the cigarette was incandescent. When he exhaled, some of the smoke curled back and up into his nostrils and was inhaled a second time. In a matter of seconds, the cigarette was almost gone. He finally relinquished it to an ashtray, the long ash intact. In later years, when I smoked, I was never able to duplicate that astounding feat.

"Would you believe that?" My father had picked up his newspaper again. "Look at this picture, hon. Christine Jorgensen had something they call 'sexual reassignment surgery' in Denmark. You ever hear a word like 'transsexual' before?"

"From George to Christine," my mother said matter-of-factly, not skipping a beat as she flipped the pancakes. Mom could be like that. She was very pregnant that December with my second sibling, due to arrive in early February.

I had tiptoed into the kitchen unannounced. "What's 'transsexual'?" I asked innocently. That time Mom did drop the spatula.

"I didn't know you were here," Dad spluttered. "I thought you were in the living room watching television."

"I was, and I just saw a neat commercial for *Mr. Potato Head.* I never saw a commercial for toys on TV before. Can I have one for Christmas?"

"Add it to your list for Santa Claus," my father responded noncommittally, snapping his newspaper as he turned the page. My shoulders slumped briefly, but I brightened as I ran back into the living room. Saturday morning was TV Nirvana for me: I had *Space Patrol, Captain Video and His Video Rangers, Tom Corbett: Space Cadet*, and *Sky King*. It was electronic drugs and I was high again in a minute.

I was eating a fried baloney sandwich with a glass of milk at lunch time. My three-year-old sister Sandy was making faces at me when our mother wasn't looking. Mom was paging through a *LIFE* magazine. When she held it up, I could see the cover. It looked like a picture of a scene from *Space Patrol*. I read titles proclaiming *"Beginning LIFE's Greatest Series of Science Stories in Pictures and*

64

Text—The World We Live In, Part I: The Earth is Born."

"Hey, Snork!" my mother called to my father. I never did find out where she got that term of endearment for him. "This would be a great gift for you-know-who."

My sister and I froze, barely daring to breathe, hanging on every word. For me? For Sandy? And what was it? My father came into the room, took one look at the picture she was holding up to him and quickly dismissed it.

"Honey, it could get him started toward a great career in science," Mom suggested.

"But did you see the price tag? $49.50. That's astronomical. We could never possibly afford that."

Sandy and I sank helplessly in our chairs, dreams of an incredible Christmas gift dissolving before us. And Mom had said "him." It would have been for me. I vowed to recover that magazine when my mother put it down, to find out what exactly was never going to be under the Christmas tree with my name on it.

I helped my mother after lunch by drying the dishes and then I spirited the magazine away. There it was—a full page advertisement. It practically glowed with radioactive excitement, describing in detail the gift that every modern boy would die for:

Gilbert U-238 Atomic Energy Lab
Contains
. U-239 Geiger Counter
. Electroscope
. Spinthariscope
. Wilson Cloud Chamber
. 3 Low Level Radiation Sources:
   - alpha particles
   - beta particles
   - gamma rays
. 4 Uranium-Bearing Ore Samples
. Nuclear Spheres for Making a Molecular Model

. *Prospecting for Uranium* - book
. *Gilbert Atomic Energy Manual*
. *Learn How Dagwood Split the Atom* - comic book
. 3 C Batteries

And a partridge in a pear tree. I almost wept. The gift of the century callously torn from my feverish hands. Much later I would secretly thank my father for sparing me from leukemia and siring two-headed babies, but at six years old I was heartbroken. Then, of course, it would be only two or three years before I got the *Porter Chemcraft Chemistry Set*, filled with enough toxic chemicals to contaminate the water supply of a small city and make a modern-day attorney salivate. (No, I didn't burn down the house with it, but I did stink up the garage pretty well.)

I went back to the living room, but the television set wouldn't turn on. "Hey, Dad, the set is on the fritz again," I called out.

It seemed every few months one of the tubes burned out. Dad had become a master at fixing the old Philco. He was in his bedroom still putting away all the election paraphernalia from the fall's activities. He was Registrar of Voters for our little town, and he and Mom had also volunteered for the Eisenhower campaign. We still had enough red, white, and blue *I Like Ike* bumper stickers left to wallpaper the entire house. I gave *I Like Ike* buttons to all my friends at school, and I still had a jar full of them on my dresser. I just could never remember if I was an elephant or a donkey.

Dad came into the living room and pulled the set away from the wall. "Hold this bag," he told me, as he proceeded to pry large vacuum tubes from inside the box. When there were three or four tubes in the bag, he said, "OK. It must be one of these. Let's go."

It was a short trip in the maroon 1950 Ford to the little village of Plantsville and Taylor's Market. Taylor's smelled like oiled wood and newsprint. It's where I went for *Action Comics* and *Mystery in Space* and *Detective Comics* and *Tales of the Unexpected*. Superman and Batman were only two of my many heroes. The market also had a machine for testing vacuum tubes, and after a couple of tries, Dad, like a latter-day Archimedes, exclaimed, "Eureka! There's the culprit!" New tube in hand, we zipped back home, and Dad completed the surgery. "I love you, Dad," I said, as the cathode ray tube winked into glorious black and white.

Some days later, school finally let out for Christmas vacation. It hadn't snowed yet, but the sky was a hopeful gray, and I could see my breath as I walked home from school. The trek from Holcomb Elementary was about a half-mile, up over the hill on Old Turnpike Road and down to the intersection with Carter Lane. There was a decided bounce to my step. As I think back on that day, I wonder if any other joy comes close: school is out, Christmas is coming, and snow is on the way. The Kids' Trifecta.

My sister and my mother had been home baking nutbread, while my father was still at work in Meriden at the International Silver Company. The windows of the house were steamed up from the baking, and the aromas when I opened the door made my mouth water. Nutbread was a Czechoslovakian recipe that my mother had learned from my grandmother, and of all the relatives in the family, Mom did it best. Walnuts ground into a thick paste were spread lovingly over the flattened dough. Softened raisins were sprinkled over this, and the dough was rolled into long loaves. With a brief brushing of milk over each loaf, they were baked in the oven until golden brown. The pinwheel results could not be sliced until Christmas morning, but this rule was modified later when we were old enough to attend midnight Mass on Christmas Eve. Then the first slice was served with coffee after Mass before we went to bed.

"Happy Christmas vacation, Stevie," my mom said to me with a smile. "Now, be a good boy and change out of your school clothes, while I make you a sandwich. You can wear your dungarees." As I ran out of the kitchen, she called after me, "Make sure to change your shoes, too. Put on your PF Flyers."

I scrambled up the stairs two at a time. As I changed, I slowed down long enough to put my pants on a hanger in the hall closet. I looked at the top of my desk to see if I had anything to stuff into my pockets. I spied the book I had gotten for my birthday—*The Secret of Thunder Mountain, by Fran Striker, Author of the Lone Ranger Books: A Tom Quest Adventure*. It was actually the sixth book in the series of eight, but it was my introduction to Tom Quest. It would not be long before it ignited a passion in me as I competed with my friend Tommy to see who could read them all first. One of the lesser known tragedies of my young life was the fact that I never found a copy of volume four, *The Secret of the Lost Mesa*. It was just never there at the Ben Franklin store whenever I looked. Of course, seeing that cover reminded me of something else.

"Hey, Mom!" I called as I ran back down the stairs. "Is *The Lone Ranger* on tonight?" I was leaping three stairs at a time on the way down. "Da da dun, da da dun, da da dun dun dun," I sang. The Lone Ranger's theme song was the perfect anthem for a hyperactive kid. It would be many years before I learned it was the William Tell Overture, and longer still before I would actually believe that. It was the Lone Ranger's song. Period.

As I chomped into my peanut butter and jelly sandwich, my mother said, almost apologetically, "Your father and I have to do some last minute Christmas shopping on Saturday, so you're going to have to go to the movies. I've asked your cousin Terry to take you. The Whites across the street will watch Sandy."

"What's playing?" I asked, in my most disinterested voice, pretending that this wasn't the best news yet in an already perfect day.

"Lash La Rue," she answered.

"*The King of the Bullwhip*?" I almost shouted, unable to contain myself any longer.

"His newest one. *The Black Lash*, I think." Decades later, my cowboy hero would mentor another hero, teaching the man who would become Indiana Jones how to use a bullwhip. What a wonderful world!

I had died and gone to heaven. Saturday afternoon at the

Colonial Theater in downtown Southington was as good as it gets. Thirty cents bought you a whole afternoon of cinematic delight. The show would start at 12:30 and often didn't get out until 6:00 PM. There would be previews of coming attractions, a serial (*Commando Cody,* if we were lucky), two or three cartoons (*Tom and Jerry* was the current favorite), and three feature films. And penny candy at the little concession stand inside: Black Crows and Jujubees and Jujyfruits and Squirrel Candy and Mary Janes and Sugar Daddies and Good & Plenty. Within minutes of show time, the whole theater would be bouncing in a sugar high. As I leaned back in my chair, absolutely overwhelmed by my good fortune, I looked out the window. It had begun to snow.

God must love little boys.

On the Sunday before Christmas, we went to ten o'clock Mass at St. Thomas Church down on Bristol Street. It was a dark, wonderful church, a little scary with its high ceilings and statues and stained glass windows. Two altar boys led Father Kennedy into the sanctuary, where they knelt and responded to his mysterious Latin invocations.

"*Introibo ad altare Dei,*" said Father Kennedy solemnly.

"*Ad Deum qui laetificat iuventutem meam,*" answered the altar boys.

I looked over at the Missal my mother was holding. It had the English translation written under the Latin.

I will go in to the altar of God, to God who brings joy to my youth.

"I want to be an altar boy," I announced to my mother.

"Shhh," she whispered. "You can be an altar boy, but you have to wait until you're ten years old."

That seemed an eternity away, but I had a goal. As my father and mother and sister and I prepared to leave after Mass, my mother stopped me and my sister and looked at us intently.

"What is Christmas?" she asked.

"The day Santa Claus comes!" my sister and I exclaimed,

jumping up and down as we shouted it out.

"But what else is Christmas?"

Sandy looked perplexed. Then before I could respond, she blurted out, "Jesus' birthday!"

"Yes, honey, you're right," my mother said, smiling and stroking my sister's hair. "Let's not ever forget that."

I gave my sister the Evil Eye. She had just scored some serious Christmas points that I was sure had not gone unnoticed by Santa. I didn't know if there was any way I could recoup my loss. I sat sullenly in the car all the way home.

I'm not sure how I survived the crescendo of anticipation as Christmas Day approached. By Wednesday afternoon, Christmas Eve, I had already listened to my two favorite Christmas songs at least five hundred times. I had driven my father to the edge. I think he was contemplating cutting the plug off the RCA Victor 45 record player or maybe just sitting in the garage with the car running. How many times can a grown man hear Jimmy Boyd singing *I Saw Mommy Kissing Santa Claus* before he begins to doubt his sanity? And for a chaser, how about Spike Jones and his City Slickers singing *All I Want For Christmas Is My Two Front Teeth*? That way lies madness. But what did I know? I was a kid in the throes of Santa Psychosis.

I was also a nervous wreck. I had to be extra careful around my sister, terrified that if I pushed her or pinched her or did anything I'd like to do, Santa wouldn't come. I could imagine myself pleading to the white-bearded, red-suited old guy, as he backed away from my house, "I've been good! I've been good! Dear God, I've been good!" But Santa, his face stern with disapproval, would disappear into the falling snow, the sack of toys on his back forever tied shut.

By the time we got ready for bed on that longest night of the year, I was so wired I was sure I must be giving off sparks. Sleep? Are you crazy? Santa Claus is coming!

Sandy and I dutifully prepared Santa's snack of milk and cookies and set it on the little end table next to the lamp. We took one last loving look at our glorious Christmas tree, shining through our picture window into the dark night beyond. I thought of it as a beacon, its red and blue and yellow lights guiding Santa and his reindeer to our house as surely as the lights on an airport runway.

Did I sleep that night? I must have, because soon my sister was tugging at my pajama sleeve.

"It's Christmas morning! Wake up! Wake up!" she whispered.

I noticed it was still dark outside, but I had been prepared for that. I had hidden my parents' electric lantern under my bed. I pulled it from its hiding place, and my sister and I crept downstairs. She clutched her Raggedy Ann doll to her chest. Halfway down, once we could see into the living room, I turned on the lantern.

The beam lit up a cornucopia of gifts. And the milk and cookies were gone. "Santa's been here," I said, with as much relief as excitement. The living room was awash in a flood of ribbons and bows and gaily colored paper. Presents of all sizes and shapes littered the floor around the tree. It took my breath away.

I shined the light to the mantel over the fireplace. The stockings we had hung were bulging with booty. I knew it was too early to risk awakening Mom and Dad, but it would be OK to empty our stockings before they got up. We tiptoed into the living room and turned on the Christmas tree lights. It was hard to suppress a gasp at the treasure trove before us. Sandy and I took down our stockings in reverent silence.

There was the obligatory new toothbrush in its cellophane wrapper, along with a tube of Ipana Toothpaste. The next lump to emerge from the stocking was a deck of Bicycle Playing Cards. We would bring those to Point O' Woods Beach next summer for games of Go Fish and War. Then came the Pez Candy, in a dispenser that looked like a cigarette lighter. I levered one of them into my mouth, the first one of the day. I felt the next lump between my fingers and pulled it out of the stocking. Kilgore Perforated Roll Caps. But did Santa know that my cap gun was broken? Was there a new cap pistol in my future? I looked hopefully at the horde of presents. Finally, I took the last of the gifts from my stocking: two packs of Lucky Strike Candy Cigarettes. I opened a box and drew out one of the red-tipped beauties. I hung it from the corner of my mouth, with a grownup sneer on my lips.

"Oh, Stevie!" my sister admonished.

"I'm practicing," I smirked at her. "In a few years I'll be able to smoke a real one."

Just then the living room lights came on. "What are you kids doing up so early?" my father asked.

My sister and I looked at each other, dumbfounded. Was that a trick question? "Santa Claus has come!" we shouted in glee.

"OK, OK," he said with a knowing smile. "Don't open anything else until I get your mommy up and make some coffee."

The wait seemed interminable. Sandy and I fidgeted in our eagerness to dive into our loot. Finally, my mother and father, coffee cups in hand, walked into the living room and sat on the couch. With a ferocity usually reserved for life and death combat, my sister and I attacked our presents. Paper and ribbons flew. Boxes were torn open. It was an orgy of unalloyed avarice.

I honestly don't remember what my sister got except for a very special cloth doll that was as big as she was. The doll had long legs and elastic loops on her feet. With those loops, my sister attached the doll's feet to her own and then danced with her through the house, pirouetting through the kitchen and the living room in unabashed joy.

As she did so, I was tugging on a pair of red and brown leather cowboy boots. I had already perched the black felt cowboy hat on my head and put on the shirt with the leather tassels. Now I opened the box from my grandparents and pulled out a Kit Carson Double Holster and Pistol Set. I was speechless. I strapped it low on my waist, the way Lash La Rue or Hopalong Cassidy would. With the cool devil-may-care attitude of a professional gunslinger, I loaded each pistol with a roll of caps and slid them back into the holsters. Before my father could stop me, I whirled on him and shouted, "Slap leather, cowpoke!" In a blur of six-gun savagery, the guns were in my hands.

Bang! Bang! The sound of the caps echoed in the small room and the pungent smell of burnt gunpowder filled my nostrils.

"Stop!" my mother shrieked, almost spilling her coffee. "Outside only with the caps."

"OK, little lady," I said, in my best Texan drawl. I holstered my trusty six-shooters and drew a candy cigarette from my shirt pocket. I put it to my lips and said, "Just let me know if there's any varmints you want taken care of."

My father rolled his eyes and shook his head back and forth. "Did you drop him on his head after he was born?" he whispered to my mother.

There was one more package to open—*To Stevie From Santa*. It was big and heavy. I tore into it with trembling fingers and held my breath.

Space Patrol Moon-Base Destroyer, the box proclaimed. The playing board was thick and heavy, like a dart board, with a painting of an interplanetary outpost on it. Then there was an object about the size and shape of a cigar box. It was actually a kind of periscope, except when you looked into it, it gave you a view of the floor at your feet, where you would put the game board. At the other end of the periscope were six slots where you positioned the rocket destroyers. When you pulled the release levers, the rockets would plummet to the game board, and you would score points depending on what structures of the moon-base you hit.

Each rocket destroyer was made of colored plastic with a lead core and was about three inches long. They weighed about two or three ounces apiece. Protruding from the nose cone of each rocket was a needle about two inches long, so it could pierce the target.

There was no Safety Warning declaring, *May skewer your foot. May enucleate your best friend's eye. May puncture your sister's skull.* It was 1952 and you celebrated Christmas at your own risk. So there I stood for the next three hours, a six-year-old cowboy playing Space Patrol with a potentially lethal weapon. A weapon, I might add, that I would take outside once the snow had melted in the spring to see if I could impale a bird or a squirrel. Life was good.

That afternoon, with the flotsam and jetsam of Christmas still knee-deep in the living room, I sat down on the couch, sated and spent. My mother sat down next to me. She took my hand and put it on her swollen belly.

"Feel that?" she asked.

I felt the baby kick and drew back my hand as if I had received an electric shock.

"I think you're going to have another sister," she said. And then, with a leap of logic I could not follow, she declared, "Don't ever forget the *creche*."

That was a new word she had taught me this year, along with *Nativity*. We had a little creche on top of our television set—little figurines of Mary and Joseph and the Baby Jesus, complete with a little cow, two lambs, and three shepherds. It was a toy compared to the big one in our church.

Every year St. Thomas would set up its creche inside the communion rail on the left side of the sanctuary. The statues of the Holy Family were almost life-size. I recalled that on the first Sunday of December, instead of leaving church immediately after Mass, my mother and father had brought Sandy and me down the aisle for a closer inspection of the Nativity scene. I looked from the baby in the manger to the enormous Crucifix suspended above the altar. I was surrounded by the icons of my religion, and my six-year-old brain was overwhelmed.

"Why did they kill him, Daddy?" I whispered. My father looked at me with an expression I did not understand. Then he smiled, or at least I think he did, and we all walked out to the car.

On that Christmas Day, as I sat on the couch beside my mother, she said, "When this baby is born, you're going to have to help me with her. She won't be able to do anything on her own. You'll have to help me feed her and change her and hold her." Then she riveted me with her gaze. "The Maker of the Universe loved us so much that He gave it all up and became a helpless little baby just like your sister will be."

I squirmed uncomfortably. "Why, Mommy?" was all I could think to say.

"Ah," my mother said, as she relaxed and sat back. "That's the mystery that we spend our whole lives pondering. It's not about being President of the United States or having atomic bombs to drop on people or driving the fanciest car or having a million dollars in the bank..." She pursed her lips and nodded her head. "Or even getting the most Christmas presents." She smiled, running her fingers through my hair.

"I'll always remember, Mommy," I promised, and in some inchoate way I began to grasp a profound truth:

How dangerous Christmas is.

The Man Who Stole the Stars

As they drifted into the July sunlight streaming through the open vent, the dust motes ignited like sparks from a spent firework. The mask on my face provided some protection from the allergens, but I still shook with spasms of sneezing. We were in my late, eccentric grandfather's attic, cleaning it out prior to putting the house on the market. It was an old elephant of a house, built around 1920, filled with high ceilings, dark wood, and creaking staircases. The proceeds from the sale would be my inheritance from a man who had been a profound mystery to our family.

"This goes to Goodwill," I said, as I slid the heavy trunk of clothes toward the hatch.

"Look what was behind it," my wife Jen said, blowing the dust from a leather-bound book. "There's some kind of numbers written on the cover. Looks like '*x equals minus b plus or minus the square root of b squared minus 4ac over 2a.*' What the hell is that?"

"That's the formula for solving a quadratic equation. It's the way my grandfather signed his things. I told you he was pretty weird."

She opened the cover. "It's like a journal or a diary, but only for a period of about five or six months. The year 2000. Anything special about that?"

I nodded my head. "That was the year Gregor left my grandmother and took a gay lover, Anton Werner. Just about destroyed her and my father. The family never recovered from the shock. I was the only one who would talk to my grandfather after that, and I did it on the Q.T. so nobody would hassle me about it."

"I remember you saying something about that. How old was he?"

"About 75, I think. Never too old to meet the love of your life, huh?"

"It sounds like he hurt a lot of people."

"He did. And he was really sorry. He tried to help me understand what his life felt like before and after he left his marriage. He introduced me to Anton, who seemed every bit as odd as my grandfather. They were made for each other." I smiled at the recollection and sang a few lines from Simon and Garfunkel's *Old Friends*.

Jen laughed at my off-key performance. "You loved them, didn't you?"

"Yeah. They were the most brilliant men I've ever met. Mathematics, physics, astronomy, biology. Then it all fell apart. They became very secretive. Stopped inviting me to come and visit. Gregor said only that they were working on a very important project, but he wouldn't tell me what it was. Neither would answer the phone or respond to my letters. I think they had a delivery service bring in their food." I shook my head. "Eight months later, Anton died of diabetes-related stuff. My grandfather lived alone in this house for the next sixteen years. A total recluse. They found his body when the grocery guy called the police to do a wellness check. Not sure how long he had been dead by then, but I heard it smelled pretty bad."

"How horrible! How could he live alone like that for so long? Why? Did you ever find out what their project was?"

"Nope. And unless he wrote about it in that book, it died with him."

"Well, we'll look at it tonight. Let's see how much of this we can take care of before supper."

Jennifer was like that. Practical. Down-to-earth. While I might feel a little spooked in the old house, imagining my grandfather's ghost walking the halls at night, looking for his lost lover, she saw a job to be done and was determined to finish.

After dinner that evening, Jen took off for a movie with two of her girlfriends. Feeling the comfort of her wild salmon soup in my belly and the relaxation of my second glass of Pinot, I opened the book.

1 April, 2000

Am I simply an April Fool? Will I ever be forgiven the harm I have done my family? Will my son ever speak to me again? But I feel Anton completes me, in my heart and in my mind. In fact, I think it was his intellect that first attracted me to him. Though astrophysics is his field of endeavor, he knows chemistry and biology and medicine. I believe he may even be my superior in mathematics. I am so blessed to have found him, even this late in life.

But what is his magnum opus, *as he calls it? He claims to have been working on it for the past five years. He says he wants to complete the first draft and then have me serve as beta reader, giving him an initial response, letting him know if it works as he wants it to. He is at the keyboard eight and ten hours a day, typing feverishly. All he will say is, "I am changing the history of the world." Obviously he has no problems with self-esteem!*

29 April

Anton says he will be finished tomorrow. He has been acting strangely—one moment laughing like an idiot and the next, weeping in despair. "When I am done with this, I will have nothing left to do," he says. "I will have completed my life's work and assured my place in history."

Can the world contain such an ego? But in bed, he calms down. He says I anchor him. Keep him from drifting off the earth. He can be tender then and thoughtful, not the raging madman who shrieks like a spoiled child if our connection to the internet is interrupted.

Tomorrow will tell the tale.

I stopped reading and poured myself another glass of wine. I wasn't sure what I felt, reading my grandfather's journal. I remembered being ten years old and looking through the bedroom keyhole at my parents making love. It was shocking but also satisfying at some visceral level. Eavesdropping on Gregor like this humanized him, made him something other than the family's vile caricature of him.

I recalled hearing that he had met Anton when both still worked at NASA, in the glory days of Apollo. After funding was cut back and popular interest waned, they both left together, thoroughly disillusioned with how political everything had become. Both assumed professorships and taught at Berkeley and Stanford for the remainder of their working lives. My grandmother, sweet innocent that she was, hadn't a clue about just how close they had become.

30 April

Anton has finished. Tonight he handed me a box containing 400 pages of single-spaced manuscript. "This is it?" I said.

"Yes."

"And?"

"And what?"

"Can you tell me about it?"

"No. Read it. Then talk to me." With that, he turned and went to bed without inviting me to accompany him.

Am I up the task? Reading a document of this size is a commitment, and I will have to put my own studies on hold for awhile. Is it supposed to be the great American novel? What if it is terrible? What if my lover does not have the command of the English language that he has of science? How then shall I speak to him about it?

I am daunted. My relationship with Anton is so precious to me I will do anything but risk that.

I called my son again tonight. His wife answered. She was polite, but he still refused to come to the phone. I fear he will never speak to me again. At times like this, I doubt myself. I wish I had not caused my family such pain.

I was beginning to get sleepy. Wine does that to me every time. I sighed at the memories of my grandfather and the family furor he had created. I confess I had seen him as just a crazy old man, but now I wasn't so sure. To see him experiencing passions that I had associated with younger men only gave me pause. *Grandpa, how did you survive such terrible loneliness after Anton's death?* Then another thought crossed my mind. *Is Anton's manuscript still somewhere in the house?*

Jennifer came home shortly after that, and we went to bed. As I turned out the light, she asked, "So how's the reading?"

"Enlightening," was all I managed before closing my eyes.

We were busy the next two days, and the journal sat unopened on our kitchen table. The task at Gregor's house was so overwhelming, we decided to hire an estate appraiser to catalog and sell everything and only do ourselves things like cleaning floors and carpets.

"Keep your eyes open for a box with a big typed manuscript in it," I told the appraiser. "I've looked in the attic and the basement, but I haven't found it."

With that, Jen and I were done. We went out for dinner to Vito's, our favorite Italian restaurant, and luxuriated in the calm away from my grandfather's house.

"What do you think we'll get for the place?" Jen asked, as she sipped her Primitivo.

"I'll bet we can get three-fifty. What do you want to do with that kind of windfall?"

"You know I've always wanted a place at the beach. Lincoln City or Depoe Bay. Would you be up for that?" She pursed her lips. "You look distracted. What are you thinking about?"

"I can't get my mind off my grandfather. Why did he stay in that house all by himself for sixteen years?"

"Maybe the answer is in his journal."

I nodded. "That's what I'm hoping."

16 May

I have read the entire manuscript. I went slowly, making editorial comments along the way, correcting spelling and grammatical errors, suggesting a turn of phrase here and there. But now that I am finished, the enormity of what I have done is haunting me. I have helped Anton with a book which will make him a pariah. I think he knows science better than he does the human heart.

The Argument Against Space Travel. *An innocuous enough title. Except it is not a novel. It is the shattering of so deeply held a myth that it staggers me to imagine the consequences. With elegant mathematics, cutting edge astrophysics, and a startling grasp of the biology, chemistry, and medicine involved, Anton has proved beyond the shadow of a doubt the impossibility of manned interstellar flight.*

Ad astra, per aspera be damned. We will never reach the stars. We have never been visited by aliens from another world. The speed of light is an absolute limit that cannot be contravened. There will never be faster-than-light travel, no folding space to flash through wormholes, no warp drive, no suspended animation from which the traveler awakes after a flight of fifty or a hundred years.

And how will people react? How will they respond to the destruction of a belief so deeply embedded in the collective psyche? The message is clear. We are quarantined from the rest of the universe, imprisoned in our insignificant solar system. Even the long-anticipated trips to Mars will lose their luster. After all is said and done, a colony there was to be a staging area to launch us beyond the nine planets. Now all will know we are locked in a closet, abandoned on an island in a sea so vast we shall never reach another shore.

And Anton has not a clue.

I sat back in my chair and exhaled. Could it be possible? Had Anton given irrefutable proof against interstellar space flight—and would the consequences be as dire as Gregor predicted? Did people really care as much as he imagined, or had dementia begun its subtle attack on his ability to reason? More than ever, I wanted to find that manuscript.

I was having trouble sleeping. I saw my grandfather busying himself in that house, washing dishes and laundry, mopping floors, trapped as surely within those walls as he claimed we are in our solar system. And now the rift beginning in his relationship with Anton. He sounded so convinced that Anton's manuscript would be destructive, would dash the hopes of countless people. What would he do?

This was a whiskey night. I poured myself a glass of Bushmill's over ice and returned to the journal.

1 June

Anton is adamant. He insists on publishing the manuscript.

"Remember Copernicus and Galileo," I plead. "Labeled heretics. Condemned by the authorities of the day. Galileo on house arrest for the remainder of his life."

"We are already on house arrest," he says. "What will change?"

"You underestimate the emotional impact of contrary ideas. Everybody will hate you. Everyone will be disappointed, disillusioned. You steal hope from them. You steal the stars! Then they will blame you when they get depressed, when they have problems at work, when they have a family crisis. When they get a flat tire for God's sake! You will be Anton, the maker of malaise, the despot of despair, the purveyor of pain."

"You sound like an adolescent girl, Gregor. So dramatic. No one cares about space anymore."

"But they do," I protest, "even if they do not know it. It is deep, deep within their unconscious, but it is there. That yearning. That reach. That driving hope, even when they look only at the ground."

But he will not listen. I know not what to do. I love him desperately, but I am appalled at the havoc he will wreak, the hurt he will provoke.

It was 2:00 AM. I stood looking out the bedroom window

at the Milky Way, shimmering like a burial shroud above the earth. I felt uneasy. Was Anton stealing something from me as well?

"What's the matter with you, honey? Come to bed."

"I can't sleep. I'm stuck in that house, listening to those two old men argue. I don't know how much is real. How much is my whacked-out grandfather. It's all so bizarre."

"I noticed you didn't eat much supper. Are you coming down with something?"

"I haven't had much appetite for awhile."

"Maybe you should stop reading that journal."

"I can't, Jen. I can't."

15 July

I have spent weeks pleading, cajoling, arguing with Anton, and now he says he is done with me. He says he cannot abide a lover who will not support him in his life's work. I overheard him on the phone with an old contact of his at the university, discussing how to go about publishing his book. What am I to do? Shall I rush like a lemming to the precipice with him? Or do I do whatever I can to stop the impending disaster?

"When my manuscript is in the hands of my agent, Gregor, I am leaving you," he announced at dinner last night.

"Shush," I said. "I have made you lamb chops. Your favorite. Eat and do not talk about such things."

"It is true," he insisted. "You are holding me back."

"I am trying to stop you from destroying yourself! Do you know how people will react when you have disillusioned them so thoroughly? Disabused them of their

myths? Do you think they will take that lightly?"

"You old fool. You make it sound like I am killing God."

"Nietzsche took care of that already. You are killing all they have left. Do you want to be the next German to wreak havoc on the world? Do you want that on your conscience? They will hate you. They will point their fingers and say terrible things. They will lampoon you in the press. Your name will be synonymous with all that is wrong in their lives and in society."

"You are daft," he said. And with that, he threw his napkin on the table and left the room without eating another mouthful.

What am I to do?

I was inattentive at work. Arguing with Jen. Thank goodness we had hired the appraiser. At least that part of my life was taken care of. The estate sale was scheduled for next weekend and we anticipated a decent return. My grandfather, daft as he may have been, had had excellent taste in furnishings. Unfortunately, there had been no sign of Anton's manuscript, which apparently had never been published. The house would not give up all its secrets, but I was determined to finish the journal in one last marathon sitting. Maybe then I could get on with the rest of my life.

11 August

Anton has not spoken with me in two weeks. I cook and serve him dinner and we sit there silently. Neither of us is eating very much. We no longer listen to music. The house is like a tomb.

His agent is coming on the 18th to pick up the manuscript. Anton has been in telephone conversation with *an editor he had used on a previous project. It feels as though the ground itself quakes beneath me. Anton will be moving out the day after he turns over the book, leaving me forever.*

I know what I must do, but it sickens me.

17 August

"You have not taken your insulin," I tell him.
"Yes, I have." His first words all month.
"I know you are leaving me, but I still love you, and I want you to be well. You missed your dose."

He knit his brows and frowned. I was counting on his occasional forgetfulness. He injected himself again.

I put the journal down. My grandfather a murderer? How could it be? I shook my head back and forth. Eccentric maybe, but homicidal? I needed a drink. A stiff one.

"I don't like the expression on your face," Jen said, as she walked in. "It's that damned book, isn't it? I'm sorry we ever found it. Please get rid of it."

"I'm almost done," I countered.

"Well, I'm going out with Julie. There's some leftovers in the fridge for your dinner. And I don't want to see you reading that thing when I get home. Clear?"

"Yes, boss."

I could see the sweat beginning to bead on his forehead and feel his body begin to tremble.
"I am not well, Gregor. Get me some orange juice. Maybe that candy in the cupboard."
"I already gave you some juice. You are just confused. Come into the bedroom and lie down. You will be

fine in a moment."

I put my arm around his shoulders and helped him down the hall. His heart was fluttering like a bird's. Just as we reached the bed, he stiffened in the throes of a seizure. His feet would no longer move, so I dragged him the last few feet and gently laid him down. His body relaxed, and he lapsed into unconsciousness.

I looked down at the man I loved so much. "You stole my heart as well as the stars, dear one." I climbed into bed beside him and drew his upper body into an awkward embrace. I stroked his hair and smoothed the grimace from his face.

How long did we lie together? By the time I relinquished my grasp of him, the sun had almost set. His chest no longer rose and fell with the gentle rhythm of breathing. His eyes were open and staring sightlessly out the window at the closing of the day.

"Did you know, Anton, that Saint Thomas Aquinas deliberately stopped writing his masterwork, the Summa Theologiae, *before he had finished it? On his deathbed he revealed that he had had a mystical experience. He said, 'All that I have written seems to me like so much straw compared with what I have seen.' Have you had that vision, too, Anton?"*

"Yes, my love."

I nodded. "There are even reports that as he lay dying, Thomas recanted and asked that his works be burned. Probably apocryphal. That dying wish was not honored." I stroked his cheek with my finger. "What is your final wish, my Saint Anton Werner?"

"Burn it, Gregor. Please burn it."

"I pledge to you that I shall."

I got up and lifted him from the bed. "You are heavier than you look. Just give me a moment to help you to the living room." I held him under the arms and dragged him down the hall. Once in the living room, I propped him in his favorite chair in front of the fireplace. In a few minutes, I had kindled a warm fire. "Let me get your book. I will be right back." I ran to his room and collected his manuscript, then hurried back to the fireplace.

I looked down at the title page of The Argument Against Space Travel, *then balled it up in my hands and threw it on the fire. "The world was not ready for this. Do you not agree?"*

"Of course, Gregor. You have always known best. Make sure to destroy it all."

One page at a time, I offered his book to the hungry flames. The living room flickered brightly with each morsel I fed to the fire. Anton looked on without emotion, the flames reflected in his unmoving eyes.

"Done." I turned to my lover and kissed him on the forehead. "It is time to say goodbye. I will miss you for the rest of my life."

A single tear trickled down my cheek as I dialed 911.

I closed the journal and exhaled the breath I hadn't known I was holding. What was I feeling? I shook my head as I struggled to extricate myself from that claustrophobic world my grandfather had inhabited. I was glad Jen wasn't home. Glad I didn't have to explain the tears in my eyes.

I poured myself another drink and felt the heat of the alcohol on my tongue and in my throat. "Your secret is safe with me, Grandpa," I said to the empty kitchen.

With a kind of grim determination, I stood up, grabbed the journal, and opened the glass slider onto our back patio. Once outside, I arranged kindling in our fire pit

88

and soon had a respectable blaze going.

Then I fed another book to another fire, a single page at a time.

Layla's Brownies

She turned in at the Green Cross sign and parked her little red Sentra in the first available slot. A brief spasm of arthritis pain in her knee made her wince. The overcast sky promised rain before nightfall.

As she walked to the front door, she chuckled to herself, recalling her first visit to HSH Cannabis Dispensary six months ago.

"Welcome to Herb Sells Herb," said the cheerful proprietor. He had shoulder-length black hair and a full beard. Both arms sported sleeves of brilliant tattoos. "I'm Herb. How can I help you today?"

"Herb? Really?"

"Yeah, it's pretty corny. It was my brother's idea. He bankrolled me to get started, so I kinda had to go along with it. No bank loans, you know."

"I know. Feds aren't very happy with recreational marijuana, are they? Cash business only, right?"

"Yep. Can't use any credit cards here. Bummer, huh?"

"You worry about getting robbed?"

The man stepped back from the counter, a look of worry creasing his face. "All the time. But we've got lots of cameras."

She smiled. "I'm Layla, and I've got no plans to pull a Bonnie and Clyde. You're safe with me."

Herb exhaled and offered his hand in greeting. "Glad to hear that. Pleased to meet you, Layla. Feel free to walk around and check out the place. I'm really proud of our emporium."

Her eyes were drawn to a display case filled with wildly shaped blown-glass pipes, whose intricate designs and colors were like Chihuly glass sculptures in miniature.

"These are so beautiful," she said.

"Those are dab rigs or oil rigs. They're waterpipes for vaporizing extracts and oils."

Layla laughed out loud. "Those are so far from the bongs we cobbled together from PVC pipe when I was young."

"When was that?"

"Way before you were born, Herb. Early seventies. When I was in graduate school."

"You don't look that old, Layla."

"Thanks. Turned the big seven-oh last week. Can hardly believe it."

"And you've smoked all this time?" His arched eyebrows almost reached his hairline.

Layla heard the incredulity in his tone and smiled at the surprised look on his face. "No, no. I stopped right after school. Didn't want to screw up my new job. Then I just got out of the habit. Kind of lost its appeal. A glass of wine is all I need now."

"Well, what brings you in then?"

"My mother. She's going on ninety-three. Chronic pain. Not much appetite. Trouble sleeping. She's tried all kinds of medicines, but nothing seems to work much. Thought I'd try this for her."

"Does she have a medical card?"

"Hell, no! She missed marijuana by a whole generation. She'd have a fit if she even knew I was in here. Jeanine would no more use marijuana than vote Democratic."

"So how would you get her to use it?"

"Well, she'd never smoke anything. But she has a

sweet tooth and loves my brownies. Back in the day, I made a killer brownie."

Herb pointed to a display case in the corner. "We've got lots of edibles. There's packs of ready-made brownies and chocolate chip cookies. Hard candy. Chewy candy. Dark chocolate bars. Take a look."

Layla strolled down the aisle, shaking her head from side to side. "Sometimes I wish I could hop in a time machine and go back to 1971. I'd tell my college buddies, 'In the future, weed is legal and there's a shop on every corner!' There is no way on this planet they'd believe me."

She stroked her chin. "I don't think I want to go store-bought. I want to make my mother my own recipe brownies. I'll just add a special ingredient I won't tell her about."

"Of course you can use oils and extracts in your baking. Or you can go the old-fashioned way. We have lots of varieties of locally-grown flower. But the rules are different for recreational and medical use. The max you can buy is an ounce a day, which is still quite a bit. Medical users can get 24 ounces per day. And I can sell you four plants if you want to try to grow some on your own."

"Oh, no. I have a black thumb. I'm death to plants. But I had a friend when I lived back east years ago. He had grow-lights and the whole nine yards. Said his secret was to give a little sugar water to the plants just before harvesting them. Called his stuff Rhode Island Red. It was pretty good, as I recall."

"Well, this will probably be a lot more potent than that, so experiment carefully. I'd recommend some of this organically-grown herb. I've been to their farm and it's really pristine."

Layla walked through the front door and into the vestibule, where the sign above the entry bell read HAVE YOUR PHOTO ID READY. She pulled out her driver's license and pushed the button.

"Hi, Layla. Good to see you again," said Herb, as he opened the inner door.

"Hey, there. I expected to see your new guy today. Had my ID all ready."

"He's out sick, so I've pulled a double. How's your mom doing?"

"I think she's turning a corner. At least, she's not complaining as much as she had been before the brownies. I took her out to dinner last night, and she ate the whole meal, even the salad. I think she's sleeping better, as far as I can tell. The best news is, I think the pain has dialed down a few notches."

"That's great. You must be relieved."

"Of course, I can never tell her I'm feeding her grass. I'd never hear the end of it. And she'd quit using it on the spot, even though it was helping her."

"Ouch! Well, I'll never tell. You want an ounce of the regular?"

She nodded and Herb rang up the order. "You remember what I told you the day we met? You know, about going back in a time machine? I've been thinking about that again." She took the bag he handed her. "Ever notice how the truth changes? Back then, weed was dangerous. It was in the same boat as heroin and meth. You could go to prison for it. It was the 'gateway drug' leading you into the hard stuff. Now it's like alcohol, for goodness sake. Ordinary as hot dogs. Shops sprouting up everywhere. It's so ridiculous."

"I guess that's why I'm glad I've got the Bible. The real truth never changes."

Layla was taken aback. "Wow. That came out of nowhere."

"Sorry. I don't usually preach at work." He concluded the sale and closed the register. "You a Christian, Layla, if you don't mind my asking?"

She pursed her lips, then frowned. "Oh, I tried it. Went to Sunday School as a kid. Youth group. But it was too hard. Trusting God to take care of me when my own father wouldn't? Not gonna happen." She turned toward the door, then stopped and turned back around. "But I confess, I do like Pontius Pilate. I think he's my favorite guy in the Bible."

"What an unusual choice. How come?"

"Because he has the guts to ask Jesus, 'What is truth?' And later, he just washes his hands of the whole mess. I think I would've done the same thing if I were in his shoes."

"Whew! That's a lot to think about."

"And by-the-by, isn't this a strange profession for a Christian? Selling dope?"

Herb chuckled. "Human beings are always trying to change their brain chemistry. Ever watch a one-year-old who's just learned to walk twirl around and around to make herself dizzy? My daughter does that. Figured it out all by herself. How about that cup of coffee you had with breakfast or that glass of wine with dinner tonight? I'm not saying Jesus would have had a toke with his friends after a long day of preaching, but that was a whole lot of wine he made at that wedding party in Cana. More than a hundred gallons."

Now it was Layla's turn to laugh. "You're a good friend, Herb. I like coming into your shop. I'll see you again soon."

94

It was a short drive to the Cinnamon Hill Retirement Village her mother had moved into four years ago. The rain pelted her car, and Layla was glad to find a parking place under the roof of the long carport. She pulled the hood of her jacket up over her hair and ran toward the door of the apartment. She heard her mother stir inside when she rang the bell.

"Coming." The door opened slowly. "You'll catch your death out there in weather like this. Come in, darling." Jeanine was wearing a long blue sweater with a wide collar. Her white hair stood out in unruly tufts across her head. Her wrinkled face smiled warmly at her daughter.

"Looks like you're about ready for another perm, Mom. I'll stop by the main office and schedule it for you on my way out."

"And you colored your hair again, didn't you? You're blonder than last week."

"My roots were showing, Mom. Can't have that, can we?" She removed her wet coat and hung it on the hook by the door.

"You're about two shades too light. You seeing someone?"

"That's quite a leap! I've lightened my hair so I must be dating?" Layla extended a plastic bag to her mother. "Brought you a crossword puzzle magazine and a book of cryptograms. Kept 'em dry." As she followed her mother into the kitchen, she added, "How are you doing for brownies?"

"I'll have the last one for supper tonight. Nobody makes them as good as you do." She scrunched up her face and said, "I don't suppose you could make me a double batch and bring them by tomorrow?"

"Sure, Mom. They're my specialty. But don't overdo it. I don't want your blood sugar getting all out of whack."

She smiled. "You went through them pretty fast this week."

A furtive look came over Jeanine's face but was gone before Layla could comment on it. "What can I tell you, honey? Brownies are my weakness. Can I get you something? A cup of coffee? Some tea maybe?"

"Tea would be nice, thanks. Chamomile. It's a little late in the day for caffeine."

As Jeanine put on a pot to boil, she said over her shoulder, "George made a pass at me in the community room a couple days ago."

"What?"

"George. We were just finishing Mahjong and he leaned over and put his hand on mine on the table. Asked me to go for a walk with him after dinner."

"Did you?"

"Are you serious? He had the nerve to pat my derrière on the elevator when we rode down to the dining room."

"So what did you do?"

"I called him a dirty old man and threatened to slap him in the face if he tried that again."

When the pot began to whistle, she poured hot water into two cups and brought them to the table. "Here's the chamomile," she said, as she offered a box of teabags to her daughter. "Then we get to the dining room, and as Thomas pushes my chair in to the table, he kisses me on the forehead! 'Why, you old geezer!' I tell him. 'You keep your lips to yourself or I'll push your front teeth through them!'"

Layla coughed to stop herself from chuckling. "They must think you're hot stuff, Mama."

"That's not all. 'I've been married once,' I say, 'and that was quite enough for me, thank you very much.' So he says, 'I'm not asking you to marry me, Jeanine, but we could be friends...' And the look on his face says it all. He's even dirtier than George! So I just got up and switched tables."

Layla laughed in spite of herself. "Wow! I didn't realize the men around here were so frisky."

"Well, I set them straight. You'd better believe it. They won't be giving me any more grief."

Layla raised the cup to her lips and inhaled the fragrant steam. "Other than that, how are things here in the village, Mom?"

Jeanine's face lit up. "Really great, honey. I've made some new friends. We get together a couple times a week. Play Mexican Train or split up into groups of four for Mahjong. Card games, too, like Hand and Foot or Canasta. We've all signed up for the trip next week to the casino." She reached across the table and grasped her daughter's hand. "I'm happy, Layla."

Her daughter smiled back. "That's so good, Mama. You deserve it."

They chatted for another forty-five minutes before Layla took her leave. "I'm going over into the main building, and I'll book you for a perm. OK?"

"Tuesday mornings or Thursday mornings are best for me."

"You got it. I'll swing by tomorrow just before lunch with your brownies."

As she stepped outside, she was glad it had stopped raining. It was a short walk to the front entrance, which was surrounded with new potted plants. A sign inside advertised the upcoming bus trip to the casino. She saw that the hair salon was closed, so she walked over to the director's office and knocked.

"Are you able to book hair appointments for the salon?" she asked the young woman behind the desk. "I'd like to schedule one for my mother."

"I'm afraid not, but I'll give you the direct number to the salon so you can call them first thing in the morning." As she wrote down the telephone number and handed it to her, she said, "You're Jeanine's daughter, aren't you? I thought I recognized you. I'm Savannah Grey." She extended her hand. "I have to tell you, your mother is doing so much better. You know, she used to hide out in that apartment of hers. Often would skip coming to meals. When I did see her, she'd be complaining about this thing or that. Now she's done a complete one-eighty. I mean, she's turned into a real social butterfly. You wouldn't know it's the same woman. Never misses a meal. Attends all the group activities and functions. She's even started her own group. They meet two afternoons a week and play card games or dominoes. Sometimes they just sit there and carry on. You can hear them laughing all over the main level. It's really wonderful."

"Thanks, Savannah. You've made my day."

As Layla left and got into her car, she thought, *Maybe some things do stay true. The old remedies are the best remedies.*

The next day, after Layla had made a quick stop to deliver the brownies, Jeanine carefully cut them into two-inch squares to make sure there would be enough to go around. At three o'clock, she put the serving platter full of the chocolate confections on the seat of her walker and proudly strutted into the main building. Several of her friends had already gathered at the large round table in the community room where they held their get-togethers.

"Ooooh!" crooned Victoria. "They look even better today!"

"I want at least two," said George, as he licked his

lips.

"Well, I've got plenty. I had Layla make a double batch."

"You're a good soul, Jeanine. And your daughter makes the best brownies I've ever tasted," said Thomas. "Won't you have one with us today?"

"Sorry, but I've never liked brownies. I just haven't had the heart to tell Layla that. And now that I know you folks like them so much, I guess I never will. You just make sure it never gets back to her. OK? As far as she knows, brownies are my favorite thing in the world. It makes her feel good to bake them for me. So let's keep it that way."

"You bet, Jeanine," said Esther with a conspiratorial wink. "We'll make sure she never finds out. You keep bringin' 'em and we'll keep eatin' 'em!"

"And mum's the word!" said George.

A chorus of "Amens!" sounded from the group.

In moments, the platter had made the rounds and the brownies disappeared.

"Mexican Train?" said Jeanine.

The Bird-Feeder

I'*m sure I can learn to type one-handed on my...on my...*
He slammed the arm of the recliner with his left fist and returned his attention to the action outside the window.

Black-capped Chickadee, he thought. *Small bird. Likes mixed woods, thickets, and neighborhoods. Spotted Towhee. Rufous sides, white belly, bright red eye. Likes open woods and thickets but does well around towns. An American Goldfinch and a Red Crossbill! My lucky day!*

Bertram Turner was convinced that if he remembered his years of bird-watching and kept mentally cataloging the ones that came to the feeder, the stimulation would strengthen his damaged brain and restore his ability to speak. *Cerebral calisthenics*, he told himself.

His daughter Anne had set up the red leather lounge chair in her den so her father could look out the bay window at the back lawn and the forest behind her house.

"Should be some interesting things to see, Dad. Deer come down here every now and then. If you're lucky, maybe some wild turkeys or a stray coyote. And Tucker just set up that bird-feeder. The little critters have begun to find it this week. You should get quite a show."

He was looking out the window now at the pink frills and lace of an ornamental cherry tree in full bloom. At the forest's edge, he saw flowering dogwood and magnolia and western crab apple. Farther away, he could make out the deep green of giant Douglas firs. But the principal attraction was his grandson Tucker's new bird-feeder, a large cylinder filled with sunflower seeds and capped with a clear plastic hood that protected it from getting hijacked by gray squirrels.

Thinking of nine-year-old Tucker made him wince. *Would I rather be Darth Vader or a zombie?* When Tucker had visited him in the hospital just after his stroke, the little boy became frightened by the hiss of the ventilator machine and asked his mother, "Is Grandpa turning into Darth Vader?" Then a week ago, Tucker came home from school early and caught Bert exercising with his walker, grunting unintelligible sounds, dragging his uncooperative right leg forward with each step. That night Tucker awoke screaming from a nightmare, claiming that his grandfather was a zombie coming to eat his brains.

I don't want to munch anybody's brains, Bert thought, *but I'd sure like to replace the one I've got with a better model.* He knew he shouldn't complain. The stroke on the left side of his brain was a piece of cake compared with his friend Zane's brain stem stroke. Zane couldn't speak either, but he couldn't move anything except his eyes. Locked-in syndrome, they called it. Bert shuddered when he tried to imagine how it felt to be imprisoned like that in one's own body.

Still, he did feel trapped. A retired college teacher robbed of his ability to speak? Is that some kind of cosmic joke? Expressive aphasia. It affected his writing as well, on top of trying to manipulate a pen with his left hand. He knew the words he wanted to say but he couldn't find them. Words were as elusive as the bright-sided Brook Trout he used to fly-fish for in the cold rocky streams of New Hampshire. The frustration made him want to scream, but he couldn't even do that. The sounds he did manage to make erupted from his throat in guttural gasps that terrified his grandson. After that fiasco, he had promised himself to practice speaking only when he was alone or working with his therapist. When others were present, he would rely on the birds. He knew they would help get his brain back on track. They were the ticket to his recovery.

He glanced at the walker parked next to the chair, a grim reminder that he would not resolve his right-sided paralysis without a lot of effort. He was beginning to get some movement from his leg, but progress was slow, and it was hard using the walker with only his left hand to grip it. His right arm and hand curled like a raptor's claw across his chest, totally useless.

Is this my punishment, God? The big get-even? He decided that counting Purple Finches and White-crowned Sparrows was giving him ample time for self-pity. *Would I have done anything differently if I had known I would end up like this?* That was the million-dollar question, the great what-if. *If I had known I would be at the mercy of my daughter, would I have treated her better growing up? And what about her mother Daphne? Would I have been kinder? Made it a marriage of equals instead of driving her away with my constant complaining?*

Of course, he knew what-if's were impossible. There were facts he had to deal with. He was here in this chair, partially paralyzed, unable to speak. But he would heal. He was determined to walk and talk again.

Red-breasted Nuthatch, he thought, *looking like a Chickadee dressed for speed. And there goes a flock of Bushtits. Busy day.*

He must have dozed because he heard Anne in the kitchen, moving pots and pans as she prepared supper. Probably saw he was asleep when she got home and didn't wake him to say hello. He sat there without moving as he heard her husband Jared come in through the garage door.

"I think we need him out of here, honey." Jared spoke in a low voice. "Look at the effect he's having on Tucker. The poor kid's scared out of his wits. And you don't owe him anything after what he did to you. Your mother

102

was smart enough to beat feet a long time ago."

They must think I can't hear them.

"Tucker's doing fine. One little nightmare is all."

"You call that little? I held him for half an hour before he calmed down. 'Grandpa's not really a zombie, is he?' over and over again. C'mon, for God's sake! What are you trying to prove?"

I hadn't known it was that bad. Poor Tucker. I love you, Grandson. I would never do anything to hurt you.

"We're all the family he has left. I don't feel right about turning our backs on him."

"He turned his back on you, didn't he? Anyway, we're not doing that to him. We'd be getting him the best treatment money can buy. That new place, Peppertree Estates. It's only about three miles from here and it has all the services he needs right there on the campus. I didn't tell you, but I checked it out. It's beautiful. And it's close enough that you can visit him every day if you want."

I don't want to live in Peppertree Estates. I want to live here, where my birds are. C'mon, Anne. Stick up for your old man.

"I don't know, darling. I've heard stories. You know. People get depressed when they're left in places like that. Sometimes they just give up on living."

"But we wouldn't be leaving him. That's what I'm saying. We would see him every day."

"It's not the same. How would you feel if someday Tucker kicks you to the curb?"

Jared harrumphed. "I'm pouring myself a glass of wine. I'll be in the den with...Grandpa Zombie and that damned bird-feeder he's fixated on."

Bert was glad the Towhee had come back. He needed to take his mind off that conversation.

"So you're awake?" Jared pulled up a chair next to

the recliner and set his glass of wine down on an end table. "How was your day? Lots of birds?" He waited a few moments, smiled, and then said, "Mine was crap. I've got a class of eighth graders I'd like to launch to the moon. Or maybe put 'em on a boat in the ocean and not bring 'em back until they're about twenty-two. I swear I only get to teach about fifteen percent of the time. The other eighty-five percent, I'm babysitting apprentice thugs and gang wannabes. I think I need to look for a private school to teach in."

Do you want to send me out on a boat, too?

"Hey, let me turn you around so you can see the TV."

No! No! I don't want to watch the stupid TV. Stop!

Jared swung the chair around ninety degrees, never once looking at Bert's face, which was contorting in displeasure. He turned on the set and called over his shoulder, "The news'll be on in a few." Then he picked up his glass and walked back out into the kitchen.

Anne came into the den with her father's supper a few minutes later and caught him struggling to turn the chair back toward the bay window. "Whoa! Careful, Dad. You'll fall and be in a world of hurt. I can move the chair back for you." She yelled into the kitchen, "Jared. What the hell? You know Dad doesn't like TV."

"Oh, sorry. I forgot."

She put the plate down on the coffee table and turned the chair back to the window. "OK, Dad. Make yourself comfortable again. I thought it might be easier for you to eat in here. I'll set your plate on this tray table. I've got some nice big napkins we can set over you in case you have any spills." She set one napkin on his lap and tucked another under his collar to protect the front of his shirt.

You don't want me eating in front of Tucker, do

you? Well, I can't blame you. I can make things pretty unappetizing. He pursed the left side of his lips. Man, I'd kill for a glass of red wine about now, and to hell with what the doctor says.

When Anne was satisfied with the arrangement, she said, "Take your time. I'll bring you in a glass of water and then come back after we've eaten to see how you're doing."

Bert gave her his half-smile. *Thank you, honey.*

She went back into the kitchen to retrieve his water. Then she brought the serving bowls to the family at the dining room table.

"How come Grandpa isn't eating with us tonight?" Tucker asked.

"You know he gets really messy sometimes," his father said. "Chokes. Spills things. He's getting better with his left hand, but your mother and I thought it would be easier on everybody if we gave him more time and privacy."

"OK." Tucker helped himself to two large meatballs and plopped them on his mound of penne pasta. Then he spread a generous pat of butter on a slice of warm Italian bread. "It smells good, Ma. I can't wait."

Jared led the family in the saying of Grace and then everyone began to eat.

Meanwhile, Bert navigated a forkful of pasta to his mouth, only to have it derail into his lap at the last second. *This is such fun. So glad it's a white napkin.* He was more successful with a piece of meatball. As he fussed with his fork, he eaves-dropped on the conversation in the dining room.

"I'm not so sure Grandpa should be living with us, Tucker. What do you think?" It was Jared's voice.

"Is it because of me? Because I had that nightmare? I'm OK now. Honest. It won't happen again."

"No, no, it's not because of you. It's just that your mother and I want to put family first. Your grandfather is alone all day here. If he were in a place like that new Peppertree Estates, he'd have friends around him all day long. And the doctors and nurses are right there."

"Your father and I just want the best for everybody, that's all."

"But I love Grandpa. Please don't send him away. He needs us."

Wow, kid. Way to go. You're on my team.

"Well, we're just thinking about it. We haven't made up our minds yet."

Right. Famous last words. Well, you predicted it, Mr. Dylan. The times they are a-changin'. I better make sure the door knob doesn't hit me on the way out.

A half-hour later, he had managed to eat most of what was on his plate. The red-splotched napkins showed the wounds of battle. His mood had turned morose. He found himself thinking of Daphne fifteen years ago. His body had worked perfectly, but his brain didn't, even back then.

"You make it sound like I don't do anything right." She had removed her apron and hung it on the hook by the stove. Her long dark hair fell over her slumped shoulders. Her eyes looked as though she were about to cry.

"Can't you do a simple thing like cook a supper without dirtying every dish in the house?"

"Don't you like my cooking?"

"That's not what I'm talking about. The kitchen is a disaster."

"But I made you beef bourguignon."

"I can't talk to you." He shook his head and stalked out of the kitchen. "Did you vacuum today?" he

*called from the living room, as he dropped into his favorite
chair, newspaper in hand.*

*"Yes," she said. Then under her breath she added,
"And three loads of laundry. And I showed two houses and
wrote up an offer, too."*

*"Well, you didn't do a very good job. There's still
some popcorn kernels in the corner from your daughter the
other night."*

*Bert heard the door to the garage slam and the
sound of her car starting up.*

Anne walked in and startled him from his reverie. "I've got
a warm wash cloth to clean you up, Dad. Here, let me get
those napkins. Looks like you enjoyed your dinner." She
fretted over him for a few minutes and then handed him his
evening paper. "Need anything else?" He waved her away
with his left hand.

Later, he heard the family in the TV room. He hated
the canned laughter of the sitcoms. Before he knew it,
Tucker was running in to kiss him good night.

"Sleep well, Grandpa."

Bert raised his left hand and stroked the boy's
cheek. *Good night, champ. Thanks for backing your old
grandpa.*

Anne had given her father the downstairs bedroom
so he wouldn't have to negotiate the stairs. Getting ready
for bed was an ordeal. He insisted on doing it himself,
despite Jared's offers to help him get out of his clothes and
into his pajamas. Brushing his teeth with his left hand was
a pain in the ass. Flossing was out of the question. He
avoided looking in the mirror at his drooping face.

A half-hour later, he lay in bed staring at the
ceiling, cursing his rebellious body. *I was a total shit to
Anne when she was growing up. Made fun of her teeth.*

Wouldn't let her use makeup at sixteen when all of her friends were. Hounded that kid Aiden out of her life. His eyes misted over. *Wouldn't let her try out for any of the high school plays. Told her it was too distracting. She needed to keep her mind on homework and prepping for college.* Tears had begun to flow. *I never made her feel pretty. Never told her I loved her. And then I...*

Sleep wouldn't come. How was Anne managing to care for him after all he had done to her?

He heard the sounds of a breeze outside, like whispers in a crowded theater before the performance begins. A full moon had risen, casting eerie shadows of moving branches on the wall by the bed. Then the distinct hoot of an owl.

Great Horned Owl. Yellow eyes. Large ear tufts. Hunts mostly at night.

He shuddered at an odd thought. *Are the birds a help or a hindrance? Are they distracting me from what I'm supposed to be doing?* The curse of being a retired second-rate Psychology professor at a second-rate community college was that he had memorized all the Psychology 101 he had taught his undergraduates. Erik Erikson's Eight Ages of Man—the eight stages of psychosocial development—bullied their way into his awareness. He knew he had done a terrible job with stage seven—middle adulthood. That was the stage where parenting was the primary task and care, the main virtue. He imagined a large red *F* stamped on his report card. *I'm sorry, Anne.*

Nonsense! No use getting maudlin. I did what I had to do. It was for her own good. The owl hooted again. *Wingspan forty-five inches. Varied diet. Mostly small mammals.*

He was awakened by sounds from the kitchen and the rush

of the upstairs shower. The sun had risen on a perfect spring morning. A light breeze was blowing, filling the air with the pink and white snow of petals from the flowering trees.

He struggled out of bed and began the laborious job of showering. Anne had put a plastic chair in the stall and that helped. Still, it would be the better part of an hour before he was dressed and ready for breakfast. With the time pressures of school and work, Anne had taken to leaving a plate for him that he could warm in the microwave at his leisure. He wouldn't see the family until Tucker got home from school at about three-thirty.

By eleven o'clock he was ensconced in his chair at the bay window. He had missed the busy early morning feeding, so traffic at the bird-feeder was light. He looked at his watch. His speech therapist was due at one. Time to relax and catch a cat-nap after his poor sleep the night before.

It seemed only moments before the doorbell was ringing and Sheri arrived. She knew to wait until Bert could make it to the door.

"How's my favorite patient today?" said the petite blonde-haired therapist, who was younger than his daughter. She was pretty in a pixie sort of way. Her effusive cheerfulness sometimes drove Bert crazy.

"Argh," he said, sounding like the punch-line from a pirate joke.

"OK. We'll work on that."

Bert fought to make his mouth and tongue move properly. He utilized all her strategies, but still felt he wasn't making enough progress.

"Be patient with yourself, Mr. Turner. Your brain is healing, but you have to give it time."

I don't have time. They're going to send me away.

"Let's try this exercise, shall we?"

And so it went. An hour later, he was exhausted and glad the lesson was over. Once Sheri had left, he made it to the kitchen and poured himself a glass of iced tea. He placed his beverage on the seat of his walker and shuffled back to his perch in the den.

I'm back, birdies. Everything all right? Oh, oh. Something else is watching my bird-feeder. On a low branch in the thicket by the forest's edge, he spied a bird about twelve inches tall. *Sharp-shinned Hawk. Watch out, birds! Danger! Danger!* A Dark-eyed Junco flew toward the feeder. With a flash of wings, the hawk swooped in and snatched the bird in its talons. In the blink of an eye, it disappeared with its meal back into the woods. Silent. Unforgiving.

Bert hung his head. *That was about how quick I got rid of Anne twenty years ago.*

"If you're not willing to live by my rules, get out!" The heated exchange had been simmering for months, but finally boiled over when Anne came in at eleven o'clock from a date. "Curfew is ten o'clock."

"But Dad, I'm eighteen years old. Ten o'clock is for kids."

"And what's this?" He shoved the pill dispenser into her face.

"My birth control pills? You went through my room? How dare you!"

"I dare, all right, you little slut. You think I'm going to support you staying out late to have sex with your boyfriend?"

Anne turned toward her mother, who was cowering in the corner, her left eye swelling and already turning black.

"I hate you!" she shrieked at him, raising a defiant fist.

He slapped her hard across the face, the blow rocking her head back. She lost her balance for a second, but regained it.

"Fuck you," she said, in a voice barely above a whisper. With that, she turned on her heels and ran to her room.

She came downstairs a few minutes later, dragging a large suitcase. Her mother stood by the front door, weeping.

"Natalie is picking me up. I'll call you when I get settled." She glanced toward the living room, where her father sat reading the newspaper. "I'm outta here." He refused to look up and acknowledge her. Those were the last words she spoke to him, the last words he would hear from her in twenty years.

Tears poured down his face. *Forgive me, Anne. Please, please forgive me.* With his left hand, he wiped at his cheeks. The motion was awkward and angry. *No. I don't deserve your forgiveness. I'm unworthy to be sitting here in your house.* He whimpered unintelligible sounds.

Erikson's eighth and final stage indicted him. *Maturity—I'm supposed to reflect on my life and accept it. But how can I accept what I've done? I've physically and mentally abused my wife and my daughter. I've made a shipwreck of my life and lied to myself about it.* He threw his head back and forth, as though trying to shake off the despair that was settling over him like a dark shroud. *Anne, how can you be so gracious to me?* His shoulders heaved as sobs dammed up for decades burst like a flash flood from deep within him.

His grief became a great, inarticulate wail against

every selfish impulse, every disappointment, every missed opportunity, every failure in his life. His body shook in spasms of remorse.

An hour later, he sat like a dead man, exhausted by the purging. As he stared out the window at his birds, busy in their last feeding of the day, he had a brief glimpse of hope to counter his despair. He remembered the final truth about Erikson's stages: the outcome of any stage isn't fixed but can be altered by later experiences.

When Anne got home from work, the first thing she saw was the piece of paper and the ballpoint pen on the coffee table. "You've written something, Dad? Really? That's wonderful! A breakthrough!" She held up the paper and examined it. In a barely legible scrawl, her father had written the single word, *SORRY,* followed by the letters *P E OK*. "You're sorry?" she said to him.

He raised his left hand and stroked her hair. *It was the first word I could find. The word I lost so many years ago.*

"Is P E Peppertree Estates? Are you saying it's OK if you go to Peppertree Estates?

"Argh," he said.

She leaned over his chair and embraced him. He felt her tears warm on his cheek, her breath sweet on his neck.

And when I can find all the words, Anne, I will tell you how beautiful you are and how much I love you.

Soul Mate

The curtains drawn over the windows filtered the light of the rising sun, swapping the morning outside for a twilight within. He sat facing his wife at the kitchen table, the dregs of his coffee cooling in his cup, swirls of egg yolk drying on his plate like dabs of paint on an artist's palette. The memory of frying bacon lingered in the air.

"Your daughter can never know I am here," Greta said, in a voice that sounded rigid with determination. She pouted at her husband, fixing him with a cold stare. In the dim light, her dark hair was a scarf, wrapping her face in deeper shadow.

Harrison knit his brows and threw up his hands. "*Our* daughter, for goodness' sake. She was only a year old when I married you. You raised her. You're her mother. She loves you."

"You married a Jewish woman. She is Aryan. Police. Gestapo. If she thought I was sitting here with you, she would swoop down on me like the little *frau des Reich* she is." She squinted at her husband. "And she would arrest you in a heartbeat for harboring me."

Harrison shook his head. "It wasn't a crime marrying a Jewish woman back then. No. Katrina loves us. She'd never do anything like that."

"When has love ever been enough? She is ambitious. She would obey her superiors. Feather her nest. Children against parents, neighbors against friends. And I have heard stories about those trains. People get on them and never come back."

"You're wrong about her. She'd never betray family."

"You are so naïve, *liebling*. She thinks I am still in Berlin and you have to keep it that way. And you ought to talk badly about me when she is around. Do not give her any reason to suspect that you would like me back. That would put you at risk."

"Greta..."

"Shush. Now let me help you clear the breakfast dishes."

Harrison stood and gathered their plates. "I'm going to soak these for a few minutes," he said, as he turned on the water in the sink.

The knock on the door startled him. "I forgot. Katrina said she would try to stop by this morning." He turned off the faucet.

Greta bolted for the stairs. "Remember what I said," she warned.

He dried his hands in a dish towel and walked to the front door. "Hello, Kat. New hairdo, I see. Looks good on you."

"Hi, Dad. Sorry to come over so early. Looks like you just got up. Pretty dark in here." When he waved away her concerns, she said, "This is my partner, Peter. We just got our new uniforms. What do you think?"

Harrison extended his hand to the slim, muscular man at her side. The man's grip was firm and confident. "How do you do, Peter? Please come in. The house is a bit of a mess. Just had breakfast and haven't finished picking up yet."

"So what do you think?" Katrina repeated, as she and Peter walked toward the kitchen.

"Very professional, honey. Can I put on a pot of coffee for you?"

"That'd be great, Dad. We've got a few minutes before we need to be back." As she was about to sit down at the kitchen table, she spied the plates in the sink. "What's with all the dishes and cups? Looks like you had company for breakfast."

"Oh, no. No. Just me. I didn't pick up after dinner last night."

"But you're eating? Three meals a day?"

"Sure. Why do you ask?"

"I just worry about you. What with Mom gone and all..."

"I can fend for myself. She never was a great cook."

"I thought you loved her cooking. You'd call and brag to me about what a dinner she'd prepared for you."

Harrison tensed in discomfort. *I'm a terrible liar*, he thought. He could feel sweat begin to moisten his shirt. Greta was right. He'd have to be careful around Katrina, and so far all he'd succeeded in doing was igniting a spark of suspicion.

"I'm glad she's gone," he announced, remembering what Greta had told him. "Good riddance!"

From the look of surprise he saw on Katrina's face, he feared he had overplayed his hand. Peter coughed and changed the subject.

"So how are you spending your days, Mr. Beech? Kat's told me you're retired."

"Writing, mostly. Memoirs."

"I·bet you have some stories to tell."

"Indeed I do, Peter." There was something he didn't like about the young man's eyes. Was it arrogance he saw there? He put on the coffee to brew and sat with them at the table. "Piece of toast? Eggs?"

"No thanks, Mr. Beech. Had breakfast. Just coffee is fine."

Katrina nodded her head in agreement. "Trying to

keep trim, Dad."

Harrison avoided any mention of Greta after that, and the conversation remained pleasantly superficial. When they had finished their coffee, he escorted them to the door.

"Depending on how busy we get, we may sneak by for another coffee tomorrow," Katrina said on the way out.

Only when the door was locked behind them did he release the tension that had built up in his neck and shoulders. He could feel the beginning of a headache in the back of his skull and hoped he could head it off.

His relief was short-lived. He looked out the front window, expecting to see the car pulling away from the curb. Instead, he saw the two officers engaged in a lively discussion on the sidewalk. He didn't like the expression on his daughter's face.

He walked upstairs to find Greta lying on their bed. "Katrina isn't buying it."

She sat up and pursed her lips. "I heard. You were pretty sloppy. I told you to be careful."

"We have to be prepared for her to come back and search the house. You need a place to hide."

"Where?"

"I have some wood in the basement. I can make a false wall here in the closet and camouflage it. It won't be big or comfortable, but it could work."

"It will have to do. I cannot risk leaving the house now if she is already suspicious. She will be watching."

Harrison gathered wood and tools from the basement. The project occupied the rest of his day. Greta lay on the bed and provided what help she could, mostly encouragement.

The fickle spring sun had vanished, overtaken by gunmetal gray clouds rushing up from the south and threatening rain before nightfall.

"Finished," he said, as he backed out of the closet, the hammer still in his hand. "Come here and take a look." He gathered up leftover nails and screws and scraps of wood. "This shelf is really a hatch into the crawlspace I've hidden behind it. Just shimmy in there and pull it shut behind you. There's no light fixture, so it'll be dark. I'll leave a flashlight inside."

She embraced him. "You really love me, don't you, *schatzi*?"

"More than you know. Twenty-five years of marriage. Twenty-five good years." He relinquished his hug, then grasped her by the shoulders. He held her at arms' length and looked into her brown eyes. "You're the love of my life—my soul mate." He smiled and pecked her cheek. "Now let's go have some supper. I have two perfect pork chops."

When they had finished dinner, Harrison poured coffee and cut small slices of chocolate cake. As he raised a forkful of dessert to his lips, he said, "What do you want to do when this..." He swept his left arm in a broad gesture to take in the world around them. "when all this madness is over?"

She closed her eyes for a moment. "I want to sit outside in the sunshine without fear of being arrested. To walk down the street or enter a restaurant and not feel ashamed of who I am. To entertain friends again like we used to." She shook her head. "To live an ordinary life. A normal life."

"And here I thought you might want something on a grander scale—sailing around the world, visiting the museums and libraries of every country, seeing all the earth's natural wonders."

She sighed. "Harry, I have seen enough to know the

madness may never be over. The *Fuhrer* kills for ideas. For beliefs. He orders murder as casually as you order a steak at Benson's Market. And there will always be someone else like him, waiting in the wings, eager for his chance to take the stage."

"I'm glad we didn't have this conversation before dinner," he said. "It doesn't do much for the appetite."

She smiled at him. "Sorry, *schatzi*. I am tired. Can we go to bed?"

"Of course. Go ahead upstairs. I'll just clear these dishes."

When he joined her later, she looked peaceful under the covers, her dark hair swirling about her head on the pillow like a night sky flecked with starlight. "I am almost asleep, *liebling*. Come hold me."

He undressed and slid under the blankets, spooning her body. "You're so beautiful. I could lie with you like this forever."

"You will," she promised. With a deep exhalation, she fell asleep.

The next day, he rose early to finish cleaning up the kitchen and to set the table for breakfast. Soon the smell of coffee roused his sleeping wife, who came downstairs in her best lingerie.

"Now I have more on my mind than eating breakfast," he said, his eyes wide with pleasure.

"Come back to bed. Let me show you what I have for you." She smirked and went back upstairs.

Harrison finished setting the table. He hurried to the staircase just as a loud knock sounded on the front door. Without thinking, he opened it and found himself face-to-face with Katrina and Peter.

"I can smell the coffee, Dad. How about it?"

"Of—of course," he stammered. It wasn't until they had walked past him into the kitchen that he realized his mistake. He shut the door and hurried after them.

"You've set two places, Dad. Who are you expecting?"

"Uh... uh. No one. Just force of habit, I guess."

"Those were her dishes in the sink yesterday, too, weren't they? Do you set a place for Mom at every meal?"

She knows! he thought. *She's here to arrest Greta!* He was sure Katrina could hear the pounding of his heart.

Katrina shook her head back and forth. "I don't know what to say, Dad." She took a deep breath and put her hand on his shoulder. "Anyway, while Peter is here, he can help carry that box of books you've saved for me out to the car. C'mon upstairs, Peter."

Harrison raised his hand to protest but said nothing. *That's just an excuse to check the upstairs. I hope Greta is in the crawlspace.*

Several minutes later, Katrina and Peter came down the stairs, carrying a large box between them. Katrina grunted with the effort. "You can pour us that coffee now while we put this stuff out in the trunk."

Harrison leaned against the wall to steady himself. His heart was still racing. Greta had escaped their discovery. But for how long?

When his daughter and her friend returned inside and came to the table, he set their coffee cups before them. "Can I get you anything else?"

"Oh, no. This will be fine," Peter said.

Harrison shifted uncomfortably in his chair. He looked from his daughter to her partner, afraid they were aware of his increasing unease. *What kind of game are you playing with me? Trying to trip me up? Get me to say something incriminating?* He felt pressure on his chest and found it hard to catch his breath. He hoped they couldn't see his hands shaking.

"I'm worried about you, Dad. Is there something you're not telling me?"

Said the cat to the mouse. "What? No. No. I'm fine. Adjusting." His words were too quick, too nervous. Just then he heard a footstep upstairs. A thrill of panic surged through him, but neither of his visitors showed any sign that they had heard it, too. He picked up a napkin and wiped his brow.

"You don't look so good, Dad. Do you need to see your doctor?"

"No. I told you I'm fine, honey. Maybe I'll go back to bed and get a little more sleep."

"Well, don't let us keep you." She finished her coffee and set down the cup. "We can show ourselves out."

Once they had left, he laid his head down on the kitchen table and wept. Greta found him like that as she padded barefoot into the kitchen.

"You did well, *liebling*," she said, as she stroked his hair and kissed his forehead.

"I don't know how much more of this I can take. She knows I'm lying. It's only a matter of time before she finds you. And then what?" He couldn't stop the tears. "This house is getting so claustrophobic. I'm afraid to go outside. Afraid to leave you alone. What kind of life is this becoming?"

"You are right," she said. "We need a more permanent solution. For now, come to bed."

They spent the better part of the day in bed together, exploring their bodies like newlyweds.

"Come, *schatzi*. Shower with me," said Greta playfully.

120

"We haven't done that since the first year of our marriage."

"Then we have a lot of catching up to do. Come." She grasped his hand and pulled him out of bed and into the bathroom. They were both laughing like children by the time the water got hot. The shower stall filled with steam, cocooning them from the world outside. As their caresses became more urgent, they made love in the warm, wet spray.

"I can't live without you," Harrison said, as they were toweling themselves dry. "I won't let them take you away."

"Of course." She nodded and looked into his eyes. "There is a way."

Once they were dressed, she took him by the hand and led him to the garage. "Leave the door closed. Start the car and open all the windows. We will fall asleep in each other's arms. There will be no pain. We will be together forever."

Harrison looked shocked at first, but he couldn't refute her logic. He opened the passenger side for Greta and watched her get in. Then he went round and slid behind the wheel. With a pang of regret, he started the engine. "Hold me, my love," he said to her, as he buried his face in her hair.

He felt terrible pressure on his chest, as though someone were pummeling him with rapid blows. Then his nose was pinched closed and someone blew air into his mouth twice before the pounding began again. He opened his eyes, wild with fear, and gasped for breath. Katrina was straddling him.

"You look like you've seen a ghost, Dad," she managed, out of breath from the exertions of CPR. Now that her father was breathing on his own, she stood up. Perspiration stained her shirt. "Peter called the paramedics, and they'll be here any minute. For now, just breathe."

"She's gone! She's gone!" he shouted.

"Who?"

"Your mother! Greta! She's gone forever!" He sobbed.

"She's been gone for eight months, Dad." She knelt beside him and cupped his face in her hands. "You remember. The Tegel Airport bombing in Berlin. Your anniversary trip to Germany to see Mom's family. You went to all the museums and landmarks—even the old prison camps from World War II. Then on the way home..." Her breath caught in her throat. "There was nothing you could do. The explosion was so violent they never found..." She felt a tear trickle down her cheek. "Dr. Feinstein has been treating you for post-traumatic stress and depression. When I went upstairs to get those books, I checked your medicine cabinet and saw that you hadn't been taking your pills. So I called his office for advice. He wants to see you. It's been such a crazy day, this was the first chance I had to come back and check on you again. Thank God I got here in time."

"You're not Gestapo, are you?"

"Just ordinary Portland Police, though some of the local anarchists might think of me as Gestapo." She smiled at him, then bent over and hugged him. "I need you to stick around, Dad," she whispered in his ear, her tears warm on his cheek. "I love you so much. You can't be doing this kind of thing."

The ambulance zoomed down the street and came to a screeching halt out front, lights flashing, sirens triggering a chorus of howls from all the dogs in the neighborhood. The paramedics rushed in and fitted an oxygen mask over his face. They did preliminary checks of his blood pressure and oxygen saturation. Then they slid him onto a gurney and wheeled him outside to the open doors of the transport. As they were lifting him into the vehicle, he motioned for his daughter to come closer.

Through the awkward baffle of the mask, he said, "I loved your mother. More than life itself."

"I know, Dad. I know."

A Show of Hands

(A 100-word short story)

Nothing was happening. On his third lap around the lonely cemetery, doubt curdled his confidence. Perhaps he had missed something. In his own defense, he could not rehearse a unique event.

At last, a thousand hands began reaching up through the dark, moist earth, reminding him of ghostly Casablanca Lilies blooming in the silver moonlight.

"About time," he muttered, his relief quickly distilling into annoyance.

Men, women, and children were writhing to the surface, clotted with dirt, like cicadas emerging from their long sojourn underground.

"What took you so long?" the angel complained. "I blew the trumpet twenty minutes ago."

Crow Man

He was never sure if he had trained the crows or they had trained him. He was convinced they recognized his face when he went out for his morning walk. They knew he had a pocketful of unsalted peanuts—gourmet treats for scavengers. He couldn't go more than fifty feet before they flew to him, landing on lamp posts, in branches of nearby trees, even setting down in the street not twenty paces ahead of him. When a crow cocked its head or uttered a low *caw*, he imagined its asking him, "So where's my breakfast?" Per their accepted protocol, he would toss a peanut into the street, and the crows would rush to it, jockeying to be first in line to collect the tasty morsel. It reminded him of his childhood, when he had to compete with eight siblings to snag that extra slice of toast. You were fast or you went hungry. Of course, the crows had no idea they were feeding him as much as he was feeding them, helping him emerge from his profound discontent.

It had begun a few days earlier, when he was rummaging through a small chest of keepsakes he hadn't opened in years. Now that their four children were grown, he and his wife Penelope were in the process of down-sizing—moving from their 4000-square-foot home in Salem to a 1500-square-foot beach cottage in Lincoln City.

"When in doubt, throw it out," Penelope had insisted.

"Easy for you to say," Jude replied. "That philosophy gives you permission to go shopping again. Besides, why can't our new home accommodate all my memories?"

"They aren't memories if you haven't bothered to

look at them in thirty-plus years. They're debris. Like those boxes that have sat unpacked in our garage since our last move. Do you even remember what's in them?"

"Important stuff."

Penelope snorted her reproof and continued packing up the kitchen.

He sat on the bedroom floor with the box open before him. This wasn't debris. Each item he touched flooded him with stories from his past. As he lifted the framed set of quartz arrowheads, he was transported to the potato farm in Rhode Island, where he and his son had gathered them for a school project 29 years ago. Then there was the shark tooth he had found on Black Point Beach in Connecticut when he was in the fifth grade. It was the summer he first discovered his interest in girls and how they were shaped. The key chain with the trout fly embedded in a disk of plastic brought back the summer he had learned to drive in his family's Ford Fairlane. He shuddered as he recalled the head-on collision that he walked away from unscathed. What about the woodchuck skull, shiny with shellac, its jaws hinged with two bent common pins? He had found it on an afternoon hike in upstate New York, while taking a break from the oppressive private school he attended. Or the 1969 ticket to Woodstock, a concert he never attended after walking seven miles to get there, finally overwhelmed by the smell and the mud.

Then he found it. The crow call. It was a black tube about an inch in diameter and almost five inches long, with a plastic reed in the mouthpiece. As an adolescent in Connecticut, he had hunted crows with his friend Hank. Hank's call was made of polished cherry wood, a good deal fancier. Crows were considered *varmints* back then—pests —the polar opposite of their protected status today. He and

Hank would pack up their shotguns, their decoys, and their crow calls and head out to the farms off East Street. They would hide at the wooded edge of a meadow after positioning the two crow decoys and the owl decoy in the branches above them. From their study of *Sports Afield*, *Field and Stream*, and *Outdoor Life*, they knew that owls and crows had a blood feud—neither able to tolerate the presence of the other anywhere nearby. Hunkering down in the brush, he and Hank would take turns blowing their crow calls, hoping to lure an unsuspecting crow within range of spotting the owl decoy in the tree. According to hunting lore, that was supposed to make the crow blind with rage and an easy target as it came hurtling in to attack the raptor. Alas, no self-respecting crow ever flew within range of the 12 gauges. He and Hank hadn't counted on how intelligent their quarry was. They did attract an owl once to the crow decoys, and it scared the bejeebers out of them as it swooped in after its hapless victims.

Jude raised the crow call to his lips and let it rip. Penelope shrieked as the ungodly sound echoed down the hallway to the kitchen.

"What the hell was that?" she cried, dropping the serving platter she was in the process of packing.

"Sorry, honey. I forgot how loud this thing is. It's my old crow call."

"Well, we have one less plate to pack."

Jude became thoughtful. *I wonder if I've still got it? Could I call crows if I didn't have a gun in my hands? If I had something to feed them?*

The words rattled around in his brain. *Have I still got it? Not just calling crows, but everything else. Maybe the better question is, did I ever have it?*

He recalled those adolescent dreams, those high school commencement addresses, urging the graduating class to take over the world with their ambition and their energy. He didn't see much evidence for having done that in his own life. Now that he was looking down the short tunnel to retirement in a month, he wondered if he had accomplished anything.

He had worked at Sharington Office Furniture for 37 years. The early years were the hardest, working his butt off peddling desks, chairs, and file cabinets throughout Oregon, Washington, and Idaho. Often he was on the road for three or four days a week, sometimes more. He would never recover those days he missed at home, days he might have spent watching his children grow up, cuddling his wife before bed, vacationing with his family. "I do it for you and the kids," he had told Penelope, time after time. Had she ever believed him? Had he?

Twelve years into it, he was finally promoted to an administrative position in the company, supervising the sales crews, monitoring inventory, hiring and firing. Though he was no longer on the road, he was working 70- and 80-hour weeks. Eight years later, he had climbed to Vice President of Sales and Advertising, and there he stayed for the rest of his tenure. He had topped out. The coveted position of company President would forever elude his grasp, available only had the current stake holder suffered a heart attack or stroke. And that man's health had remained robust for the duration of Jude's career.

In the grand scheme of things, how many file cabinets matter? How many desks and chairs does it take to reach critical mass and generate meaning in a life? A thousand? A million? *Was I—am I—a success?* He shook his head and frowned. *We raised four good kids—or Penelope did. They're all gainfully employed. Nobody's in prison or drug addicted or beating a spouse. Isn't that enough?* The truth was, he felt old and unnecessary.

He put the crow call into his shirt pocket and sighed. He looked toward the kitchen, where he could hear Penelope rattling around. Her blonde hair had begun turning gray, but she remedied that every month. Even at seventy, she had retained her striking good looks, and she exercised faithfully to maintain her slim figure. Penelope and he were as comfortable together as that old leather jacket he slid into every fall—stretched in all the right places, broken in, familiar in its feel and smell. But the passion had not fared so well, guttering out like an old candle a decade before. Had it been eight months since they last made love? Ten? It just seemed like so much work to get started. And what he used to call his "blue steel hard-on" had gradually softened, especially after that prostate medication he had taken for a couple of years to manage his PSA.

He slammed his fist on the floor. "What self-pitying crap!" he said aloud.

"What?" called Penelope from down the hall.

"Nothing. Just talking to myself." He felt the crow call in his breast pocket and stood up. *I'll learn to talk crow.* He pursed his lips and nodded. *That's something, isn't it? An accomplishment?*

After he had done all the packing he was going to do for the day, he poured himself a beer and Googled *crow* on his laptop. *Know your adversary*, he thought. He was struck by their keen intelligence, especially their problem-solving and tool-using skills. He learned about their family communities and territorial boundaries, favorite foods and common behaviors.

He decided upon a simple strategy. *Babies learn to speak by imitating their parents*, he told himself. *I'll mimic any crow sounds I hear. If I get one to come in closer, curious about this funny-looking, white crow babbling like an idiot, I'll throw out a peanut. Maybe they'll associate my jabbering with free food. The old Pavlov ploy.*

He took a trip to the local market to get peanuts. Around and around the produce department he went, searching for the elusive legumes. Mothers with children in their baskets were hustling to and fro, stocking up on apples and bananas and potatoes, tossing grapes to their fidgeting toddlers to keep them at bay. *Is everyone younger than me?* he moped. He finally cornered his prey on a low shelf beneath bulk canisters of grains and tree nuts. Purchase completed, he returned home and went into the backyard to practice blowing the crow call.

"What a godawful racket!" Penelope said, as she leaned out the glass slider. "If the neighbors complain, I swear I'm gonna tell them my husband has gone bat-shit crazy."

"That, my dear, was a crow concerto. I call it '*Caw*.' Very nuanced."

She laughed. "Well, Mr. Crow Man, please fire up the barbecue. I've got some salmon I'd like you to grill for us tonight."

He arose early on Sunday morning to begin his experiment in earnest. Prime feeding time was just after sunrise. The late spring weather was still cool, so he put on a light jacket. Then he filled a small plastic bag with peanuts and stuffed it into his pocket. He perched a black baseball cap on his bald head and started out.

The neighborhood was still as the sun reached over the horizon, its beams captured briefly in the dissipating mist. He heard birds declaring their territory and calling to mates from the trees and the shrubbery. The air was sweet with blooming rhododendrons, dogwood, and azaleas. A squirrel hopped across the street in front of him and bolted up a gnarled oak tree, lashing its tail and scolding him for his impertinence.

He withdrew the call from his pocket, inserted one end in his mouth, and blew three slow caws. Several minutes later, he repeated the invocation, feeling like a priest from the century before, speaking Latin to his uncomprehending altar boy, awaiting a response to his arcane antiphon.

Five minutes later, he heard four caws in the distance. He imitated the sound, and was rewarded by a response, closer now. Could it be this easy?

It wasn't. The crow flew high overhead and kept on going. Undaunted, Jude maintained his four-note symphony as he continued his walk through the quiet tree-lined streets. *Anybody listening?* he wondered. He heard more crows in the distance, but they seemed to be arguing with each other and paid him no attention. *I'm a stranger on their turf. I'm not a friend yet.*

Forty-five minutes later, he returned home and began to cook breakfast. *Learning any new language is a process*, he assured himself, as he cracked two eggs into a frying pan. He remembered a line from a favorite book of his in his twenties—*I can think, I can fast, I can wait. Soon the crows will discover that the white man brings gifts.*

That thought startled him. *The white man brings gifts.* How many Native Americans had succumbed to that siren song? He felt as though he were free associating as he munched his toast and eggs and drank his coffee. Wasn't there a Crow Indian tribe? What might he learn from a people who called themselves after the bird he was determined to befriend?

Penelope bustled into the kitchen and poured herself a cup of coffee. "I'm taking off with Angela. Lots of yard sales today. Then we'll probably go out to lunch."

"But I thought you were clearing stuff out, throwing away anything you hadn't used in a year. Now you want to get more?"

"Beach-themed stuff for the new house. It has to be nautical. You'll see." After a few more sips of coffee, she pecked him on the cheek and headed toward the door. "Have fun today."

He blew her a kiss as she left, a waft of her sweet fragrance lingering in the air behind her. After a final swallow of coffee, he cleared his dishes into the sink and went back to his computer. In moments, he was lost in the history of the tribe whose name in their own language was *Apsáalooke*, or *Absaroka*, Children of the Large-Beaked Bird. They hunted bison on foot and later on horseback, using arrows or guns and even *buffalo jumps*, driving the animals off cliffs.

The more he read, the more mesmerized he became. Through the lens of his own failures, he romanticized a life from a simpler time, where success was measured not by the number of widgets manufactured and sold, but by bravery in battle and the meat brought home to feed family and community. He imagined a life stripped to its barest essentials, and it drew him into a world of his own making. He saw himself stretching bison hides over long poles, fashioning his own tipi. It was he who wielded the knife and skinned the buffalo he had shot with his own bow. He who protected the tribe's horses from raiding bands of Lakota and Cheyenne. He who volunteered for the Sun Dance...

Not that. He stopped reading abruptly. He pushed his chair away from the desk and closed his laptop. Not that.

He picked up his crow call and went into the backyard to practice.

He and Penelope had timed moving into their cottage in Lincoln City with his retirement, so he wouldn't have to be commuting back to Salem. That gave him a month to establish a relationship with his black-feathered friends and be welcomed into their family. Then he would do the same thing in the coastal town. Since it was becoming daylight earlier and earlier, he determined to arise each day with enough time for a half-hour walk in the neighborhood.

The morning was overcast. There had been some light rain overnight, and droplets fell off the leaves overhead with each breath of wind, tapping on the pavement as though it were raining still. The air was redolent with the smells of wet earth and mown lawn. Fifty yards ahead, he could hear crows squabbling, and he tried to match their volume, speed, and dialect. In an instant, a large black bird came rushing toward him, cawing loudly. Jude fumbled for a peanut in his pocket, all the while keeping up his tune on the call. He held the peanut high so the bird could see it, then tossed it into the center of the street behind him. He kept walking forward, afraid that if he stopped, the crow might get suspicious. Forty feet farther, he looked back over his shoulder and saw the crow pecking at the peanut to free the food inside. Jude was elated.

Over the course of his walk, he was able to attract one more crow to his bait. *It's working. They're beginning to accept me. But would it work better if I did the Sun Dance?*

He quickly banished the thought. *That's crazy. What am I thinking?* The little that he had read about the Crow's annual religious ceremony frightened him.

When he got home, he was tempted to look up more about the Absaroka on his computer, but decided he couldn't be late for work. Even though his career was drawing to a close, he had to give it his best. But it was becoming harder to concentrate. What would he do when he no longer had work to provide him with a schedule and a routine? With a reason? He hadn't hunted since his days with Hank, and he hadn't fished in decades. He was never much for watching sports, and never played any himself except for his brief and unexceptional season on the freshman track team. He had no hobbies. How much time could he spend reading? Would he succumb to the inanity of daytime TV?

More than that, he was becoming obsessed with the Crow Nation. Whenever his attention wandered, he was there sitting before his tipi, knapping arrowheads from quartzite, fletching shafts, making bows. Then he would shake his head as if awakening from a dream and return to the task at hand.

When he got home that night, Penelope was excited. "I've ordered that new bed for the beach house and it arrives on Wednesday afternoon. I'll drive out there tomorrow morning with another car-full and probably stay through the weekend to get things organized and cleaned the way I like. You be OK on your own till Sunday night?"

"Yeah, I'll be all right. There's plenty of frozen stuff for me to eat. I'll keep plugging away at packing my crap."

She hugged him. "We're gonna be fine, you know. Don't look so sad. You'll like being retired. I sure've been enjoying myself these last six months away from that nuthouse."

"But you have your art and you already have a bunch of friends at the coast. What am I going to do?"

"I'm sure you'll figure it out, honey. Just give yourself time."

The next morning, while Penelope was still asleep, he was out making the circuit. The early morning sun felt good on his face after the gray of the previous day. He responded to a five-caw report and soon two crows landed in a tree off to his right.

"Were you guys here yesterday?" he said. "Here's some breakfast." He tossed two peanuts into the street and before he had gone ten more feet, the birds glided down from the tree like shiny black kites, the tips of their wings upturned, their feathers fanned open. One cawed three times, and Jude did likewise. "You're welcome."

He continued his walk and more crows made his acquaintance. "Word has gotten around, huh? The funny-looking crow has snacks? Well, step right up. I got lots more."

Twenty minutes later, his pockets empty, Jude returned home, feeling what he could only describe as *success*. He had befriended the crows. They had accepted him.

That night, alone in the house after supper, sipping his second glass of Zin, he went back to the Crow Nation. Disinhibited by the wine, he began to read more about the Sun Dance, the tribe's most sacred ceremony. Not a lot was written about it, and some of what he found was contradictory. One site said it was held in late spring or early summer, when the buffalo congregated after the long winter. Another said it was done in late July or early August, after the buffalo hunt. All agreed that the Sun Dance was a spiritual quest, a personal sacrifice for the benefit of the family and the community.

As he continued reading, the darkness that had settled outside the house seemed to enter into him. He read about the practitioner of the Sun Dance fasting from food and drink for many days before submitting to the tribal elders, who would pierce the skin of his chest and insert a skewer of bone through a flap of flesh. The skewer would be tied with a leather thong to a cottonwood pole, an umbilical cord attached to the Tree of Life. The man would dance toward the pole four times and touch it with his palm. Then he would lean back against the rope and hang from the pole, seeking the Sun Dance vision, until his flesh finally tore and freed him. The torture could last for hours.

Jude took a deep breath and shuddered. His mind was seared with frightening images that both repelled and attracted him in equal measure. For a moment, he felt detached from his body, as though he were viewing it from above. In a flash of recognition, he recalled the horror he felt as a young child the first time he beheld an icon of Christ hanging from the cross.

He closed the cover of his laptop and stood up. *I can't go there*, he thought. But it was the vain musing of a man about to succumb to a temptation he is too weak to continue fighting. He felt himself slipping toward the edge of the abyss.

Although he did not usually shower before bedtime, he felt an intense need to cleanse himself. He scrubbed furiously at his skin, while standing in the hottest water he could tolerate. After toweling off, he slid into bed and turned off the lights.

He lay staring up at the ceiling, then tossed and turned restlessly for the next hour, unable to get comfortable. When at last sleep came, he was with the Crow, being welcomed into the tribe. Then he was with Jesus in Gethsemane, praying for the cup of suffering to pass. Sometime during the night, he saw Penelope at the coast, looking at him as though he were a stranger she didn't recognize. As the morning sun awoke him, he felt the calm of a decision made.

He got up and dressed, then called in sick to work. *I must fast*, he told himself, as his stomach grumbled in complaint. He put on his light jacket and cap and refilled his pocket with peanuts.

As he began his walk, he felt lighter than he had in weeks. Gone was the worrying about his retirement and what he would do with himself. Gone was the discontent that dogged his days. He had a reason to continue living. He was learning his place in the universe.

The sun shone through a lace curtain of mist. The whole world felt alive. He was Adam on the first day in the Garden.

"*You're late*," said the crow that flared its wings and fluttered to the street just ahead of him.

"I know," Jude replied. "I'm sorry. I had a tough night. I'm better now."

"*You know what you must do.*"

"Yes. I just have to figure out how."

"*There's a cottonwood tree in the thicket behind your house*," said another crow, who flew down to join his brother. "*We can show you.*"

"Thank you. Please take these gifts." He tossed them each a peanut and continued on his way.

A block farther down, another bird landed on the streetlight he was approaching.

"*Good morning, Jude. Do you have something for me?*"

"Of course, my friend." He withdrew a peanut and dropped it in the street.

The crow glided down silently and strutted toward its snack. "*You're committed now.*"

"I know. I've begun my fast."

In another block, a half-dozen of the birds, shiny as anthracite, swooped around and around him. The chorus of their cries felt like a homecoming. He opened his arms wide and smiled in appreciation. By the time he completed the loop, all his treats were gone, and he made his way home. He waved a final time to his tribe and entered the house.

The final pieces of his plan were falling into place. He showered quickly, then got into his car to drive the three miles toward downtown. On the right he saw the sign proclaiming *Body Art: Tattoos and Piercings.* In smaller print beneath, he read, *Your Body is Your Temple.* He pulled into the small lot by the shop and entered.

He wasn't sure what he had expected. The reception area was brightly lit, and the walls all around were hung with images of flowers and fairy queens, dragons and angels—pictures he presumed the local artist was happy to inscribe permanently on Jude's skin. A glass case on the right displayed the surgical steel studs and rings and barbells for piercing lip, tongue, eyebrow, nose, navel, nipple, or genitalia. He was sure the black-curtained doorway on the far wall led to the artist's studio.

"May I help you?" the young woman behind the counter asked. "I'm Isadora." Her ear lobes were stretched around inch-wide rings. Her V-neck T-shirt revealed a single rose growing up from between her breasts and blooming at her throat.

Jude wasn't sure how to ask. He shifted his weight from one foot to another. He blurted out, "Do you know the Sun Dance?"

"The Plains Indians? Lakota? Crow? Of course. Piercings go back hundreds of years."

"How would I... how would you..." His face felt hot and his breathing labored.

"Do that kind of piercing on your chest? It's not hard, but I hear it hurts like hell. Never tried it myself, but I have friends who've done it. We call it suspension piercing. From the back, the chest, the belly. It's a thing. Have you seen the videos on YouTube? Place downtown rents a hall once a month and it's packed with people who can't wait to be hung on the ol' meat hooks. A real party with music and booze and all. Of course, it's not the Sun Dance way. That's sacrilegious for a non-Native. Hell, they don't even let outsiders watch the Sun Dance. It's too holy for us. So why do you wanna go and get pierced like that for? Aren't you kinda old?"

"I... um." He didn't have the words. "I just have to."

"Well, my guy Blade does the body work. He's real good. Trained as an Army medic in Afghanistan." She reached under the counter and pulled out two metal hooks about six inches long and the diameter of a pencil. "Fish hooks for whales, huh? Stainless steel, but you can get 'em in titanium if you want. We use two of these instead of the single skewer of bone the Natives used. Anyway, I just do tatts. Blade's been pretty busy but I'm sure we can fit you in." She looked at the computer on the counter top. "How's Friday morning at 11:00 sound?"

"Perfect."

She entered his information into the shop's database and handed him an appointment card. "If you change your mind, just give me a call."

Jude put the card in his pocket and left. Next he went to a leather shop and purchased a leather thong about twenty feet long. He had the owner slice the last twelve inches of it to create a fork, so he could tie it to both hooks.

Jude spent the rest of the day fending off his hunger and his thirst. The thirst was harder. All he could think about was drinking a tall glass of cold water, ice cubes tinkling against the rim, droplets of moisture condensing along the sides. To distract himself, he looked up suspension piercing on YouTube and was appalled by what he saw. It felt more like he was watching pornography than witnessing something spiritual. When at last he fell asleep that night, he was back with the tribe, ushered into the sweat lodge. His throat and stomach ached. He knew the steam would purify him.

He was groggy the next morning when he began his walk, but the sounds of his brother crows cleared his mind. Colors got brighter, smells more intense. He lifted his arms as the tribe swarmed around him, loudly calling his name. He threw great handfuls of peanuts into the street in thanksgiving.

"*Follow us,*" their elder said. "*We'll show you the cottonwood. Mark the trail so you can find it again.*"

He returned to the house and retrieved a ball of string from the garage. Then he walked out back, where the crows beckoned him into the woods. Using his pocketknife, he cut and tied little swatches of string to branches every ten or twenty feet. At first the brush was dense, whipping at his face and scratching his arms. Gradually, it opened up, and it became easier for him to walk. After another hundred yards, he came to the cottonwood.

"*The Tree of Life,*" the elder said, as he flew off with his brothers deeper into the forest.

Jude knelt in the soft earth, looking prayerfully at the tree. It was a smallish specimen with heart-shaped leaves, the trunk perhaps twelve inches in diameter. He got up and walked to it, stroking the rough gray bark with his fingers. He touched a point about six feet off the ground and decided he would attach his tether there.

The rest of the time until his piercing passed by in a blur. His hunger actually diminished, though the dull pain in his gut remained. He found it more difficult to speak as his body continued to dehydrate. His head throbbed and his body had trouble moving as he wanted it to. At times he felt a dizziness that threatened to impair his ability to drive. It was harder to think.

When Friday dawned, he was relieved. His tribe swarmed him again.

"*Courage, brother,*" one called.

"*For tribe and family,*" said another.

"*Fulfill your destiny, Jude,*" intoned the elder.

He arrived at Body Art early. Isadora checked him in, ran his card, and gestured to a chair in the waiting area.

Thirty minutes later, the black curtain parted and Blade walked toward him, extending his hand. "Don't worry," he said. "I use sterile procedure. I scrub before I work." He had great sleeves of tattoos encircling both muscled arms.

Jude shook his hand and smiled weakly. "I'm ready."

"You don't look so good, Jude. You feeling OK?"

"I'm fine, really. Just a little anxious, I guess."

"Well, come on back here and we'll get started."

Blade pointed to what looked like a large dental chair and urged Jude to have a seat. "Take your shirt off, man. Now let me take a look at the victim—I mean, the patient." He smiled and handed Jude a safety razor. "You're a pretty hairy dude, so you better do some shaving. I'll put one hook here and the other one there."

While Jude occupied himself scraping the hair from his chest, Blade slid clean OR blues over his clothes and began to scrub his hands and lower arms. "So you a fan of the Plains Indians?" When Jude didn't respond, he said, "Had a buddy tried the Sun Dance a few years back. Wanted to find himself after the war, you know? He did it all alone out in the woods instead of in the safe group downtown. Ended bad for him." He finished washing and pulled on a pair of latex gloves. "My sterile procedure may be overkill, but I don't think you can be too careful, you know? Once a nurse, always a nurse, I guess."

Jude closed his eyes and tried to distract himself. He saw images of his tipi and his bow and his horse. He wrinkled his nose at the smell of the Betadine antiseptic that Blade rubbed on his skin. *For my family and the tribe*, he kept repeating to himself. He prayed for strength to harden his resolve and endure his destiny. *I can do this. I will succeed.* The searing pain made him catch his breath.

In a few minutes, it was over. "Here's some antibiotic ointment and sterile bandages." The artist pointed to the wounds and the steel. "Wash both areas gently every day, then use the ointment with new bandages to keep 'em from getting infected. You don't wanna leave 'em in very long. They probably won't bleed much, but if they do, just clean 'em up with warm water and put more ointment and bandages on 'em."

Jude stared down at his chest and the steel hooks that hung from his flesh. Oddly, he remembered the last business conference he had attended and the badge he had pinned to the front of his shirt. He swung his feet over the side of the chair and felt a moment of vertigo. Blade put a hand on his shoulder to steady him.

"You'll be OK, man. Let me help you with these bandages, then you can put your shirt back on. Can I sign you up for the group? We're actually meeting tomorrow night."

"No thanks." Jude watched himself walk out of the shop and get into his car.

Inside the shop, Blade pulled out his cell phone and called the local police station. "Yeah, Barry, it's me, Blade. Yeah, it's been a long time. Hey, listen, man. I got another one. Just like Sandoval. No, no, I still think I could've saved Sandy's life if he hadn't taken off like that. Anyway, would you do a wellness check on this guy? Jude Lane. He worries me. Wouldn't talk to me during the op. Doesn't want the group. Looked like shit. I'm not sure I should've let him drive. Seemed pretty whacked out. I'm guessing he hasn't been eating or drinking anything for the last few days, maybe more. This Sun Dance thing for an old guy and a non-Native can be a kind of suicide thing. Know what I mean? Yeah, once a nurse, always a nurse. Anyway, better bring an EMT with you. Sure. Hey, thanks. I owe you big time. Buy you a beer if you come around." He gave the officer Jude's address and ended the call.

Jude wasn't sure how he got home. He found himself in the garage, pushing the button to close the door and entering the house. He sat for a moment at the kitchen table, his mind blank, his breathing slow and regular. The ticking of the clock on the wall got louder and louder, mimicking the pulse pounding in his temples. A wave of detachment washed over him, and the material things around him—the table and chairs, the appliances, the walls themselves—began to lose substance, became almost invisible.

He stood up, got his leather thong from the bedroom, and stepped out through the back sliding door. At the edge of the woods, he saw his first strand of string tied to a low branch, pointing the way. *I have purpose and meaning*, he told himself, as he walked toward the string. Fifteen feet farther, he saw the next strand, as he threaded his way to the cottonwood. In the distance he could hear his tribe talking to one another, eagerly awaiting his arrival. The sky above was the deepest blue he had ever seen, contrasting with the varied greens and browns of the forest around him. The air was honeyed with the fragrances of blossom and earth. Everything fit together.

In minutes he reached the Tree of Life. His brothers and sisters sat in the branches like sentinels, nodding their acknowledgment of him. The forest became silent. Jude knelt briefly and shed his shirt. Then he removed the bandages from his wounds. He walked forward and tied one end of the leather rope to the tree. With fingers that felt more nimble than they should have been, he tied the strands of the forked end to both hooks. He touched the tree with his palm, walked backward the length of the tether, and approached the tree again, touching it with as much love as he could muster. After he repeated this twice more, he walked backward until the leather was taut, pulling on the hooks. He felt a flash of searing pain.

Slowly, he arched away from the tree, leaning backward, pulling harder against the hooks in his chest, putting more weight on the leather rope binding him to the world. His brain shrieked in agony. His head fell backward as his arms opened, cruciform. As a magnifying glass compacts a beam of sunlight, the ritual focused all his life onto a few square centimeters of his flesh, where the pain howled like a hurricane.

Time lost all meaning. Had he hung there minutes? Hours? Pain was all that was, swelling to fill his whole body like a surging tide. Every nerve fiber in his exhausted frame vibrated like a struck tuning fork. When he could endure no more, he emptied himself, wailing in utter abandonment.

The darkness swallowed him.

A bubble of light burst like a nova before him, banishing the blackness. He sloughed off his old discontent as a snake sheds its skin. Where once regret and disappointment had lingered, only gratitude remained. His hunger and thirst and pain were gone, replaced by an ecstasy that knew no words. Lifted up by joy, light as a crow feather. He was one with himself and his family and his tribe. Touched by the Holy. Wrapped in the Divine.

"It's OK, Mr. Lane. We've got you now. You're going to be all right." One of the paramedics started an IV drip, while the other tended to the wounds on Jude's chest.

"I'm Matthew, Mr. Lane. That's Jason with the IV. I'm gonna put a pressure dressing on your chest for now. We'll leave it to the doc at the hospital to do the suturing. You tore pretty bad, so it's gonna take a lot of stitches. You OK with that?"

Jude nodded his assent. He saw a policeman standing nearby, jotting down notes on a small pad.

"I'm Officer Barry Hempford, Mr. Lane. You were pretty hard to find, but our dog did a good job sniffing you out. I'm glad we got here in time. I don't know how long you were unconscious. The guys say you're very dehydrated. How are you feeling?"

"I feel new," Jude said, his voice a dry rasp. "Happy."

Matthew interrupted him. "We're gonna slide you onto this gurney, Mr. Lane, and then we're gonna belt you down pretty tight. It'll be a bumpy ride outta here."

In moments, Jude felt like a mummy wrapped in white sheets. The men snugged the strap around his hips to avoid any further abrasion to his chest.

"Hang on, man," Jason said. "Here we go."

As the stretcher lurched through the underbrush, Jude heard his tribe singing in the branches of the cottonwood.

His own heart sang in reply.

Eye of Newt

An Epilogue to the novel *Seal of Secrets*

W hat a lovely day for a murder," Sterling Friese said aloud to the empty house. Outside, the sun had just risen, painting the top of cottony fog in the lower valleys with a patina of gold. He opened the window and heard the rhythmic crashing of surf four blocks away. The salt air was cool and fresh.

As he cleared away his breakfast dishes, he began to sing the Simon and Garfunkel tune, *Feelin' Groovy*. The pop station he had listened to Friday had played the *moldy oldie* on his way home from Pacific Crest University, where he taught undergraduate biology. If all went according to his plans, the faculty committee would recommend him for tenure by the end of next week. Too bad Dean Wasserman refused to get on board, but Friese had found the solution to that problem.

Friese told himself that he simply had spent too much time and effort working toward tenure to let a self-important twit like Wasserman derail him at the last minute. After all, Friese had published frequently over the past six years, and his work on Post-Darwinism was getting some real recognition in the scientific community. He had a full teaching load and good evaluations from his students. He served on several faculty committees and had even attracted some much needed funding from several large corporations in Portland. Yes, he had several affairs with female students, but they were always most discreet and were completely unknown to all but Wasserman. How the dean had found out would remain a mystery to him. But so be it.

Besides, Friese loved living in Driftwood. The small coastal town suited him perfectly. His house in the hills above Highway 101 was small, but more than adequate. He could glimpse the ocean from the small deck off his upstairs bedroom, and it was a favorite rendezvous for the young ladies who came to sip wine with him and discuss their latest examinations.

With the last dish rinsed and settled in the dishwasher, he began his preparations in earnest. He opened the refrigerator and removed the plastic cup that held the little creature he had captured on his walk around Coos Pond yesterday.

"You will be my Angel of Death," he whispered to it. "You will sacrifice yourself for the greater good."

A broad smile creased his face, as he recited the chant from the ugly witches in Macbeth.

"Eye of newt, and toe of frog,
Wool of bat, and tongue of dog,
Adder's fork, and blind-worm's sting,
Lizard's leg, and howlet's wing—
For a charm of powerful trouble,
Like a hell-broth boil and bubble."

He began to laugh, his raucous guffaws filling the confines of the small kitchen. Once he calmed himself, he continued talking out loud, as if providing himself company—or an audience for his genius.

He left the kitchen to tidy the house for his expected guest. He dusted the tables, ran the vacuum, cleaned the sink and the toilet.

"Mustn't get careless," he told himself when he returned to the kitchen. He completed the initial phase of his work for the evening and wrote out a brief shopping list. Then he slipped on a light jacket and his Ivy Cap and got into his modest Toyota. "When my tenure is assured,

I'll get more suitable transportation," he promised himself. His bed-time reading of late had been Lexus, Audi, and BMW catalogs.

In moments he was at Hook, Line, and Sinker, the area's best local fish market.

"Good morning, Professor Friese," said the red-faced man behind the counter. His white apron already had stains written across the front of it, the signatures of a hard-working man. "You're out and about early for a Sunday morning. Good to see you again."

"Good to see you, too, Paul. Have you gotten any line-caught salmon in? You didn't have any when I checked last Wednesday."

"Your lucky day, Professor. Came in late yesterday. Beautiful fish. Copper River. Look at the color." He held up an 18-inch long fillet, its flesh a radiant red.

"Wonderful, Paul! Please wrap it up for me."

At the grocery store, he picked up a bag of baby Yukon Gold potatoes, a bunch of fresh asparagus, and a bottle of his favorite Pinot Noir. It would be a gourmet dinner and just the right send-off for his erstwhile friend, Dean Wasserman.

When he returned home, he hummed a tune as he filled his coffee maker. His preparations were complete. He had set the stage for his perfect murder.

2. Monday Morning

"So are you going out with her or not?" Tony Esperanza challenged his partner once again.

"We had dinner and a movie is all," replied Charley Whitehorse.

The two police officers were the sole staff of the small PD in Driftwood. Behind their backs, residents joked about how different they were. Esperanza was a tall, muscular man who had completed a successful stint in college football. Whitehorse was a short, slim member of the Kalapuya tribe, who had been heckled about his height for as long as he could remember. His scars were mute testimony to the brawling that had always been a part of his school curriculum.

"Charley, it's been a whole year since that case was closed. We're not investigating Chloe or her daughter anymore. Kaitlynn is doing her time and will probably get out early for good behavior."

"Yeah, but—"

"But nothing. The chemistry between you guys is obvious. Chloe's had the hots for you ever since you took her to the hospital after Raven bonked her on the head. You guys were made for each other. Take the leap, for God's sake!"

"Since when are you a matchmaker?"

"Since my partner started dragging his feet like some dumb-ass high school kid."

Whitehorse changed the subject. "Want a cup of coffee?"

Esperanza threw up his hands. "I give up. Do what you want. But don't come moping to me if that chick loses patience with your hard-to-get routine and takes up with somebody else. You've got your chance and you're blowing it."

Whitehorse knew his partner was right. What was he afraid of?

The phone rang and Esperanza picked up.

"Hey, Tony. This is Pamela over at 911. Just got a call about a dead guy. One of the deans from Pacific Crest. Sounds like natural causes. I've sent the EMT's but you'll probably want a quick look before they wrap it up. Got an address for you. Home of a professor Sterling Friese."

Esperanza wrote down the address and concluded the call. "C'mon partner. We got something to do on this Monday morning besides shuffling papers back and forth."

"What's up?"

"Dead guy over on Urchin Lane. College type."

"Foul play?"

"Naw, doesn't look like it. You disappointed?"

Whitehorse smiled. "I'm the Tracker, remember? I like to sniff things out."

"You're the most paranoid sonofabitch I know. How could I forget?"

"Hey, I'm a necessary part of this operation. We're on a shoestring here."

"Don't I know it. Well, let's saddle up. I'll drive."

It was a short trip to Urchin Lane, perched in the eastern hills above the town. They were delayed twice by garbage trucks blocking the narrow streets.

"Trash day today," commented Whitehorse. He noted all the gray plastic bins with their lids locked down —protection should they be blown over by the often fierce coastal winds or should the town's healthy raccoon population take an undo interest in someone's garbage.

They parked behind the emergency vehicle in front of the small beige house.

"Nice neighborhood. Not far from Chloe's." Esperanza smiled at Whitehorse, who frowned in response. Then a look of bewilderment shadowed his face. "Hey, what are you doing, partner?"

Whitehorse had undone the latch and lifted the lid of the trash bin at the curb. "I'm just a curious sonofabitch." He turned his face away for a moment. "Pretty ripe." He turned back to the bin. "Now look here. Looks like a perfectly good coffee pot our resident threw out."

"What the hell's the matter with you?"

"You have no expectation of privacy in trash left out at the curb for pickup. Police can rummage around in it all we like without probable cause or a warrant." He rattled it off as if he were quoting from a legal brief.

"I know the law, doofus. But why are you doing that now?" Esperanza's voice was an aggravated whisper. "We're here to check out a dead body. Natural causes. That's all."

Whitehorse refastened the lid. "OK. Let's go in."

3. Sunday Evening

"Welcome, Dean Wasserman. So glad you could make it." Friese extended his hand to the man at the threshold.

The dean shook his hand. "You can call me Arlon, but know that this doesn't change my opinion. I will do everything I can to persuade the committee to reject you for tenure."

"Arlon, I understand. But this isn't the time for unpleasantness. I wanted to show my appreciation for six good years at PCU. I've prepared a dinner that should be a real surprise. Let me take your coat and pour you a glass of wine."

The scowling man removed his tweed jacket. With his bushy eyebrows and white hair in wild disarray, he looked like a parody of Albert Einstein.

"This is my favorite Pinot. What do you think of it?"

"It's good, but I've had better."

"I'm sure you can afford better than I can on my salary, but I did get us some very nice salmon today."

The man harrumphed. "You know you'll have a year to find another job. Where will you go?"

"Oh, I'd like to stay in the Pacific Northwest. I really like it here. I'd never go back to LA." They sipped their wines in silence. Friese could feel his boss's discomfort and relished it. He smiled broadly. "The potatoes are almost done. I'll put on the asparagus and the salmon."

Fifteen minutes later the two were sitting down to dinner. Friese refilled their glasses and served generous portions of fish and vegetables.

"This is excellent, Sterling. You're quite a cook." Arlon raised another forkful of salmon to his lips. "Too bad you can't keep your dick in your pants."

"What?"

"You know what. How many undergraduates have you beguiled into your bed? Are you keeping score? How long before one of them brings a lawsuit against you and the school?"

"I assure you, Arlon. My trysts are always discreet, always consensual."

"Are you so naïve? How can the university support your tenure with these shenanigans going on? At least if we fire you we'll have some leg to stand on in court."

"But you're the only one who knows about my so-called shenanigans."

"I won't be after the tenure committee meets on Friday."

"Well, I'm sorry I've disappointed you. In all other respects I believe my conduct at the school has been exemplary—teaching, research, publications, fundraising."

"Don't you understand? We have a reputation to uphold. And a multimillion dollar lawsuit could cripple us."

Friese put down his fork, wiped his lips with his napkin, and stood up. "Let me start the coffee. I have a very fine tiramisu—store-bought, but outstanding, nonetheless."

"I may be too full," Arlon protested.

"Nonsense. Just a morsel to sweeten the palate with your coffee."

Friese listened to the sound of the coffee maker and wondered why he felt no compunction about the murder he was about to commit. *Because I've earned my tenure. The school owes me. The dean is an old dog, out of touch, holding the whole department back. I'm doing the school a service.*

"Do you take cream and sugar?" He brought the china cup to the table and set it before Arlon.

"Yes, please. Just a bit." Arlon sipped the steaming liquid. "Unusual flavor, but I like it."

"It's my own special blend. And here's a small piece of cake."

Friese watched his adversary drink the coffee. He sampled the tiramisu and stared at the coffee in his own cup. The minutes ticked by. The play was nearing its denouement.

"I feel odd," Arlon said. "My lips are tingling. My tongue is getting numb." He put a hand over his mouth, as though he were about to vomit.

"There's a bathroom right down the hall." Friese guided the man, who lurched to the toilet and fell to his knees, retching violently into the bowl.

"I can't get up." He reached for Friese's arm.

"That will be the muscle weakness setting in. Let me help you to the couch in the living room." He grabbed the slight man around the shoulders and aided him to the sofa, where he fell in a heap. "Here we go. Let me swing your legs up and put a pillow under your head. Mustn't put our shoes on the furniture, so I'll just take them off for you."

Wasserman made unintelligible sounds, as if no longer able to speak.

"Is this my doing, you ask? Of course it is, Arlon. I can't let you ruin my life, can I? Don't you think there should be consequences for that?" He shook his head back and forth. "What is it you say? What other symptoms can you expect? Well, I'd be surprised if you weren't feeling a skull-splitting headache about now. And very soon you'll slip into a paralytic coma, unable to move a single muscle." He smiled at the man stretched out before him. "But the real beauty of it is, you'll remain totally conscious. Trapped in your own body. Aware of everything around you. Waiting helplessly to breathe your last. That's what will get you finally. Your diaphragm will stop working and you'll suffocate. Till then we can have a chat about life, the state of the world, the future of Pacific Crest University, finding a dean to replace you."

He walked out into the kitchen to pour himself another glass of wine, then walked back into the living room. He slid a chair over to be closer to the dying man, whose eyes bore into him.

"Hate me? I hope so. I've hated you for years. Your pettiness. Your weakness. It'll be good riddance, I say. The department will bloom in your absence." He took a sip of his wine. "Did you know that police don't call the Medical Examiner's office for deaths that occur at home unless they think there's something suspicious? And they're not usually suspicious if there's no sign of visible injury. Nothing to suggest an overdose. The victim—you, in this case—is over 50 and has seen a doctor in the last year or two. Even if a Medical Examiner were called, I have it on good authority that they do not detect a poison they aren't specifically testing for, and they rarely test for poisons." He smiled again. "And tomorrow is trash day. I'll toss away all the incriminating evidence and the city will dispose of it for me. Dear Arlon, I may have just committed the perfect murder. Or will have, at any rate, once you stop breathing."

Friese's gaze took in the whole room. "I think I'll buy a bigger house when I get tenure. At least a better car than that heap I'm driving. If you will excuse me, I'll go clean the kitchen." He stood. "I'll call 911 in the morning. Rest in peace, Dean Wasserman."

4. Monday Morning

Whitehorse rang the bell and introduced himself and his partner to the auburn-haired man who opened the door. There was a rugged handsomeness to the man's features and suggestions of finely-honed muscles.

"Hello, officers. I'm Dr. Sterling Friese. Please come in. The EMTs are almost done." He ushered them down a short hall into the living room, where two uniformed men were examining a body on the couch.

Whitehorse observed the position of the body and the pair of shoes on the floor. "Dr. Friese, can you tell us what happened?"

"As I've told these men, I had Dean Wasserman over for dinner last night. I had some beautiful Copper River salmon I was dying to share with him. We finished with tiramisu and coffee, and shortly after that the dean began complaining that he didn't feel well. I told him he probably had a little too much rich food and suggested he come in here and relax. He took off his shoes and lay down on the sofa. I went about the business of cleaning up the kitchen. He was snoring by the time I finished, so I decided not to disturb him. He's slept over here before, so I thought it wouldn't be a problem. When I got up this morning, I found him like this."

One of the men bending over the body turned to the policemen. "Hi, Tony, Charley. No signs of injury. No history of drug addiction, as far as we know. No pills lying around. Heart? Brain aneurysm? Hard to say without an autopsy, but I don't know if the family would want that."

"Most assuredly not, if I can speak for them. His brothers have visited the university before and we've all gone out for dinner together. I remember one of them commenting about the amount of red meat the dean ate. One of them said something like, 'With a history like yours, you should be eating a more heart-healthy diet.'"

"See?" the EMT said.

"Pity," said Friese. "This was a special dinner celebrating my being granted tenure at the university. Well, technically not yet. This Friday. But the dean confided in me that it was already decided in my favor."

"Tenure?" Esperanza pursed his lips. "Does that mean like you can't be fired?"

Friese shook his head. "No, it's actually more like finally getting into the union. I can't be fired without just cause." He smiled. "Which never happens, so maybe it's like I can't get fired. Salary goes up. Benefits improve. I have more freedom with my teaching. Lots more job security."

"The golden ring, huh?"

"You could say that. I've worked six long, hard years to achieve it."

"You must be pretty proud."

"It's my life, Officer Esperanza. And with my tenure, I'll extend my teaching of biology to the graduate school as well."

Whitehorse was looking at the paintings on the wall. "You have quite a collection of wildlife pictures. Are they prints or originals?"

"Originals all. By a sweet student of mine several years back. That one is *Puma concolor*, the cougar or mountain lion. Did you know it is both nocturnal and crepuscular?"

"Crep—what?"

"Crepuscular. Having to do with twilight. It is active primarily at night and during twilight hours. Very secretive and usually solitary. Second heaviest cat in the New World after the jaguar."

Friese sounded as though he were lecturing his students. He pointed to another painting. "That, of course, is the bald eagle. *Haliaeetus leucocephalus*. Did you know it builds the largest nest of any North American bird? Up to 13 feet deep and more than 8 feet across. The nest can weigh a metric ton."

"Fascinating, doctor." Whitehorse looked to his colleague and back to Friese. "May we have a look around your house? We don't mean to intrude."

"Be my guests."

Whitehorse and Esperanza walked out into the kitchen. Whitehorse examined the counters and looked under the sink into the empty garbage can. His partner followed him down the hall, where they looked in on the professor's study. A large painting of a lizard-like creature was prominently displayed over Friese's desk. Then they entered his bedroom, tastefully done in muted colors, a collection of songbird paintings splashing brightness on the walls. The bed was neatly made, the closet door shut, the sink in the bathroom immaculately clean.

When they returned to the professor, Whitehorse looked at him with a curious expression on his face. "I understood you to say that you served coffee to your guest last night, but I don't see any coffee maker in your kitchen."

Friese nodded. "I can be a real klutz. Would you believe I poured our coffee and then dropped the damn pot? Broke into a thousand pieces on this tile floor. I'll be out to buy a new one today."

Whitehorse chuckled. "Did the same thing myself not three weeks ago. Only my pot was full. What a mess!" He scratched his chin. "Before I forget, I couldn't help but notice the painting over your desk. Lizard?"

"Just a local salamander. Quite common actually. It was my student's first effort."

Whitehorse heard the sound of a large truck out front. "Dr. Friese, I have to step outside to confer with Officer Esperanza for a moment. We'll be back in shortly."

The two police officers went outside and Whitehorse ran to the garbage truck just before it picked up Friese's bin. "Please leave this," he told the driver, who nodded and gave him an OK sign with his fingers.

"What are you doing, Charley?" Esperanza sounded confused.

"There may be critical evidence in here."

"Evidence for what?"

"Murder, Tony."

"For Chrissakes, Charley. What the hell are you talking about?"

"He said he broke his coffee pot into a thousand pieces and it's sitting whole in his garbage can. What else is he lying about?"

"And that's grounds for accusing him of murder?"

"There's other stuff, too. Did you see Wasserman's shoes? They were both together, tucked under the edge of the couch and pointing in. What do you do with your shoes when you sit back in a comfy chair and take them off?"

"Jesus. I throw them toward my bedroom. Then I hear it from my wife."

"Don't most people leave their shoes pointing out, so they can slip back into them when they get up? Friese took those shoes off Wasserman, and then the neat-freak carefully stowed them under the sofa."

"Charley, I think you've lost it. I haven't heard anything yet that sounds like murder or a motive for one."

But Whitehorse was on a roll. "And that painting over his desk. All morning long that guy has been trying to impress us—spouting Latin names for animals, carrying on with odd facts and figures. But we come to that one and all he says is it's a local salamander. No highfalutin name. No way-out facts. He's dismissive. Why?"

"How should I know, Charley. I swear you're from outer space."

"We need to call the Medical Examiner."

"Amy in Newport? And tell her what?"

"We want her to look at the body for suspected poisoning and see if there's any residue in the garbage. What kind of poison. How it was administered. I'll give you dollars for donuts it had something to do with the coffee."

"Sweet mother of mercy! Are you out of your mind? What do we tell Friese?"

"Tell him it's just standard procedure to have the M.E. take a look when somebody dies in somebody else's house. I don't care. Just keep him preoccupied so he doesn't see me putting his garbage in your trunk."

"What? No, no, no. You're not gonna stink up my car because you're bored with a death by natural causes. No way."

Whitehorse smiled like Sylvester the Cat with a mouthful of Tweety Bird. "Friese poisoned Wasserman. I'm sure of it. We just have to prove it."

"And if Wasserman's family comes after us for

having an autopsy done on a far-fetched hunch by a policeman with an overboard imagination? I'm depositing that one like dog shit on your front door mat."

"Understood."

"But why, Tony? Why? This had all the makings of a perfectly nice, normal day."

"Like you said, brother. I'm a paranoid sonofabitch."

5. Tuesday Morning

Pacific Crest University perched atop Cascadia Head, high above the western ocean. Founded in 1973 during the Governorship of Tom McCall, the school was known for its commitment to Oregon's environment. It was a model of so-called green engineering, boasting the smallest carbon footprint of any comparable university in the country. As such, it attracted a world-class faculty.

News of Dean Wasserman's sudden and unexpected death swept like a firestorm through the college community. Classes were suspended on Monday and a somber and poignant memorial service was held that night in the school's ecumenical chapel. On Tuesday, the normal class schedule resumed. Whitehorse had a destination.

At times like these, the policeman was glad to be living in a small town. Being on a first-name basis with a local judge made getting a warrant a matter of an hour instead of a day or more. He had to search Wasserman's office at the university before the family came in to empty it.

"Sorry, Charley," Judge Harowitz said. The tall gray-haired man was sitting in his chambers taking a much-needed coffee break between cases. "Do a better job of convincing me. You want a search warrant for Wasserman's office to look for evidence, but where's the probable cause that he was murdered? You admit that the EMT's saw nothing about his death suggestive of anything but natural causes. You say Friese lied about breaking his coffee pot. Big goddamn deal. How is that evidence that a crime was committed? I know you've got a good gut instinct, but this is quite a stretch."

"Judge, Friese lied about why he got rid of his coffee maker. I think the poison was in the coffee. That's why he threw the whole thing out." Whitehorse tried to hide the exasperation he was feeling.

"What poison?"

Whitehorse sighed. "I don't know. I just started going through Friese's garbage—don't worry, it was at the curb. Haven't found any receipts or containers for chemicals or pills. It's still a mystery."

"And what do you expect to find in Wasserman's office?"

"Motive, Judge. Wasserman had something on Friese. I'm sure of it."

"This is because we're friends, Charley, and we have lots of cases under our belts." Harowitz shook his head back and forth as he signed the warrant. "But it's flimsy. If the college or the family put up a stink about this, I'll rescind it in a heartbeat."

"Thanks, Judge."

Back at the PD, Esperanza tried to dissuade his partner from going to the university, to no avail. "You're like a goddamn dog with a bone," he declared. "Have at it. I'll mind the store."

Whitehorse parked in the student lot to try to avoid drawing too much attention to himself. The grounds could not have been lovelier. Every effort had been made to spare the majestic Douglas firs that surrounded the lecture halls, nestled in the forest as though they were an organic part of it. Whitehorse thought of the schools he had attended, and none were like this.

Entering the Administration wing, he registered at the office and obtained a pass so he could visit each of the facilities on the campus. "And here's my warrant to search Dean Wasserman's office," he told the young woman behind the desk. Her red hair caught the sun streaming in the window behind her, creating a brilliant halo around her face. "Where is Dean Wasserman's office exactly?"

"Please give me a moment, sir. I'll have to inform Chancellor Brady about the warrant." As she placed the call, he saw her smile turn to a frown.

"The Chancellor said he would send over Campus Security to escort you."

Whitehorse thanked her and waited. In moments a young man in a blue blazer walked briskly up to him. The man offered his hand. "I'm Philip Effling with Security. Come with me, please."

Outside a light breeze had come up, carrying a sweet fragrance Whitehorse couldn't identify, mingled with the salt air of the sea. He smiled to himself as two young coeds sauntered by. "Good morning, ladies," he said. "What a beautiful college you have."

"We love it," the dark-haired one said as they continued walking.

"Is this more standard procedure?" The voice behind him caught him off guard. He turned and saw a man in a gray sports jacket and driving cap. He carried a brown leather briefcase. His eyes were chips of ice.

"Dr. Friese. Good morning."

"I see you've made the acquaintance of Campus Security," he said, nodding toward Effling. "What's this all about?"

As loath as he was to alert Friese to the nature of his visit, it was unavoidable with Effling there. "I've come to search Dean Wasserman's office. I have a warrant." Was that a flash of fear he saw in those cold eyes?

"How dare you! What can you possibly hope to find? I'm reporting this to the Chancellor and Dean Wasserman's wife immediately. This is harassment, pure and simple, and the school and the family won't stand for it."

The man's arrogant tone rankled him. Despite his better judgment, Whitehorse said, "I know you did it. I just have to find out how and why." His voice was soft and menacing.

"What did you say?" Effling's face looked bewildered.

"It's nothing, Philip. We have an overly zealous policeman with an overly active imagination. I'll put a stop to this nonsense as soon as I can." With that he turned and hurried toward the Administration wing.

Effling shrugged and gestured to the building ahead of them. "The dean's office is in Ranier Hall, right over there. Please come this way."

They walked in through the large glass doors and stopped briefly at the desk. Effling addressed the student sitting there. "This man has a warrant to search Dean Wasserman's office. We'll be a few minutes." He turned back to Whitehorse. "Come along."

They walked down a long corridor and stopped just before the end. "Here we are," said Effling as he unlocked the door. It opened on a modest room, with bookshelves dominating two walls and a large bay window looking out over the lower reaches of the campus toward the forest beyond. A mahogany desk sat before the window, and two burgundy leather chairs in front of it provided the only other seating. The far wall was an array of oak filing cabinets.

Both men entered, and Effling stood stiffly to the side, arms folded across his chest.

"Are you going to stand there watching me?"

"Chancellor Brady has directed me to do so."

Whitehorse shrugged and got right to work, first going through the contents of the desk. He found a ring of keys he presumed would open the filing cabinets. The two drawers on either side contained individual files on students, their test scores and examinations, the papers they'd written. Whitehorse presumed these were Wasserman's current students.

He opened the laptop on the desk and went to the dean's email account. He began to look through recent messages. Several had the subject heading, *Tenure Committee*. He clicked on the most recent.

Arlon, looks like we're pretty well agreed on recommending Sterling for tenure. The vote on Friday will confirm it. He's been a real asset to the university. See you Friday.
Jonathan.

Whitehorse saw the little arrow indicating that Wasserman had sent a response. He opened the *Sent* file.

Jonathan, I have some information which may change your mind about our dear Professor Friese. I look forward to Friday's meeting.
Arlon

Whitehorse rubbed his chin. So Friese had lied again. The dean hadn't come to him to celebrate his upcoming tenure, but perhaps to break the news that it was going to be denied. He picked up the keys and went to the filing cabinets.

He opened them one after another. Although there were no visible identifiers on the outside of the drawers, each was dedicated to a particular faculty member. The drawers contained performance evaluations, copies of research articles that the professor had published, class evaluations, medical histories. Wasserman kept very detailed records on each of the people in his department.

After several tries, he found Friese's drawer. There in front was a large manila envelope addressed to Dean Wasserman from Invictus Investigations. "Bingo!" he said aloud.

"What?" The security officer moved closer to Whitehorse.

"I think I've found what I came for." Wasserman had hired a private investigator to check Friese out. From the size and heft of the envelope, Whitehorse guessed it contained photographs.

"Don't open that!" came an authoritative voice from the doorway. "I'm Cheryl Fairweather, attorney for Pacific Crest University. Your search warrant has been voided by Judge Harowitz. Please put that envelope back where you found it." Her tone suggested she was accustomed to being obeyed. Standing next to her were Sterling Friese and a man Whitehorse assumed was Chancellor Brady.

"You must understand, Officer Whitehorse." The chancellor spoke in a commanding voice. "The Wasserman family are the biggest patrons of Pacific Crest. Their foundation provides the scholarships that fund the education of many worthy students and supports the building and updating of our facilities. We must respect their wishes, and they insist that this witch hunt be stopped before it besmirches the reputation of our community. Upon examination, your so-called 'probable cause' is seriously lacking, so the warrant has been rescinded and the autopsy canceled in progress. Mr. Effling will escort you from the premises."

Whitehorse had nothing to say. He looked at Friese, who appeared to be gloating at this turn of events. The self-importance in those eyes made Whitehorse grit his teeth and want to smack him hard across the face.

"Oh, and lest I forget," said Friese. "As we spoke with the judge about the warrant, he mentioned the garbage you stole from me. Turns out I never put my can out to the curb. Perhaps some overly helpful neighbor or policeman? At any rate, Attorney Fairweather has entered a motion to suppress any of the nonexistent evidence that you supposed was in there. Inadmissible in court. Too bad." He clucked his tongue and smiled. "Please come back sometime under better circumstances, Officer Whitehorse. Why not audit one of my classes? I extend you an open invitation."

"Thank you, professor," the policeman managed to say. He walked out with Effling by his side.

6. Wednesday Morning

"Sorry, Charley," said Amy Cranston, the Medical Examiner, over the phone. "I just didn't have enough time before they shut me down. And it was a needle in a haystack anyway. I didn't know what I was looking for. That's a tough gig for an M.E."

"It's OK, Amy. I understand. Wish I could've given you more help. I still don't know what the poison was. And I didn't know how political it would get." He sighed. "Thinking I could mess with a money place like Pacific Crest without stirring up a hornet's nest. So the sonofabitch walks."

"Looks like it."

"Well, thanks again, Amy. I hope our paths don't cross again any time soon."

"You and me both. Take care."

It was hard for Whitehorse to let it go, hard to know a murderer was loose because he wasn't smart enough to catch him.

"Lighten up, Charley," said Esperanza. "It's not your fault. That family knows the Governor and the Mayor and everybody on the city council. And they have big pockets."

"That doesn't make it right."

"No, it doesn't, partner. No, it doesn't. Hopefully we won't have anything more serious than a couple of traffic stops for the next few weeks."

"That'd suit me fine. But I'm gonna look through his garbage one more time."

"Jesus, Charley! It was ripe when we lifted it. It's gotta be gag-a-maggot by now. Besides, you know we can't use it."

"I gotta do it, Tony, if only to convince myself I didn't miss anything."

"I can't stop you, but your time would be better spent asking Chloe out for a date."

"You're probably right, though I hate to admit it."

7. Wednesday Evening

Whitehorse pulled latex gloves over his hands and walked out onto his back patio, where he had spread the contents of Friese's garbage on a disposable plastic tarp. The sun was still high enough above the horizon to illuminate his work area. It was a futile effort, a last gasp in a case he had already lost. Hope of finding anything significant had long since left him.

He had already set aside the sauce pan and the tongs that had been right on top. A coffee maker, a pan, and salad tongs—all in perfect shape. Why had Friese tossed them? The other hard items were easy—chicken bones, a bone from a rib-eye steak, a plastic cup. What was left was a slurry of food debris and wet paper napkins. He gently pushed his fingers through the mess, stopping occasionally to stifle his gag reflex. And there it was.

A salamander. Not a brightly colored one as he had seen in Friese's painting. This one was dull gray, about five inches long.

This has to be mean something, he told himself. *It can't be coincidental.*

Just then the phone rang. He stripped off the gloves and pulled the phone from his pocket. "Chloe? What a surprise."

"Hi, Charley. I really enjoyed that dinner we had. Has it been two weeks already? Three? Anyway, I got to thinking I might be an old lady before you get around to calling me again, so I'm calling you."

"I'm sorry, Chloe. I enjoyed our time together, too. It's just that I've been really busy." Even to him his excuse sounded hollow.

"So do you want to go out with me or not? Sorry to be so blunt, but with the kind of luck I have in the romance department, I have to know."

Whitehorse shuddered as he recalled the hurt Jack Wallace had caused her. He certainly didn't want to do that. And his attraction to her was undeniable. "Yes," he blurted out without thinking. "Yes, I want to go out with you."

"Good. I'm taking you out to dinner tonight. I'll pick you up in an hour."

"Wait. Wait. I'm right in the middle of something." But she had already ended the call.

168

Maybe I need a break. Clear my head. That salamander will still be here when I get back.

He entered the house and went to shower. Then he put on a pair of his best slacks and a new sports shirt he hadn't worn yet. Within an hour he heard his doorbell.

He couldn't suppress his exclamation of surprise. Chloe stood there in a short black skirt and a white sweater top that perfectly accented her natural curves. Her blonde hair stole the remaining sun as it set below the western sea.

"Hi, Charley."

"H-hi, Chloe," he stammered. "You look..."

She cocked her head, waiting for him to complete his thought.

"You're a knockout."

"Well, thank you, Charley. You clean up pretty well yourself. How about that cute new place, *Trattoria Italiana*?"

"Sounds good. Let me drive."

"Not the police car?"

"No, I have a little Honda."

As they drove down 101 toward the restaurant, Whitehorse didn't know how to initiate a conversation. He felt like the tongue-tied, dumb-ass high school kid his partner accused him of being. Finally, he said, "I'm sorry about your daughter. Sending her off to prison like that."

"You didn't send Kaitlynn to prison. Raven took care of that. And she's doing OK. Taking some college classes. With any kind of luck, she'll be out within a year. Let it go, Charley. I don't hold anything against you. Is that why you haven't called me?"

Whitehorse shook his head. "I didn't expect that thing to turn out the way it did. I just wish we could have gotten to her sooner."

Chloe patted his knee. "You're a good man, Charley

Brown. Now let's go have a glass of wine and some good Italian food."

The little restaurant was perfect. Nestled by the beach, its west wall was all glass, giving a breath-taking view of the ocean. The few tables were decked out with checkered tablecloths, a single candle, and a rose in a bud vase. The food was simple but good and the house wine, delicious.

"I'm going to be blunt again, Charley. I'd like to make a habit of this. I think we could make it work."

"I think so, too, Chloe." He turned to look out toward the darkened sea.

"What's the matter? Something bothering you?"

He sighed and turned toward her. "It's not you. This damn case I've been working on. It's closed now. I'm sure a guy committed murder, but I can't prove it, and he's getting away with it."

"Tell me about it."

And he did, unburdening himself of the weight of his failure. He told her all the details, including his garbage groveling when she had called him earlier.

"A salamander, you say?"

"Yeah. This little gray thing about five inches long. It wasn't brightly colored like the painting the perp had over his desk. That one was brown on top and bright orange underneath."

Chloe nodded vigorously up and down. "I know what it is, Charley. Remember I told you last time how Kaitlynn used to play *Guess the Animal* with me when she was around ten years old? That was one animal she stumped me with."

Whitehorse leaned forward in his chair, hanging on her every word.

"Rough-skinned newt. The most toxic amphibian in

North America. Has that same neurotoxin as the Japanese pufferfish. You know *fugu*? The dinner you play Russian Roulette with? Anyway, Kaitlynn nailed me with that one. *'But, honey, you've played with those things before. How come you were never hurt? Because you have to eat them, silly. And I'm never going to eat one of those yucky things.'* Anyway, every now and then one of the little devils dies in my water feature in the backyard. Once I fished one out that must have been there for weeks. It was all bleached out, no color left."

"Holy shit! Oh, excuse my language. That's what I've been looking for!"

"Well, Google it after you get home tonight. It's a real eye-opener."

He reached across the table and grabbed both her hands. "Thank you!"

"My pleasure, officer," she said with a smile. "And that's a sign that we're good together." She raised her glass and he joined her in a toast. "Here's to us."

After dinner they walked hand in hand on the beach until a cold wind began to blow, and they retreated to the car. On the drive home, Whitehorse felt his heart pounding as he tried to find the words to describe what he was feeling. Finally, he gave up and said, "Can I see you tomorrow?"

"I thought you'd never ask. How about if I make you some pan-fried oysters? They're kind of a specialty of mine."

"I love oysters."

"Then I'll see you at seven."

He pulled into his driveway and helped her out of the car. She turned and playfully kissed him on the lips.

"More of that to come," she teased. "But I've got to get home now, and you have some research to do."

He watched her drive away, too stunned to do anything but wave as she disappeared.

Once inside, he opened his laptop and Googled *Rough-skinned newt*. His jaw dropped as all the missing pieces fell into place. *That's how the bastard did it*, he thought. He immediately called Judge Harowitz.

"This better be good, Charley, to be calling me this late in the day."

"I've got probable cause this time, Judge. For sure. Friese killed Wasserman with poison he extracted from a Rough-skinned newt. Before they shut me down in Wasserman's office, I had my hands on an envelope from Invictus Investigations. The dean hired a private detective and got some kind of dirt on Friese. I'll bet he was going to bring it to the faculty meeting and get Friese's tenure denied. You've got to grant me a court order so I can get Invictus Investigations to hand over their file on Friese. Then we have to get the autopsy back on track."

"Charley, I don't know if you heard, but when I stuck my neck out for you last time, the Governor handed me my head on a platter. So no, I don't have to give you a court order. Besides, Wasserman was cremated this evening. Give it up. You've lost. Good night."

Whitehorse stared at the silent phone in his hands for several minutes. Then he poured himself a glass of whiskey.

8. Thursday Morning

"You're going to what?" Esperanza choked on the water he was drinking.

"You heard me. I'm going over to the university and audit one of Friese's classes."

"In the history of bad ideas, partner, this is one of the worst. What do you hope to accomplish? He could slap a harassment suit on you so fast your head would spin."

"He invited me to do it."

"Sheesh! You're impossible. Lucky you're so cute."

"Yeah, well. Anyway, the class starts at 10:00. Call me at 10:15 so I have an excuse to leave if I need one."

"Oh, this is sounding better and better. Don't say I didn't warn you if you come back with your ass in a sling."

"Thanks, Tony. I owe you."

A half-hour later, Whitehorse was walking down the corridor toward the Tom McCall Lecture Hall. Students were filing into the stadium-style seating, fussing with notebooks and pens. Friese spotted him before he sat down.

"Ladies and gentlemen, we have a visitor auditing our class this morning." He opened his arms and then gestured toward him. "Let me introduce Officer Whitehorse of the local police department. He's helped the university with the sad and unfortunate death of Dean Wasserman. Welcome, Officer Whitehorse."

"*Taricha granulosa*," said Whitehorse, in a voice loud enough for all to hear. "TTX." He saw the subtlest twitch in Friese's eyes. His years of looking for tells when playing poker paid off. *Gotcha, you sonofabitch*, he thought.

Friese quickly recovered. "Class, what animal has our officer just given the Latin name for?"

"The Rough-skinned newt," said a pretty young woman in the first row.

"And what's special about them?"

"Tetrodotoxin—TTX—the same neurotoxin as found in pufferfish, the Blue-ringed octopus, and Moon snails. It binds to the channels that allow sodium ions to pass into and out of nerve cells, essentially shutting them down. The typical Rough-skinned newt contains enough to kill twenty or thirty people."

An apple for your teacher? Whitehorse thought.

"Audrey is one of my brightest students, Officer."

A trophy, you bastard?

"May I ask a question of your class, Dr. Friese?"

"Of course."

"Hypothetically speaking, if you wanted to use a Rough-skinned newt to kill someone, how would you do it?"

A titter of laughter erupted around him. A young man in a dark T-shirt and blue jeans stood and turned toward Whitehorse. "You'd have to make your victim eat a newt, and I'm guessing that would be hard to do." More laughter.

Whitehorse fixed his eyes on Friese, who looked decidedly uncomfortable. "Would this work, do you think? Since TTX is water soluble and heat stable, could you boil a newt to extract the poison from its skin? Of course, you wouldn't want to touch that water afterwards. You might use a slotted spoon...or salad tongs to remove the newt? Then use the poisoned water for the victim's Kool-Aid or... put it into a coffee maker for a killer cup of coffee? What do you think?"

Friese gave a nervous laugh. "Are you teaching my students how to commit murder, Officer Whitehorse?"

"Of course not, professor. Like I said, this is purely hypothetical." Just then, his phone rang. "Forgive me, Dr. Friese. I'm afraid duty calls. Thank you and your students for your time."

"Do come back again, Officer Whitehorse, when you can spend more time with us." He had withdrawn a handkerchief from his pocket and wiped his brow.

"Thank you, professor. I will. I have so much more to learn. And congratulations on your upcoming tenure. I understand you're a shoe-in now." He smiled his biggest smile at Friese, whose face had turned ashen.

"I'll catch you later, professor," he said as he left the auditorium. "Promise."

The Bethesda Pool

Tall Douglas firs filtered the early rays of sunlight, casting a tangled web of shadows on the crystalline pool below. A giant gray boulder, glacial orphan from eons past, presided over the cold, deep waters. The rock was half again as tall as a man and seven times that around, flat on the top, and an easy climb on the northeast side. His son had dubbed the monolith *Lunch Rock* decades ago, when they sat on it in the cool stillness and munched peanut butter sandwiches and bright, crisp apples. Then, as now, the silence was broken only by birdsong and the occasional splash of a silver- and pink-sided trout catching an unwary insect for its own repast.

The fisherman approached the pool from the downstream side, his felt-soled waders moving slowly and quietly over the stream's rocky bottom. Since the fish were typically small, he had opted for his ultralight fly rod—five feet of quick graphite that could throw a four-weight double-tapered line as gracefully as a ballerina doing a pirouette. A 4x leader was as light as he could manage, a size 16 fly as small as he could still see to tie on, given his increasing cataracts and the arthritis that was claiming his fingers.

He paused, inhaling the loamy fragrance of the air and listening to the busy murmur of the stream. The moments spent fishing were time away from the rest of his life, respite from the telephone and the television and the traffic. He was at peace in his temple.

He tucked his rod under his arm while he withdrew a case of flies from his ancient vest. Over the years he had given up trying to keep the names of his flies straight. He simply picked a pattern that looked *buggy* and tied it on. Of course, tying it on had become quite the challenge of late. He squinted over the top of his bifocals and coaxed his stiff fingers to pass the monofilament leader through the eye of the hook and work it into an improved clinch knot. Finishing his terminal gear had become as much an accomplishment as catching a fish. Growing old was certainly not for the faint of heart.

Releasing the fly, he false cast enough line to lightly drop it at the lower end of the pool. He stripped in line to prevent drag from spoiling the fly's natural drift. Nothing. He lifted the lure from the water, gave it a quick snap to dry it, and dropped it a little farther up the pool. A dimple on the surface rewarded him, as a nine-inch Rainbow trout rose to the feathered barb. The man raised his rod tip to set the hook and reveled in the little fish's spunky acrobatics. It swooped up the pool, then raced back, finally leaping into the air in a frantic attempt to free itself from the stinging hook. In moments, it was in his net. He held it in his left hand, felt the cool, throbbing life of it, then removed the fly from its jaw and watched it zip away to deeper waters. He felt complete.

Temporarily. Fishing was nothing if not deception.

He smiled at the wet and bedraggled fly in his fingers, reminding him of his over-eager Persian cat, who had accidentally jumped into a full bathtub last week. Since the fly would no longer float true, he snipped it off the leader and stuck it on the lamb's wool patch on his vest to dry. With his index finger, he poked through his collection, looking for a similar size and pattern. He tied his choice onto the leader and surveyed the pool. He waited a few minutes longer to make sure the pool had calmed down enough after his trout's recent skirmish.

With the deft arms of muscle memory, he

lengthened his cast to drop the fly into the center of the pool. A twelve-inch trout boiled under it, and the fight was on. Cavorting up and down the pool, it jumped three times before he brought it to the net. Once he released it, he knew the pool needed a longer recovery, so he decided it was time for a break. He made his way to the shore and climbed up on Lunch Rock. Removing his vest, he sat down in the soft moss on top and pulled a sandwich and a bottled water from the back pouch.

"Here's to you, Mark," he said, toasting his absent son. "Sorry you had to work today. This is still one of the best places on the planet." He heard a pileated woodpecker reply from deep in the forest.

In all the years he had fished this hole, had the rock ever disappointed him? Like an enormous Philosopher's Stone, it seemed able to transform an ordinary day—or an awful one—into something magical, something golden. When his wife had miscarried her second pregnancy, he had taken her out here with him. They had sat together, sipping a bottle of wine, and the pain had diminished, if ever so slightly. When Mark failed his first run at a driver's license, an hour's worth of fishing by the rock had assuaged his damaged pride. In fact, the fifteen-inch Rainbow he had landed that day remained their record for the pool. When his daughter Christie's callous boyfriend had broken her heart, her daddy taught her to fly fish at this very spot and soothed her hurt.

This is a place of power, he said to himself. *But will it be enough?* He closed his eyes as his day-to-day life seeped back into his consciousness, like river water through a tear in his waders. He shuddered as he recalled the man in the black suit and tie. He was ringing his doorbell to present him with the divorce papers. Even though he had seen it coming, it still felt like a physical blow. *It's too late in life for this to be happening. It can't be!* He and Genevieve had been through too much together —two children, a miscarriage, her breast cancer, the deaths of their parents. *No!*

But it was happening. She was being fair about their assets, but it still felt as though the earth shook on its axis, as though color had bled from the world, only to be replaced by drab black and white. It had been six months already, and he felt no closer to healing. He still clenched with anger when he saw a car like Genevieve's drive past him on the street. Still choked back a sob at the grocery store when he caught himself buying a special treat for her, only to remember she was no longer at home. Still wondered if he would ever allow himself to trust a woman. Still doubted he could ever love again, or even want to.

The hardest part was the emotional roller coaster. Up and down and sideways from rage to anguish to sorrow deeper than the pool he loved to fish. Or the days of numbness, when he felt nothing at all, just listened to the monotony of his breathing, the mindless beating of his heart. The tedium of daily living.

He heard Christie's voice the day he told her.

"You're what?" It was the cry of an injured bird, scared and hurting. "You and Mom can't get divorced. You have to grow old together. I'm pregnant with your first grandchild."

And all he could do was stand there, dumb, while tears poured down her cheeks. He could not comfort her as her weeping turned to fury, and she pounded her fists into his chest.

"How could you?" she shrieked.

How could I? How could I have let it happen? Surely there were signs I should have noticed. Something I could have done.

And doubt, like a cloud heavy with rain, would settle over him, its thunder rousing him from restless sleep. How many lonely nights had he spent wracked by guilt and self-recrimination? On and on it went, no end in sight, as his grief morphed into a depression that emptied him of joy.

So here he came, to his Philosopher's Stone and its Bethesda Pool, waiting for a transformation—for the angel to stir the waters and heal him.

Enough, he thought, as he shook his head. *I'm here to fish, and fish I shall.* He finished his sandwich and took a long draft of water. He put his vest back on and clambered down the rock. At streamside, the age-old question captured his attention, banishing the last of his moody distractions. *What fly to use?* Despite his success with the earlier pattern, he decided on something large and gaudy. *Just to shake things up and keep 'em guessing.*

He tied on what looked to be a size 12 or even a 10, with lots of tinsel and bright hackles. *This will land on that pool like a seaplane*, he thought. *Any self-respecting trout will dive for cover. But what the hell.* He eased out into the water, well below the pool. His false casts lengthened the line until he was able to plop the fly at the headwaters. What happened next almost made him lose his balance and fall headlong into the stream.

A summer steelhead raced from the bottom of the pool and launched itself like a Polaris missile under the fly. Its momentum carried it almost four feet out of the water, till it fell back like a breaching whale, the splash sending shock waves across the pool.

"Sweet Mother of God!" the fisherman shouted. "What the hell are you doing here? You've gotta be ten or twelve pounds and I only have a 4x leader!"

His rod bent in a perilous arc as the fish jetted

downstream. The drag on his reel screamed in protest. "Now I've gotta chase you, you sonofabitch." He held the rod high and moved as quickly as he could in the direction of the three-foot-long fish that seemed bent on making its way back to the sea. It leaped again, spraying water at the sun, revealing the fly tucked firmly in its lower jaw.

"I won't let you break off!" he shouted. As he ran after the fish, he saw the last of his fly line peel off the reel and the nylon backing zipping through the guides of his rod. "Slow down, damn you! I can't run that fast over these rocks."

As if responding to his cry, the fish paused in a pool downstream. The fisherman quickly retrieved as much line as he could while he continued his pursuit. "You're just catching your breath, aren't you?" he said. "Let me catch mine."

Then the fish changed directions and came swimming right at him.

"Goddamn it!" he called, as he reeled in line as fast as he could. The fish shot past him like a silver torpedo. "Hang on! Hang on!" The hook held. Now his drag began whining again. The fish came out of the water in the pool by the rock, its silver-speckled sides electric in the dim forest. The fisherman ran back to the pool, making a commotion in the water to try to keep his quarry from escaping in another mad dash downstream. Again it jumped, not so high this time as it tired. It thrashed on the surface as he began to retrieve more line. With his rod held as high as he could, he eased the exhausted fish to his left hand, where he grasped it at the base of its tail and lifted it from the water.

"Got you, you beauty, you creature of God!"

He stuffed the butt of his rod into his waders to free his right hand and quickly removed the hook from the fish's jaw. Then he gently held the fish with both hands under the surface, moving it forward to work water through its gills. In moments, the fish recovered enough strength to burst from his fingers toward the darkest depths of the pool.

He stood there for long minutes afterward, until his pounding heart slowed and his breathing returned to normal. For him, it had been the encounter of a lifetime—a giant fish on the lightest tackle. Body and soul basked in the pristine joy of it.

He felt something within him unclench. Like the slipping of a poorly tied fisherman's knot, the cords that had bound his heart for six months loosened.

An angel had stirred the waters.

His healing had begun.

The Yellow Card

It takes four men to make the system work, and that takes a lot of coordinating. I'm the brains of the outfit, so the job of making it all run without a hitch falls to me. Or at least it did, but more about that later. On an average week, we can gross maybe ten to twenty grand—small potatoes you might say when you split it up four ways, but none of us are greedy or needing to quit our day jobs any time soon. We want supplemental income, like when Harry's wife gets a bee in her bonnet to go to Hawaii or take a Mediterranean cruise. Or Jackson's kid graduates high school and needs tuition for college. The little scores add up. And every once in a while we hit it big. Hell, the Harthoffer estate netted us a hundred large last month, and the Mendelsohn mansion topped two-fifty six months ago. Who knew the old codger had a safe stuffed with dead presidents?

Anyway, Harry is our main man at the Post Office. Maybe the most important job of all. He's the one who gets the ball rolling by picking out our targets. He stands behind the counter, day in, day out, selling stamps, mailing those godawful packages for people who couldn't find their way around a roll of Scotch tape, smiling politely at the octogenarians complaining that their mail is getting lost somewhere. That's a fifty-cent word, huh? *Octogenarian*. Got it from a crossword puzzle yesterday. Yeah, anyway, somebody comes in and files that yellow card with him—*Authorization to Hold Mail*.

The way we figure it, stopping mail one or two weeks is about right. Anything less, and if they have a damn dog, the owners might leave it in the house and pay somebody to come over every day and feed it. A week or more and they'd probably board the mutt or farm it out to some unlucky friend. And Harry knows all the neighborhoods. He can look at an address and know right away if it's in a place that makes all our hard work worthwhile.

Jackson is our first-boots-on-the-ground guy. The scout. Also, his brother-in-law is quite the fence when we come back with jewels. Anyway, he walks up to the front door, carrying a sealed cardboard box, like he's making some kind of delivery. If there's a dog, it starts barking. And man, Jackson has like a sixth sense for security cameras. Know what I mean? It's like he can spot them from a mile away. If he doesn't see any outside cameras, he lays the package down and takes a quick look through a window. Any security box is usually right inside the door so it can be disarmed as soon as somebody walks in. At least the old-fashioned ones. Now they can do all that shit with their cell phones.

That's where Joe comes in. Joe works at Global Networks—the biggest TV, telephone, and internet provider in town, and the shop that gobbled up all the home security systems in our little burg. What with that big hack last year, GN got some really bad press, so now it upgrades its systems every week on a randomized schedule. That means for thirty minutes a week, the security systems are down. Only certain employees know about that and our boy is one of them. And he seems more than happy to share the intel with the team—for his cut. In extreme cases, like when the Steinfeldts were gone last year, and the upgrade occurred at an impossible time to manage, Joe turned off security for that particular house. House, my ass. Castle was more like it. 20K square feet? Gimme a break! Anyway, the trouble with that is it leaves a computer record, and then Joe has to hack his own company and change it before anyone is the wiser. It can be pretty dicey, and he'll only do it for exceptional cases. I guess he thought the fifty grand he got for the Steinfeldts was an exceptional case.

Now we come to my area of expertise. Let me take a bow first. Yeah. They don't call me Fingers for nothing. I haven't met a lock I couldn't pick, a home safe I couldn't crack. Not those big mothers in the banks with the time locks and all that shit. Simple home safes. Simple door locks. It's a talent I learned from the old man before the cops took him out. I couldn't've been more than ten when he taught me to pick my first lock. By fifteen, no house in town was safe. But he held me back. Afraid I'd get caught and sent away to that Youth Correctional Facility in Woodburn.

"They got murderers in there, son. Rapists. Very bad dudes. You definitely don't want to go there."

Who was I to argue? The place sounded plenty scary to me. My father, bless his soul. Never carried a gun. Never hurt a fly. Never trashed any of the houses he burglarized. I never understood why the cops went so berserk when they finally caught up with him after all those years. Filled him so full of holes he had to have a closed casket. I was glad my ma was already gone by then and didn't have to go through that shit. It would've broken her heart.

So I didn't really start my life of crime, such as it is, till the old man was pushing up daisies.

It was just one of those things, you know, those random things that put everything into perspective. Something just clicks and you see the world different. I was in the Post Office two and a half years ago, wanting to put a hold on my mail for a drug trip down to Mexico, and

I met Harry. He had this look in his eyes like *I-hate-my-friggin'-job-but-I'm-pasting-a-smile-on-my-face-because-my-boss-is-friggin'-watching-me.* Know what I mean? It was the look I wore on my face when I did my aide shifts down at the nursing home.

"So, Harry," I said, reading the name badge pinned to his shirt. "Pleased to meet you." I handed him the yellow card. "Did I fill that out right? You can see my name is Tom, but my friends call me Fingers."

"You filled it out perfect...Fingers." He reached over the counter and shook my hand.

It felt like he was—what do they call it—a kindred spirit? "Hey, you wanna go out for a beer later? I'm kinda parched."

"I'm off..." He looked at his watch. "in ten minutes, at 4:00 P.M. What's your watering hole?"

"How about Taps down on Commercial?"

"I'll meet you there."

The rest, as they say, is history. It's like it was Karma or something. The planets lined up. We got talking, and one thing led to another. Before we really knew what was happening, the ideas started popping like Orville Redenbacher in a microwave. The team started coming together.

"I know a couple guys I did a little time with a few years back. Joe works for Global Networks, and he can help us with all the security and alarms shit. Jackson can be our front runner."

Sorry. I didn't tell you that part. I did get arrested once. Luckily, I was old enough not to get sent off to Woodburn, so my old man didn't have to roll over in his grave. It was only burglary and it was my first offense, so I got off easy. I told myself I wouldn't get careless like that again. But I got a really smokin' tattoo outta the deal. Some of those guys inside are real artists.

So anyway, two weeks ago the whole thing goes tits up. I mean ass over teakettle. We pieced it together later to see what went wrong. It was a real cluster f—oh shit, I'm not supposed to be using that word anymore. No more f-bombs according to my new girlfriend Shari. She says I have a real potty mouth. Afraid I'll spout off in church when she takes me there on Sundays. "You gotta clean up your act," she says. "You wanna go out with me, you gotta talk nice."

I swear I'm trying my hardest. Hell, I'm gonna propose to her after our next score. Make an honest woman out of her. More or less.

Anyway, Harry sends me the text. *87814. 2340 Rainbow NW.* That's the mail hold—August 7 to August 14 —and the address. What I don't know is that Harry is hurrying—his supervisor is breathing down his back, afraid he's getting on Facebook at work. So Harry hits a wrong number. The real address is *2240*, but he sends it off without checking it when his boss gives him the evil eye.

I forward it to Joe, who shoots me back a text an hour later. *8101530.* Looks like just a string of numbers, doesn't it? Joe's pretty clever about his shit. In case anybody looks over his shoulder, it's not obvious that he's telling me the system upgrade for that neighborhood is on August 10 at 3:30 in the afternoon. That Joe's quite a guy.

So Jackson gets Joe's text from me. August 10 he's on deck for his scouting mission. Only Jackson's truck is in the shop. Seems he let his son borrow it the night before and he got in a little fender bender. 4500 effin' dollars for a scratch! Do you believe that shit? Anyway, his son claims it wasn't his fault and Jackson is letting the insurance companies battle it out. So he borrows his wife's car and wouldn't you know it. He gets pulled over for a blown tail light! What the f—you know what I mean. So now he's running late. Instead of taking his time, he runs up to the front door, rings the bell once, takes a quick look through the window, and goes back to the car. *No dogs. No cameras*, he texts. *Didn't even see a security box inside.*

I gotta move. I'm two blocks away, waiting for the all clear from him. It's 3:30, and even with no visible box and Joe feeding us the intel, I've learned to play it smart and always make like there's an active system. I pull up out front, walk slowly to the front door, casually casing the joint. Neighborhood's quiet. Nice houses around, though this one isn't quite up to snuff. No kids playing outside. Door is under a little canopy, shrubs around. Good work environment for me. I pull out my tools and have the door open in about a minute. Just before I step inside, I pull on my black ski mask. Just in case they have an independent nanny-cam thing going.

I'm careful. The trick is to be really neat. You don't want to disturb anything. You don't want some suntanned bimbo with a boob job just back from an island vacation knowing right away her house was broken into. If you're careful, they might not realize it for a day or two, and that throws the whole time line thing off when they call the cops.

So I head to the master bedroom. If there's a safe, it's probably in there somewhere. That shit about wall safes behind paintings in the library? Mostly Hollywood crap. People buy safes and park them in their closet, along with the jewelry box. Although you might be surprised how many people keep their jewelry boxes in the bathroom. I guess it's so the old lady can check out what the earrings and necklaces look like in the mirror. And we don't do appliances. You know, computers and TVs and shit. Too bulky and awkward getting them out of the house. So I never even look in the living room.

I zip into the master bath and I'm greeted with a shriek that scares the holy crap outta me. There in the bathtub is this gorgeous blonde bombshell with melons the size of cantaloupes, screaming her lungs out.

"Lady, lady, pipe down!" I say. "I'm not gonna hurt you. I'm just here to pick up your contribution to Good Will. The mask is because I had surgery on my face and I didn't wanna scare you." That seems to confuse her for a second, but she only shuts her yap long enough to reach for the cell phone I see on the bathroom counter.

"Don't hurt me! Don't hurt me!" she wails.

And wouldn't you know it. She fumbles with the goddamn phone and drops it into the tub. Quick as a bunny, she fishes it out of the soapy water and tries to shake it dry.

Anyway, I want to be helpful, so I pick up the hair dryer lying there and turn it on. "Don't worry," I say as I rush over. "I think we can save it." But I'm such a klutz, I trip on the damn bathmat and down goes the hair dryer into the water right between her legs. There's a loud ZAP! and she arches back like I just stiff-armed her. Thank God she isn't jumping around like that poor dope in that old James Bond movie. You know the one where he kicks the fan into the tub and sparks fly everywhere? Anyway, the circuit breaker goes off and stops all that action, but she's still out like a light and slides under the water.

"No, no, no!" I shout. I reach in and grab her under the arms and slide her out of the tub. I don't think she's breathing, so I straddle her and start doing CPR. OK, I'm distracted, what with the melons and all, but I sure as hell don't want her to go and die on me. And yeah, a little mouth-to-mouth, but it's all on the up and up. This is me being a decent guy.

She chokes up a mouthful of water and opens her

eyes and I jump off her like she's a bomb about to explode.

"You tried to kill me!" she screams.

I put my hands over my ears, sure she's popped an eardrum. "Hey! I just saved your life! You would've drowned in your own goddamn bathtub. What would your husband have said then?"

"He divorced me six months ago!" She's still shouting.

"Then he's a goddamn asshole! He's thrown away the most beautiful woman I've ever seen!"

"I'm lying here on the floor in my birthday suit and you're still wearing a mask." She lowers the volume a tad.

"Oh, shit." I grab the robe that's hanging on the door and hand it to her. Then I help her up. "I'm sorry about your phone. That was my fault. I'll buy you a new one."

She cocks her head and squints at me. "But you came here to steal stuff, right? Now you want to replace my phone?"

"I don't take appliances. I'm only after cash and jewels."

She laughs out loud and it's the prettiest sound I've ever heard. "Well, you're a little late, my gentleman burglar. My ex made off with most of that. I got the house, but as you can see, it's the cheapest one on the block. You got the wrong place."

"This is 2340 Rainbow, right? How come you're home? You were supposed to be away all week."

"You got the right address," she says, nodding her pretty little head. "But no way can I afford a vacation. I'm lucky I've got a pot to piss in."

"Damn. I wonder where Harry went wrong. He's usually better about this stuff."

"Harry?"

"I shouldn't have said his name. He's part of the team. We all work together. Four of us. Takes a lot of coordination."

"I'll bet. And you call this coordination?" She purses her lips. "I see you're not carrying a gun. Got a knife in your pocket?"

"Hell, no. I'm strictly a no weapons kind of guy."

"And you're not going to hurt me?"

"I'm pretty much a pacifist. Don't even know any martial arts. Truth is, you could probably beat the shit outta me if you tried, so please don't."

She laughs again, and I know I'm in love. Even her wet hair is beautiful. When she speaks, my heart starts pounding like Metallica's drummer is doing a number on it.

"Can I get you something to drink? A beer? A glass of wine?"

"I should probably be going. The guys are gonna be wondering where I am."

"They can wait. This is the most fun I've had in six months. Take your mask off and come with me to the kitchen." She sees me hesitate. "I can't call the cops, remember? C'mon. If you know your way around a barbecue grill—the ex was kind enough to leave me that relic—you can fire it up and throw some hot dogs on it for us. I think that's the only meat I have in the fridge. I'm on a tight budget."

I pull the ski mask off.

"See? I knew there was a handsome face under there. I'm Shari, by the way."

"Tom. Actually, Fingers. Nobody calls me Tom."

"Fingers, hmmm? Sounds interesting."

She leads me by the hand to the kitchen, sits me down at the table, and pops the tops on two brewskis. "So tell me all about your gang of four," she says. "Given the major screw-up today, it sounds like you need a full-time events coordinator." She smiles a smile that could melt a gold bar.

"And I know just the girl for you."

The Barista

The sameness of the mornings made it easier. She and Parker had a routine that suited them both.

After lying awake for several hours, she got up, had her first cup of the day, and jumped into the shower. At precisely 7:20, she woke up Parker, and while he was rubbing the sleep out of his eyes, she zipped to the kitchen and poured him a bowl of cornflakes. She was careful to leave the carton of almond milk on the table so he could pour it himself when he got there. The one day she poured it, the cereal got soggy before he could eat it, and Parker threw a fit. That end-of-the-world disaster almost made her late for work. *Never again*, she promised herself.

While he ate, she did her hair and makeup, though she was getting remiss in that department lately. Some days she only ran a brush through her hair in the most perfunctory way. *How long has it been since I had my roots done?* she wondered. No moisturizer or foundation. No lipstick. Just a little something to hide the wrinkles under her eyes. *Why bother?*

Then back to the kitchen to round up Parker, get him into the bathroom to brush his teeth, and shoo him to the bedroom to get dressed in the clothes she had laid out the evening before.

"You woke me up last night, Mommy. I heard you in the living room."

"Mommy's been having trouble sleeping, sugarplum. But I'm all right."

"Do you miss Daddy?"

"I have to be honest, sweetie. He's a little too mean to miss."

"I know. I just wish he was different."

"Me, too." She stroked his hair and ran a finger down his cheek. "I'm sorry I didn't protect you better."

"It's OK, Mommy. You can hardly see the scar anymore."

With a sigh, she gathered up her keys and purse. "So how's the fourth grade treating you? Are you liking your teacher?"

"Mrs. Miller's great. She tells us animal stories every morning. Did you know there's a fish in the ocean called the Sarcastic Fringehead? It's got a giant mouth and it's really ferocious."

"You're kidding, right?"

"No. Really. She showed us on YouTube."

"OK, Jedi. Let's get cracking. Your bell will be ringing soon."

The weather outside was unseasonably warm for the Oregon coast. The breeze had languished for the last week, and the fall rains had not yet begun. Jackets and windbreakers were still stowed in closets, in favor of light shirts and blouses. The sea was calm.

Soon Parker was buckled into his booster in the back seat of the aging red Corolla, and she was starting the car. "There's a parent-teacher meeting coming up sometime this week, isn't there?"

"I think so. Mrs. Miller's having us draw extra pictures to show with our work. I think the note's in my backpack."

"Thanks, honey. I'll check."

It was a short trip to Driftwood Heights Elementary School. She pulled the car into the line by the sidewalk and watched in the mirror as Parker unbuckled himself. "You be good, mister." Her heart ached as she watched her little boy run to the open front door of the school. *I'm sorry, buddy. For everything.* She shook her head and put the car in gear.

She dreaded the fifteen minutes it took to get to the store. Alone in the car, the memories rose in a dark, noisome tide. Her shoulders slumped as though the recollections were a physical weight pressing her down, squeezing the breath out of her. Reaching the store, she bounded from the car in relief.

And there he was. Tricia saw the man almost every morning, sitting with his back against the wall of the SaveLots grocery store. She would pretend he was invisible and walk straight through the automatic doors. Panhandlers and homeless people made her uncomfortable —self-conscious—as though she had left one too many buttons open on the front of her blouse, or she had a big fleck of green salad stuck in her teeth. She felt justified for her discomfort after reading the recent article about them in *The Beachtown News*. The story claimed they were organized into shifts, took turns at the most productive corners and stores, pooled their resources. *They're nothing more than con men*, she thought.

Just as the doors swung open to admit her into air conditioned safety, the man called out.

"Hey! Yeah, you lady." His voice was a dry rasp, brittle fall leaves skittering down a sidewalk.

She stopped and turned. His cardboard sign read: ANYTHING WILL HELP. His grizzled face was framed by shoulder-length brown hair, matted and oily. The tattered black AC/DC T-shirt barely rolled over the top of his dirty jeans, which were punctuated by large holes over both knees. She took a cautious step toward him, as though she were approaching a dog that might bite her.

"I can't give you any money." She made it sound like an apology.

"Did I ask you for money?"

"No." She felt scolded. The stitch in her breath warned her she might launch into one of her panic attacks. "I have to check in and start pouring coffee." She pointed to the embroidered badge on the breast of her green and yellow uniform. "I work at The Coastal Coffee Cup inside."

"Good. Bring me out a small one. Black."

"I-I..." she stammered.

"C'mon, lady. Nobody's gonna miss one cup of coffee. Consider it your good deed for the day."

She turned and ran into the store.

"Whoa, Tricia. You look like you've just seen that horror movie I warned you about—the one with that scary clown in it," said the redhead behind the counter of the coffee bar. She was three years younger than Tricia and had a face and a body that would stop conversations when she walked into a room. "Are you all right?"

"You know that homeless guy out front, Sammy? The one with the sign?" She pulled the loop of her apron over her head and began tying the straps behind her back.

"Yeah. Creeps me out. I've called Security a few times but he always manages to leave before they get here."

"Well, this morning he talked to me. Told me to get him a cup of coffee. It's not like he even asked for it. More like he demanded it."

"You give him one this morning and he'll hit you up every day. I'm calling Security right now." She picked up the store phone.

"Thanks. I like your hair, by the way."

"Got it cut after work yesterday. Sylvia at that new Hair Heaven in the mall." She chatted briefly into the phone, then put it down. "First two pots are brewed." She turned and addressed the thirty-something man in line at the counter. "How can I help you this morning?" She wrote his name and his order on the cup and handed it to her partner.

"And we're off and running," Tricia said, as Sammy put two more cups into her queue.

Morning hours were the best because they were the busiest. No time to worry if her ex's child support check had cleared. No time to fret over whether she had passed her last chemistry exam at McCall Community College. No time to brood about matriculating into the nursing program at Pacific Crest. She was even able to push memories of Palmer to the back of her overworked brain.

At the stroke of ten, she pulled off her apron. "I think I'll sit right there at the table in the corner for my break." She poured herself a small cup of coffee, added some sweetener and cream, and winked at her friend. "When do you suppose we'll be able to afford the kinds of drinks we make for our customers?"

"Not on our paychecks!" Sammy laughed.

Tricia took her cup and settled in the corner with a sigh. She took a sip, then closed her eyes, luxuriating in the aroma and the heat of the coffee. When she opened her eyes, she was startled to see the panhandler sitting across the table from her.

"Came in the other door. Left my sign outside."

"Wh-what do you want?" Tricia felt a premonition of panic rising in her again. She looked around the little dining area for anyone she could ask for help. A mother sat sipping her drink, staring at the screen of the phone in her hand, absently rocking a stroller that cradled a sleeping infant. A young girl was busy typing on her laptop, three empty cups in a row on the table before her. Sammy was engrossed in serving her next customer.

"I'll take that coffee now, if you don't mind. Black." He smiled. "Relax. You look like a deer in the headlights, for Chrissakes. I'm not gonna hurt you. You don't need to call Security. I just want a cup of coffee."

"S-sure." Tricia leaped to her feet and hurried to the counter. "It's him!" she whispered. "The homeless guy!" When her friend reached for the phone, Tricia waved her hands. "No, don't. I don't want to make a scene. Let's give him a cup of coffee. If he doesn't leave after that, then we'll call."

"Whatever you say, Trish. Just give me a sign if he starts to cause trouble." She poured a cup of coffee, pushed a lid down over it, and handed it to her. "I'll keep an eye on you."

"Thanks." She returned to the table and set the beverage before the stranger.

"See. That wasn't so hard, was it? I'll be on my way after I finish this." He popped the top off the cup and took a sip of the steaming liquid. "I like to be able to smell my coffee."

Tricia did not respond. The silence between them lingered like the heat of the Indian summer day outside. She finally remembered to drink her own coffee. The man looked at the name tag pinned to her shirt.

"So...Tricia. Tell me about yourself. Looks like you hide your depression pretty well. Does anybody else know?"

"What?" Her eyes grew wide.

"About your depression. I've seen you—maybe a hundred times. Just before you turn away to pretend I'm not there, I see that look in your eyes. You know. Far away. Tired. Worried you maybe won't make it through the day. Sometimes just kinda lost."

"I'm not depressed." She shook her head back and forth. "Where do you get off saying that? You don't know me."

The man pursed his lips. "I'm an observer. I see things." He took another sip of coffee. "This is delicious, by the way." He set his cup on the table. "So what's your story?"

"I don't have a story. I work at a coffee shop. And I'm not in the habit of talking to strangers."

"You sound annoyed. Are we really strangers after all this time?"

She was about to get up and leave, when he motioned with his hand. "Humor me. I sit alone a lot. Would it help if I told you a little about myself first?"

"Help what? Look, I've got a job to do. I can't be sitting here gabbing all day."

"You're not gabbing. You're making a connection with one of your customers."

"I'm sorry. No offense, but I don't want a connection with you. I have a family to take care of. Bills to pay." As an afterthought, she added, "And I don't take handouts."

"Fair enough." He nodded. "I don't like taking handouts, but I've had a real hard time holding down a job since my last tour."

"Tour?" She knit her brows.

"Afghanistan. Wish they wouldn't use that word 'tour.' Makes it sound like I was on a bus or something having fun."

"What happened to you?"

"The usual—guns, bombs. Nothing a little medication can't help—when I remember to take it. But then I get to drinking and all bets are off." He laid his hands on the table. "So that's a bit about me. Now tell me a little about yourself."

She looked at her watch. *Is this the only way I'll be rid of him?* she thought. *So be it. The sooner I get this over with, the better.* "OK. OK. But then you have to leave."

"Promise."

She took a deep breath, stalling for time, wondering where to start.

"Tell me about the family you grew up in."

She frowned. "Well, it was pretty hard on my mom. She babysat neighbor kids to make a little extra cash. Dad worked as a mechanic at a garage in town. Didn't make a lot of money, but always found enough for his whiskey. He was a weekend alcoholic. Know what I mean? Started drinking Friday after work and went straight through till Sunday. Late Sunday was the worst. He'd beat on her something terrible. I used to sleep in the closet, afraid he'd come into my bedroom in the middle of the night."

"I'll bet you married to get out of the house?"

"Yep. Went from the frying pan into the fire." She shuddered at the grim recollection. "Al turned out to be even worse than my father. He'd fly into rages. Break stuff. Slap me around. I was kind of a regular at the ER. They thought I was a real klutz—walking into doors, falling down stairs."

"How bad did it get? Any broken bones? Stitches?"

She leaned toward him and pulled back her hair on the left side of her face. The upper part of her ear was missing. "He Mike Tysoned me during one of his binges. Got himself sentenced to a year for that one. I thought about fixing it, but the surgery was too expensive. Besides, I needed to remind myself what really bad decisions I can make when I'm not careful. Anyway, it gave me the chance I needed to file for divorce and get the hell out of there."

The man exhaled noisily. "Jesus. There and back

again, huh? Got any kids?"

"Parker is the light of my life." For a brief moment, her face brightened. "Just turned nine. As sweet as honey. Made me pancakes for my birthday two weeks ago. Doing great at school, as far as I know. I get to meet with his teacher this week." The smile vanished. She lifted her coffee cup but set it back down without drinking from it.

He waited a moment. When she said nothing further, he looked into her eyes. "What's the matter?"

"He had a brother. Doesn't remember him much anymore. Parker was only three when Palmer died." She choked on the words. "Rare genetic disorder, the doctors told me. Died the day before his first birthday." A single tear trickled down her cheek. She wiped it with a napkin. "So if I look a little depressed to you, maybe I got my reasons." Her words were tinged with bitterness and despair.

"How do you bear it?"

"Bear it? I live day to day. Hope I get my child support. Hope I get into nursing school so I can dump this dead-end job. Cry myself to sleep when Parker can't hear me."

"Anything else?"

"What else is there?" she snapped. "Everybody dies in the end. Right?"

"Full of sound and fury, signifying nothing..."

"What?"

"Macbeth."

"You're quoting Shakespeare at me? Who the hell do you think you are anyway?"

"I'm nobody." He opened his arms and shrugged his shoulders. "Like I said, never been much good at holding down a job. I get hittin' the sauce and before you know it, I got hell to pay. But Father Jimmy down at the Mission—

he's real good to me. Always finds me a bed when I need one. Even paid for my last rehab." He nodded. "I guess I got a lot going for me. I'm pretty happy."

"Happy?" Tricia stared at him in disbelief. "How can you possibly say that? What on earth do you have to be happy about?"

He smiled broadly. "That's easy. I'm not being shot at anymore, for one. But mostly, I know who I am, and I know where I'm going." He took a final sip of his coffee. "That's the trouble with you. You don't know."

"Look, what I know is I gotta get back to work. You keep your part of the bargain and leave."

As she stood up, he reached for her arm. "Wait. I know what your problem is. I gotta tell you."

"Let go of me!" She pulled back, but he held fast. Her heart pounded and the room began to spin. She gasped for breath. As she broke away, her foot caught the leg of her chair, and she fell to the floor, the chair clattering down on top of her.

The man extended his hand to help her up. "I'm sorry. I didn't mean to hurt you or anything. Are you OK?"

When she regained her feet, her eyes bore into him. "Yes, no thanks to you. Now leave me alone and get out of the store."

"I will, just like I promised. But I gotta tell you. You know what your problem is?"

She harrumphed and brushed at her pants and blouse. "So tell me, Shakespeare."

"You're homeless."

"What?" Her face contorted in surprise.

"You're lost, like a ship without a port. You got no anchor."

"What are you talking about?" She backed away, staring at him as though he were suddenly speaking a foreign language and threatening her with a gun.

A policeman came running toward them, looking like a lineman about to sack a quarterback. His face was hard as granite. He had his hand on the pistol strapped to his side. "Stop right there!" he yelled, as he drew close. He positioned himself between the man and the woman and looked at Tricia. "I'm Officer Esperanza, ma'am. Are you all right? Has this man hurt you in any way?"

"No. No, I'm fine. I just tripped on a chair when he grabbed my arm."

"Do you want to file a complaint?"

She shook her head. "I just want to get back to work, Officer."

He turned to the man and frowned. "I've had reports about you before, sir. I'm going to have to ask you to leave the premises immediately and not come back. Otherwise, the store will file formal charges, and I'll have to take you in. Do you understand?"

"Sure thing, man. I don't want no trouble." He raised his hands in mock surrender.

"Please come with me to the door."

The man fell into stride next to the policeman.

Tricia watched them walk away, stunned by what had happened. As her breathing returned to normal, her mind whirled in confusion. Before they disappeared out the door, she called, "Who are you?"

The man looked over his shoulder and smiled. "I'm a stranger, remember? But I'm also a child of God. So are you." He began to laugh, and the policeman put a calming hand on his shoulder. "And don't forget what they say about showing hospitality to strangers!"

Looking at the Sun

Do you love me, Patrick?" The question hung in the air for the briefest of moments, like a soap bubble from a child's wand. She heard it—that hiccup of silence. She tucked a lock of black hair behind her ear and tilted her head toward her husband. They had been on different pages for a long time.

"Of course I do." It seemed to her more protest than affirmation. He took another sip of his morning coffee and grimaced. "Hell, we had three more kids after our...happy accident."

She turned and looked out the glass slider toward the sea. Her voice was soft, wistful. "Was that love or boredom, do you think?"

"Jesus, Julie, sometimes I can't figure you out. Can't we just enjoy this? It's a goddamn total eclipse of the sun. We're never gonna see this again in our lifetime." He put down his coffee cup and opened his arms wide. She knew he spoke with his hands when he got excited. "Hell, they say the zone of totality is only seventy miles wide. On the surface of a globe that's like a line drawn with a ball point pen. Do you realize what a privilege it is to be among the few who will be able to look directly at the sun without any kind of protection?"

Julie pursed her lips. "Why don't we ever look at us?"

He sighed. "Do you want another cup of coffee? I need a warm-up."

"No thanks."

She looked toward the coffee table in the living room, where her photo journalism book, *Hell Hath No Fury,* lay untouched since last year. Her portrait of the

204

suffering of the Cuban people after Hurricane Indira had swept the island won accolades for its courageous humanity. Buried amid the epic devastation were intimate family stories she had unearthed and shared with the world. Her efforts earned her the Pulitzer Prize and months of breathless nightmares. Had Patrick even read it?

He was so absorbed in his own work, writing code for the Wunderkind Gaming Company, that he had time for little else. His creation, *Chrysolite III*, had won Video Game of the Year and he had just accepted an invitation to present at Comic-Con 2018 in San Diego.

She watched as he frowned at the coffee pot and poured the dregs into his cup. He turned off the machine. "You know, it will actually get dark," he called over his shoulder. "Crickets will start chirping. Bats will be flying. Then in two minutes, it's daylight again."

She opened the sliding door and walked out onto the deck. The cool air felt moist on her cheeks. "It's still pretty foggy. We may not see a thing."

Patrick drew near and stroked her back. "Aren't you the optimist."

"Just saying. The marine layer hasn't shown its face for the last three days and now it's back. It may not be your lucky day. Will you be disappointed?"

"The weatherman says it'll clear up and I believe him. We'll be fine."

"But will you be disappointed if it doesn't and you don't see it?"

"Forget it. I'll be in the house cooking myself a couple of eggs. Let me know if you want anything." He entered the kitchen and pulled the slider closed behind him.

Julie listened to the rhythmic roll of the surf. There were almost no traffic sounds. She and her friends had been surprised that the *tourist Armageddon*, predicted by every news channel, had not overwhelmed the sleepy coastal town. She figured those news reports and the fickle weather had scared the tourists away. The dilemma now was that every store and restaurant was hopelessly overstocked with food and paraphernalia that would never be purchased. Merchants' losses could be catastrophic.

All for what? A two-minute glimpse of the sun blacked out by the moon? Surely there were more important things? *I don't get it,* she concluded. She inhaled deep breaths of salt-laden air, relishing the smell and the taste of it. She loved the ocean and their little beach house. She just wasn't sure she loved Patrick.

She walked back inside. Patrick was at the stove, cooking some scrambled eggs. Another pan held four strips of bacon that were filling the house with the classic fragrance of breakfast. *Patrick must have recharged the coffee pot, too,* she thought.

"It smells awfully good in here. Is there enough for me to have some?"

"Sure, honey."

"And when does the eclipse start?"

He looked at his watch. "In about a half an hour. It'll be total a little after ten."

He finished his cooking and set two plates on the table. "More coffee?"

"Please."

They ate in silence. Julie was surprised at how loud the kitchen clock sounded. "Almost forgot to make the beach house mortgage payment last week. Remembered on the due date and did it over the phone so we didn't get stiffed with any penalties." She bit off a piece of savory bacon.

"I told you to make it an automatic withdrawal. Then you wouldn't have to worry about it every month."

"Yeah. You're right."

When they were done, Julie cleared the dishes into the sink and poured herself another cup of coffee. She waved the pot at her husband, and he nodded back. With a deft twist of her wrist, she poured him another cup. "You're cut off now, mister, or you'll be bouncing off the walls."

"Yes, Mommy," he said, as he took an exaggerated slurp from the mug in his hands.

We are good together, aren't we? Or is that just wishful thinking on my part? She took a sip and burned the tip of her tongue. *At least the sex is still good. But is sex enough to sustain a relationship? And do I trust him?*

"So, loverboy, how's Suzy?"

He looked surprised. "How would I know? She's in another office. I rarely see her."

"I thought you said you had lunch with her last week?"

"Oh, yeah. I forgot. She's doing fine. Likes her new position."

Her suspicion meter turned on, but she didn't have enough energy to pursue it. *I guess that's diagnostic,* she decided. She began to feel as though she had been filling out some kind of marital satisfaction inventory, and she didn't like it.

"Where's the glasses anyway?"

"Right here." He reached into their kitchen junk drawer and withdrew two pairs of eclipse glasses from a protective envelope. "Try 'em. You can stare right at the sun and not hurt yourself."

"You're sure?"

"Guaranteed." He looked at his watch again. "Let's go back out on the deck. It'll be starting any time."

He moved two chairs into position and they sat side by side. Tattered clouds scudded across the sky, dimming the sun but not blocking it out. "Here we go! Look at that! See the notch forming at the edge?"

The excitement in his voice reminded her of their son Danny, their boy naturalist. Anything to do with bugs or birds, snakes or stars, was his bailiwick. He and his brothers had gone to their friend Carson's house, a few miles inland and farther from the marine layer. "We'll have a better chance to see it," he had claimed. Not to mention that Carson's parents always seemed to have a good supply of corn dogs and Oreos on hand.

"You sound just like Danny."

"I saw two partial eclipses growing up, but never a total. It's like I've waited for this moment my whole life."

It's like the way I felt on our wedding day, she thought. *All of my life distilled into that single minute when he slid the ring on my finger and said the words that knit us together.*

She stood in the sanctuary of St. Matthew's, the church she had attended since her baptism as an infant. It was as familiar as visiting the house of an old friend. First Confession at age seven, when sin was as foreign to her as the reckless lives of the movie stars she overheard her mother talking about with her coffee klatch. First Holy Communion a week later, decked out in the white dress and veil of an angel come to earth. Confirmation at twelve, when she had just been introduced to the mysteries of being a woman. Now marriage at twenty-one. These sacraments, these visible expressions of some invisible grace, were mileposts along her life's journey, anchors that kept her safe and gave her direction.

Today the candles burned as brightly as they always had, while smells of paraffin and incense perfumed the air. Father Kelleher, long-time family friend, stood before them, his smile as warm as the August day outside. She felt herself falling into Patrick's azure eyes, afraid she might faint at any moment.

"Till death do you part?" the priest asked.

"Till death do we part," she affirmed.

Those words stuck in her mind like a cookie crumb caught in her throat. She coughed.

"What's the matter?"

"Nothing. Just remembering stuff."

"Like what?"

"Our wedding day. How handsome you were."

"Still am."

She smiled. "Still are." She held the glasses up to her eyes and saw the bite the moon had taken out of the sun. *Shadow overcoming light. Or tedium taking joy?*

"It's begun!" His elation was almost contagious. "What cosmic coincidences! The moon being just the right size, just the right distance from the earth and the sun. It fits perfectly." He was so enrapt he didn't see the single tear on her cheek, and she brushed it away with her finger.

We fit perfectly once, the right size and distance. When gravity didn't pull so hard. Can we ever get it back? Do we want to? She sat without speaking, glasses shielding her eyes. The notch grew larger.

Patrick started to laugh. "It's beginning to look like Pac-Man. Hey! I just remembered. Look at this." He ran back into the house and came out with their colander. Lifting it high above his head, he pointed to the deck floor. "See what it's doing? Each hole becomes a pinhole camera and projects the sun's image." Like gold doubloons with chunks taken out of them, little eclipses littered the deck.

He put down the colander. "C'mon with me. We've got plenty of time before totality." Without waiting for his wife to respond, he grasped her hand and hurried her off the deck, downstairs, and outside. "We'll take a quick walk down Sand Dollar Avenue. There's a lot of oak trees there."

Hand in hand they marched the two blocks to the tree-lined street. "This'll knock your socks off, honey."

She gasped when they walked under the canopy of branches. "How?"

"Just like with the colander. Little openings between the leaves make tiny pinhole cameras. Hundreds of 'em." He swept his arm in a graceful arc, presenting her with a treasure trove of crescent suns at their feet, an extravagance of riches.

Astonished, she held her breath as she surveyed the lights in the shadow. *How profligate nature is,* she mused. *I guess his enthusiasm is beginning to affect me after all.* She stopped thinking for a moment and kissed him on the cheek.

"Now let's get back to the deck. It's getting close to the time. I have to show you Baily's beads."

"What's that?"

"Right at the moment of totality, the sun is a thin little ring with what look like tiny sparks along the edge. Believe it or not, those sparks are sunlight peeking through the valleys between the mountains on the moon. Then the corona erupts around the disk and we get to look at the sun without glasses for almost two and a half minutes. It's once in a lifetime, darling."

Once in a lifetime, she mused. *Like our wedding day was supposed to be. Can I reignite that spark? Does he even know?*

As though he sensed something was not right, Patrick stopped and looked into her eyes. "You're not very excited, are you?" He took a deep breath. "I know you haven't been very happy with me." His face darkened. "For a long time."

"We never really talk anymore." She spoke with a resignation born of tired, empty days and nights of troubled sleep.

"We've been talking all morning." His voice sounded petulant, a little boy defending himself.

"That's what I mean." Her lower lip quivered but she held back her tears.

"What? I don't understand."

"We don't talk. You lecture me about the sun. Or you give me a dissertation about North Korea or how the Seahawks are doing this year. Do you remember why I was upset about my friend Corinne? I told you during the game last Sunday and you never even looked up from the TV. Last night I said I wanted to visit her in the hospital sometime today and when I mentioned it this morning, you looked at me with that expression you get when you think you're hearing about something for the first time." She shook her head. "We're like a jigsaw puzzle missing a piece, and I don't even know where to look for it."

"What do you want from me?" He sounded desperate and frustrated.

"I'm not sure I know anymore. Acknowledgment? Recognition? Why do I feel like we're becoming strangers?"

"We made love two nights ago."

"We had good sex two nights ago," she corrected. "I'll give you that." She looked at the man-boy she had married fifteen years ago. She loved the feel and the smell of him, but needed something more.

Patrick stepped forward and wrapped his arms around her. "I don't know how to make us better," he whispered in her ear.

"I know. Let's go back so you can show me Baily's

beads."

They walked back to the house, hand in hand. Neither spoke. She felt a nervousness in his grasp, not the cocky self-confidence he usually flaunted. *At least he's being honest,* she thought.

The last time she had felt that disquiet in his hand had been when he walked her down the aisle at church at the end of the ceremony.

Husband and wife. Outside on the church steps, the sun beat down on them, making her white gown dazzling. People began clapping and throwing confetti and rice and she felt his body tremble. She knew he was scared. They had just pledged their lives to each other and both grasped the enormity of their endeavor. Both already had friends who had been divorced. But that undefended vulnerability soon succumbed to congratulations and well-wishing, wedding cake and alcohol.

She tightened her grip on his hand and leaned into him. "We'll make it work," she whispered, uncertain from where that affirmation had come. "We'll just have to be patient with each other."

At the house, they hurried back out onto the deck and put on their glasses.

"It's almost time," Patrick said, as the sun began to wink out. "There! It's total!" He pointed to the heavens. "Those little flashes of light on the edge of the ring. From the mountains of the moon to you, darling." The sun was gone and a different light, like the shimmering petals of a flower, grew around the black disk. "That's the corona. It means 'crown.' It's an aura of plasma way hotter than the surface of the sun."

"My gosh, it's cold. Did you feel the temperature

drop?"

"At least ten degrees, maybe more. And look. There's bats. Lots of 'em."

Crickets had begun chirping in the underbrush, and streetlights turned on in the deep twilight. Julie found it hard to take her attention away from the dark disk hovering in the sky. She wasn't prepared for how overwhelmed she felt, sitting there, staring at the sun. A cleansing emotion welled up from deep within her, as tears poured from her eyes.

"It's so beautiful," she breathed. "I didn't know."

Patrick kissed her. "I've saved the best for last. Just keep watching."

As the seconds ticked by, Julie was transported. Her heart pounded and her breath quickened. She felt as though she weren't a part of her body any longer, as though she were lifted high above it, separate but whole.

"Here it comes. Totality is ending." The edge of the sun burst from behind the moon. They got a quick glance and turned away from the brilliance. "They call it the 'diamond ring.'" He grasped her left hand, raised it to his lips, and kissed it tenderly. "With this ring," he said, his voice cracking and his hand trembling, "I thee wed...and promise to thee...my faithfulness."

Julie wept.

Homecoming

I'*m the Hammer of God, you Butcher Bird," he hissed, "come to send you to Hell." But before he could unleash his .50 caliber machine guns, another 190 appeared on his tail. "Damn. You guys don't play fair, do you?" After a quick look through his canopy at the sky above him, he pulled back hard on the stick and took the Mustang into a steep climb. The 190 hesitated for a heartbeat, and that was long enough. The cocky pilot flipped his plane upside down and completed a loop that put him behind the outclassed German plane.*

"Like some lead for lunch?" he taunted, as he let his guns roar. The hail of bullets sheared off the left wing of the Focke-Wulf, *then slammed into the engine. The American banked right as the 190 exploded in a massive fireball. "Now where'd your buddy go? I got something for him, too."*

First Lieutenant William Hammer was playing defense for the 464ᵗʰ Bomb Group, on their way to oil refineries near Vienna. The German 190's had been punishing the Flying Fortress and Liberator crews for months, but he was determined to put a stop to that. His P-51 Mustang had the new Rolls-Royce Merlin engine, the new bubble cockpit, and two more machine guns studding the wings. The German edge was over, if his six guns had anything to say about it.

He caught sight of the German, far ahead of him. "Turning tail and going home? We're not done playing yet." He had an almost 40 mile per hour advantage over the German craft and soon closed the distance between them. The 190 went into a nose dive and the chase was on.

"You've got more cajones *than your late friend," he whispered. "But that won't save you."*

The German twisted and turned, diving and climbing, to no avail. Hammer was on him like an attack dog. The engines of both fighter planes howled in protest as their adrenaline-fueled pilots pushed them to their limits.

"Bye, bye, Birdie," Hammer said through clenched teeth. His bullets rained along the fuselage and into the cockpit of the enemy craft. Thick black smoke erupted from the engine, and the plane spiraled into a hopeless dive toward the earth below.

Hammer resumed his flight toward Vienna, searching for signs of the bomber squadron he had been assigned to protect. On the edge of the horizon, he saw an enormous black smudge roil the skies. "I hope that's the refineries and not our planes," he muttered aloud. To his relief, he soon saw a wedge of Liberators flying toward home. He pulled in alongside and accompanied them back to their base at Pantanella, near the little town of Canosa.

As he taxied to a stop, he saw his favorite mechanic running toward him. The man was easily six-foot-six, with a shock of wild red hair. His jump suit was black with grime. With deft motions that came automatically, Hammer was out of his plane and on the ground in moments. His breath made white clouds in the cold November air.

"Looks like snow coming, Wrench. What do you think?"

"Radio says six inches before 2200. That'll make sloppy runways tomorrow."

Hammer sighed and shook his head. "Sure would like to sleep in. Like that's gonna happen." He patted his friend on the shoulder. "What do you hear from the other grease monkeys?"

"Looks like the mission was a success, but we lost three more planes." The big man turned away, as if unwilling to say anything further.

"What? Who?"

The mechanic frowned. "One of the planes was the Malfunction Junction.*"*

Hammer looked as though Wrench had slapped him. "My brother is the bombardier on that plane. Christ!"

"It was flak, not fighters." The words sounded hollow.

"That's supposed to make me feel better?"

"And they saw chutes. All ten of 'em."

"Great. So my brother is down behind enemy lines in winter. And the Krauts are thicker than fleas over there. Goddamn it!" He stormed away to the debriefing tent.

"Can he hear us?" I said to the Hospice workers as they wheeled the gurney into the bedroom and positioned it beside the hospital-style bed.

"Very likely," the nurse who had been awaiting their arrival replied. "We always behave as though they do."

One of the men leaned over the gurney and spoke into my father's ear. "Mr. Hammer, we're going to slide you off this stretcher and onto your bed." My father never opened his eyes, never spoke a word.

"He's been like that for four days now," the nurse said. "No evidence for a stroke on the CT scan or the MRI, but he sure acts like it. They're calling it encephalopathy. He also has pneumonia and a collapsed lung."

With an economy of motion, the men soon had my father in the bed. They drew a sheet and a blanket over his unresponsive body and pulled up the bed rails. In moments, they wheeled the gurney out and were gone.

"I'm Lyla, by the way." The nurse shook hands with

me and my brother John. She drew her brown hair back into a ponytail and pulled on a pair of rubber gloves. "Give me a few minutes with him, will you? I need to clean him up, check his vitals, go over the discharge summary. I won't be long. Then you can come back in."

My brother and I walked into the living room and Lyla shut the bedroom door.

"How was your flight?" John asked. "You a little jet-lagged?"

He had picked me up at Orlando International only an hour earlier. I could feel the three-hour time difference from Oregon in my foggy brain. "I'm dragging all right. How are you doing? You've had to deal with the brunt of this."

"I'm OK. He went downhill pretty fast after your last visit. I walked in Wednesday morning and saw him struggling to get out of bed. He didn't make it to the bathroom in time. He was talking, but not making any sense." John sighed. "Like I told you on the phone, I called 911 right away. By the time they got him to the hospital, he had stopped talking. He doesn't seem able to open his eyes anymore, and he can't pull his tongue back into his mouth."

I sat back heavily in the chair. That man in the bed was so unlike the man I had visited a few short weeks ago. My father had always been a hero to me—a man above mere mortals, a Titan visiting the earth. Ace fighter pilot during World War II, with 23 kills to his credit. COO of a global clothing company. Humanitarian and philanthropist. But age had not been kind to him. His back had bent forward to the point that he could barely raise his head. His balance was so impaired he couldn't take a step without his walker to support him. All but one of his teeth had fallen out or broken off at the gum line, and he had refused any dental work. Knees depleted of cartilage were a source of constant pain. Now trapped in his frail body, he was unable to speak, unable to toilet himself.

"What?" It was my brother's voice.

"Just thinking about Dad. He's always been so strong."

"You're telling me...*Junior*."

I knew that epithet carried with it the venom of a lifetime of feeling second best, stuck in my shadow, never measuring up. I was the golden boy and John was the afterthought, the unnecessary appendage to a family that had already been complete before his arrival on the scene. While Dad had attended my every sporting event in high school, John had been forgotten, even when his baseball team won the Nationals. When Dad picked up the tab for my university schooling, John was told there wasn't enough to go around, that they could only afford to send one kid to college. Once he had impregnated his girlfriend, John felt college was out of the question, and he threw himself into work in a forklift company, making his way up the corporate ladder. He retired with as good a salary as I had ever achieved, but with a wound that would not heal. Then six years ago, it all came crashing down. Dad became too incapacitated to live by himself, and John's wife Joanne took pity on him. Despite John's protests, she invited his father to move in with them.

"We can't send him into one of those awful nursing homes," she said. "Besides, we've been blessed with such a big house. Most days you won't even have to see him except for meals. And I'll be a buffer between you two."

By a cruel twist of fate, Joanne was killed in a car crash four months later, and John became Dad's sole caretaker. He would never speak to me about it, never complained, but always found some excuse not to come to the phone when I called Dad every Saturday morning. All the while, I was safely 3000 miles away.

"Do you miss Mom?" I asked.

"I guess. The old man sure does. When he was still driving, he'd go out to the cemetery almost every day of the week. Didn't matter to him that the last year of her life she didn't even remember his name. Kept yelling at him to get Billy and Johnny ready for school and wouldn't listen to him when he told her a thousand times we were all grown up."

"Full circle, huh? We wind up as helpless as the babies we started out as."

"Well, you're the religious nut. What does your God tell you about that?"

I winced. Since Dad was such a staunch Catholic, John had become something else—sometimes agnostic, sometimes atheist. It annoyed him that I had remained Christian.

"I have to believe it's all part of God's plan. Our parents took care of us, and now we get to take care of them."

"It's a bloody mess," John snorted. "What a waste."

Just then, the bedroom door opened. "You guys can come in now if you'd like."

After debriefing, Hammer went to the Mess to eat something before he crashed on his cot in the tent he shared with three other airmen. Knowing that his brother's plane had gone down had soured his mood. "You gotta make it back, Raleigh," he said to no one in particular.

As he filled his plate, he felt someone pat him on the back.

"Heard about your brother, man. Sorry."

"Thanks, Zero. But if anybody can make it outta there, it's my brother. He'll convince the partisans to lend him a blonde-haired, blue-eyed dame and a limo for the ride home. That sonofabitch'll be back, wheelin' and dealin' his way out of Hell itself."

His bravado disappeared as quickly as the steam rising from his cup of coffee. He ate a few mouthfuls of the hash on his plate, then made it back to his tent. Before collapsing on his cot, he pulled out his wallet and withdrew a small scrap of paper. He touched it to his lips. "I love you, darling. Miss you." He returned the paper to his wallet and lay down. In moments, he was asleep.

I stared at the stranger in the bed, tongue hanging out of his mouth, eyes closed. His head stirred, and he began to moan. The moaning grew louder, as his shoulders and head writhed on the pillows.

"I've given him all the pain medication I can," Lyla said. "I have to follow the doctor's orders."

I couldn't tell if Dad were moaning in pain or in frustration at his inability to speak. I stroked his grizzled head and ran my fingers down his sandpaper cheek. Dad had never gone a day without shaving for as long as I could remember, and now several days of beard growth pricked my fingers.

"We're here, Dad. Johnny and me. We love you."

John stood at the foot of the bed, arms akimbo. I didn't understand the expression on his face. Anger that the golden boy had supplanted him once again? Relief that he would likely never hear another complaint about his performance? Guilt that he had grown so cold to Dad over the years? Or hope that some kind of healing might happen before Dad breathed his last?

"It must be driving you crazy that you can't talk.

Oh, and I called your brother just before Johnny picked me up at the airport." Raleigh was a snowbird and spent summers at his original house in Connecticut. He was due to come back to Florida in about two weeks. "He sends his love and says he's sorry that he can't be here. I told him I'll give him regular updates about how you're doing."

John cleared his throat. "Haven't been shopping so I've got nothing to eat in the house. We'll have to go out. Hungry?"

My stomach growled in response. "Hey, Dad. Johnny and I are going out for a bite. We'll be back soon." He moaned louder then, whether to protest our leaving his bedside or in response to worsening pain, I couldn't tell. I felt a sudden urge to get away.

"Would you like us to bring anything back for you?" I asked Lyla.

"No, I'm fine. Got my water and my energy bars. I'll guard the fort."

We left the house and got into John's new Audi. "Looks like retirement is treating you pretty well," I quipped.

"Can't complain."

The silence deepened as we drove toward a newly opened Longhorn Steak House. Years of unspoken thoughts and feelings were like thunderclouds churning overhead, threatening lightning or hail or torrents of rain.

"How's your daughter?" I asked.

"Janice is fine. Expecting another kid soon."

"Congratulations."

"Yeah."

As we pulled into the lot to park, I turned to my brother. "Can we talk about it?"

"About what?"

I took a deep breath and exhaled in frustration.

"Nothing, I guess."

Dinner was excellent. By his second glass of wine, my brother began to relax. He told a funny story about his four-year-old grandson Carlton.

"So Janice, who's pregnant out to here, asks him, 'Cary, would you like a little baby brother or a baby sister?' And without missing a beat, he says to her, 'I'd like a baby dinosaur, please.'"

I chuckled and raised my glass. "He's quite a kid, all right."

"Sure is. I was babysitting for him a while back and we got talking about the alphabet and how he's getting ready to go to full-time Kindergarten. So I start writing down the letters on a big piece of paper—A, B, C, D, E, F, G—and he turns to me with this very sober face and says, 'That's wrong, grandpa. That's not how the alphabet goes. It's Q, W, E, R, T, Y.' Can you believe that kid? What a generation we're raising, I swear."

Feeling the effects of the wine and those few moments of good will, I went all in. "I'm sorry for how Dad treated you all those years." My breath caught in my throat as I saw the smile vanish from his face.

"You can't apologize for him. It doesn't work that way. Besides, it wasn't all his fault."

"What do you mean?"

"The part you always seem to so conveniently forget. The way you bullied me until I finally got big enough and strong enough to make you back down. I guess I've got you to thank for getting my black belt."

"That was just brother stuff. I never bullied you."

"Well, let's see. Remember the broken nose when I was in fourth grade? Or the busted wrist in sixth? Maybe you recall the time you locked me out of the house when Mom and Dad were away for the evening? I had to take a shit so bad and you just laughed when I had to go in the bushes behind the house. Or humiliating me in front of my first girlfriend? That was a good one—showing her pictures of me as a little kid in the bathtub and making jokes about my 'cute little dick.' Is that bullying enough for you? Because I got lots more."

"That's enough."

"But hey, I survived."

I hung my head. How could I have not seen it? But I realized that was the wrong question entirely. How could I refuse to see myself for who I really was? How could I blame only my dad all these years, when I was equally guilty, complicit in the myriad ways John had been made to feel inferior? Too late, I understood that the truths we hide from ourselves become more toxic than lies.

"Don't you love these warm family get-togethers?" It sounded like a taunt.

"I don't know what to say." I shook my head back and forth. "I'm sorry, but I know that doesn't cut it."

He pursed his lips. "You're right, but maybe we can decide to be honest with each other."

He called for the check and we split it down the middle.

On the ride home, it was John who spoke. "Did you know Dad always blamed himself for Uncle Raleigh's plane getting shot down on that mission over Austria?"

"What? I never heard that."

"Yeah. He got liquored up one night before he got sick and started gabbing to me about it. True confessions crap. Said he was supposed to be protecting the bomb group, keeping the enemy fighters away from them. But he was hotdogging it, like all that *ace aviator* shit went to his head. He let two planes draw him away from the group. Got more interested in scoring another notch on his gun than in defending the mission to take out the refineries. That left the group wide open." He turned into the driveway at his home. "Other German planes moved in like a pack of wolves. He said his mechanic told him that it was anti-aircraft batteries that took down the bombers, but the crews told him there were fighters there, too. Some didn't even want him flying with them for awhile. The hotshot screwed up royally."

"Why are you telling me this now?" I slammed my hand on the dashboard. "You sound like you're gloating. Like it makes you happy or something."

"Not at all. I just want you to know he's not the perfect man you imagine he is."

The weather got colder and the missions got longer. For a week, several of the men wouldn't sit with Hammer in the Mess tent between sorties. They relented only when he redeemed himself by becoming the protector they needed him to be. He had learned his lesson. But as the days dragged on, his hope of ever seeing his brother alive again faded. With that despondency came a recklessness in his flying that made him a holy terror to any German unfortunate enough to share the skies with him. "It's like I'm dead already, Wrench. What have I got to lose?" He threw himself in harm's way, risking all to defend his group, without concern for his personal safety.

On his cot every night, before sleep overcame him, he pulled out the scrap of paper from his wallet, kissed it, and spoke to the woman back home he had promised to marry. "Flo, I know you can't hear me, but I miss you so much. I hope to get back home to you, but this war goes on and on. I have to be there for the guys who depend on me. I pray you can understand."

On the 30th *day after* Malfunction Junction *had*

been shot down, his CO met Hammer as he taxied his Mustang to a stop. "Just got word from a British gunship in Zadar. Your brother walked out of the woods yesterday, all in one piece. They're bringing him back here."

Hammer couldn't stop the tears, much as they embarrassed him. His brother was alive! The yoke of guilt lifted from his shoulders. He was whole again.

There was no change in Dad's condition when we returned home. Jet lag had finally caught up with me and I bid my brother good night.

The next day I was awakened by the sounds of Dad's moaning in his bedroom. The Hospice nurses had changed shifts during the night and I introduced myself to the lanky man who stood at the bedside, taking Dad's blood pressure.

"Bill junior," I said.

"David," he responded." He nodded toward Dad. "He's been this way through the night. Sleeps for an hour or two, then gets restless. I've got calls in to his prescribing doctor. I don't think the morphine is holding him. We need to up the dose."

"Thanks." I walked to the bedside and stroked my father's hand. "It's me. Good morning." His head moved slightly and another moan escaped his lips. I turned back toward David. "We gotta do something. Keep after his doctor."

I walked out into the kitchen and put on a pot of coffee. John stumbled into the light, rubbing the sleep from his eyes.

"That's what I need. Maybe our new nurse can give me the coffee intravenously?"

I smiled at my brother. "He's trying to track down the doc. Dad needs more pain medication." As if to emphasize the point, we heard another moan from the bedroom.

"Does your God torture people? You know, like we did to bugs when we were kids. Burning them with a magnifying glass. Pulling their wings off."

I shook my head. "I don't understand pain and death any more than you do. I just know God is with us through it all."

"Right," he replied dismissively.

While the coffee continued brewing, I walked back into the bedroom. Dad had calmed somewhat, but still moved restlessly, grimacing around the tongue that refused to retract into his mouth.

"Haven't got a call back yet," David said.

I nodded and looked at the framed pictures on Dad's bureau. There was the family reunion from nine years ago. Mom was still alive and smiled at the photographer. My daughter's twin boys were making faces at each other, while another grandbaby was growing in her belly. It was a good time—a gift.

My eyes wandered to the next picture, the one Dad always called "The Kiss." It was Mom before they married, a lovely, leggy brunette sitting by a pond they used to frequent on their high school dates. At the bottom of the picture, Dad had inserted a little scrap of paper, now yellow-brown with age. A barely legible date was scrawled in pencil on it.

"Oh, my God!" I exclaimed. "That was 75 years ago today!"

October 1, 1942. *Hammer lit some candles and turned on the radio in the corner. It was Glen Miller playing Flo's current favorite,* That Old Black Magic. *He sighed. He'd need some magic all right. Tomorrow he was shipping out* to Flight School in Missouri. From there, it was to the front lines in Europe. He grasped Flo's hand and touched it with his lips.

"This is our last date for a long, long time." The words were etched with grief.

"Just swear you're coming back to me, Bill Hammer. And don't go falling for any of those French or Italian girls either. I got my claim on you, mister." She embraced him, and her bravado collapsed. Her shoulders heaved as she buried her face in his chest and wept.

"I'll come home to you, darling. I promise. We'll get married and buy a home and grow a bevy of babies. You'll see."

She pulled her face away and looked up into his eyes. "What I see is you leaving me to fight in this stupid war. What am I going to do without you?"

"Get a job at the phone company or that new doctor's office in town. Live here with your Aunt Nelle while your folks are away with that post office job of your father's in Bermuda. They'll be back in a few months. And write me letters—lots and lots of letters."

She kissed him on the lips, long and hard. It took his breath away.

"I'm gonna miss that, honey. Nobody kisses like you."

"Well, don't go experimenting. Like I said."

He saw a twinkle in her eye and an impish grin on her face, sure signs she was up to some mischief.

"Wait right here." She rushed into the kitchen. She came back with a paper napkin and ripped off one corner of it. With a quick motion of her right hand, she freshened her bright red lipstick, then pressed her lips to the scrap of paper, creating a perfect impression. "Take this with you, lover." Her tone was playful, but tender. "That way you'll *be able to kiss my sweet lips no matter where you are."*

He smiled, all the while choking down the sob that threatened to burst from his chest. To keep himself from weeping, he picked up a pencil and wrote "10/1/42" above the lipstick kiss. Then he touched it to his lips and put it in his wallet. "There. Now I'm ready for anything."

"Oh, yeah?" she said, as she took him in her arms.

The nurses changed shifts again, and the one who came on board had years of Hospice experience. One look at Dad and his medical chart, and she pulled out her phone. As she dialed the number, she took a glance up at John and me. "That morphine still isn't holding him. The doses are too little and too far apart." She turned her attention to the chart and spoke into the phone. "Yeah, this is Lisa, with my patient Mr. Hammer. I want Dr. Parkinson or his service to get back to me stat. This poor man is crying like a baby. He's in pain and we have to help him now. There's no excuse for this."

She ended the call. "Not good enough, even after the increase David got for him. But we'll get this fixed. Pronto." Her voice was gruff, no-nonsense. It sounded like she was used to getting her way.

I loved her. For the first time since Dad's crisis began, I felt like we had the right person in charge of his care. Her phone rang. She smiled and gave us the thumbs up sign.

"Now it'll be fifteen or twenty minutes before this takes effect." She finished the injection and turned back to us. "When it does, I think I'll give him a shave. Men of his generation usually like that. Makes them feel more comfortable."

"That's perfect. I'll get you his electric razor."

Half an hour later, Dad was resting, apparently

without pain. As my brother and I sat in the living room, we heard the buzz of his shaver like hornets around their nest.

"Looks like happy hour has rolled around again. Can I get you a glass of wine?" my brother said. "I didn't shop for food, but I got alcohol."

"That'd be great."

He returned from the kitchen moments later with two glasses of red wine. He handed one to me. "My current favorite."

I swirled the wine in my glass and held it to my nose. Then I took a sip of the jammy elixir. "Good stuff, bro. Thanks."

I watched his eyes take on a far away, thoughtful look. "You remember? He always called you 'My Number One Son.' I was just Johnny."

I nodded. I did remember. And I recalled my childhood self, smirking at my little brother whenever my father did that. Complicit. Ignoring the hurt on that little boy's face. The tears in his eyes. I slowly expelled my breath. "I don't expect you to forgive me, but I really am sorry. Probably sorrier than I can put into words right now. For everything."

He stared over the rim of his glass at me. "You mean it?"

"Yeah, I mean it. Hell, I dreamt about you last night. All these years it's like I've had this sliver in my mind, pricking me, making me uncomfortable. But never knowing what it was." I took another swallow of wine and shook my head back and forth.

We sat together silently after that. John refilled our glasses.

Twenty minutes later, Lisa emerged from the bedroom. "You know, sometimes people have a hard time letting go if they feel something is left undone or unsaid. If there's anything you'd like to say to him, this would probably be a good time to do it." She made eye contact with both of us. "I think he has only about ten or fifteen minutes left. That's my guess, anyway. I could be wrong."

We took our wine glasses with us and entered the bedroom. My mind was whirling, my heart racing. What would we say? The wounds went so deep. I never appreciated before what a dense fabric families are, each individual caught in the warp and woof of a cloth far bigger and more complex than any one person can grasp. If you worry a single thread, will the whole garment unravel? And should it?

Dad lay there peacefully, eyes closed, cheeks and chin clean-shaven, mouth open wide but tongue now withdrawn inside, held there by the single tooth he had left. His breathing was slow and labored.

"Hey, Dad. Bill and I have been doing a lot of talking and we wanted to bring you up to speed."

Now my heart began to pound. I imagined John spewing the vitriol of decades at our father and at me, his last chance to get even with the people he blamed for so much of what had gone wrong with his childhood. Instead, he gently lifted Dad's hand from the mattress and caressed it. "We've decided that you're the best father any two brothers could ever have."

I was dumbfounded. Could he mean what he was saying?

"That doesn't mean we don't think you screwed up occasionally."

I held my breath.

"Like the time you locked the keys in the car when you took Billy and me to that Cub Scout meeting. The cops thought you were breaking into somebody's car and almost arrested you. Or the time you forgot to pick us up after that matinee. You forgot we were there until Mom called us for supper and we didn't show up. I can still hear her screeching at you later that night. She could be pretty poetic."

I smiled at the memories, those nuggets left by the sluice of time.

"I confess I would smart a little when you called Billy your 'Number One Son.' But, hey. It made me more competitive, and that came in handy at the company I finally worked for. I wound up wrangling a heftier salary than Bill ever did with all his fancy education." He smirked at me then, but I felt something good-natured in it.

"Got me, bro."

"Bottom line is, I love you, Dad, and I think you've done a great job."

"I love you, too, Dad." I grasped his other hand. "You know John and I have our religious differences, but I gotta tell you. Pretty soon you'll be reunited with the love of your life. You and Mom together again." I looked over at John, wondering what he might be thinking. He answered my unspoken question.

"And you'll get new knees, Dad. You'll be able to dance again. It'll be some party!"

A wave of the purest gratitude washed over me, and I thanked God for my little brother.

"A toast to you, Dad." We both raised our glasses and clinked them together over the bed. Then we watched as the time between his breaths lengthened. At last his chest rose and fell one final time, and he stopped.

My brother and I wept.

Brightridge Funeral Home came for his body within the hour, and we scheduled a meeting with them for the next day to work out all the details. Over dinner that night, John surprised me again.

"You know we have to have a Catholic Mass for him, right? He went to Sacred Heart the whole time he lived here. I took the liberty of calling them when you were in the bathroom." He signaled the waiter and asked for another glass of wine. "We meet with them after we're finished at Brightridge. Since you're more up on that stuff than I am, you pick out the readings."

On the day of the funeral, John drove us to the church. We were bright and shiny in our black suits, white shirts and ties, polished shoes. Those same shoes clicked on the marble floors like the measured ticking of a great grandfather clock. It was satisfying somehow. The church had been modernized only five years before, and looked as if it could double as an art museum in New York City or LA. Not the kind of Catholic Church I grew up in, steeped in shadow, haunted by the holy ghosts of dead apostles.

I did the Old and New Testament readings, choices that garnered John's approval. The first was from Ecclesiastes:

> There is an appointed time for everything.
> And there is a time for every event under heaven—
> A time to be born, and a time to die;...
> A time to love, and a time to hate;
> a time for war, and a time for peace.

The New Testament reading was from Paul's First Letter to the Thessalonians:

> But we do not want you to be uninformed, brethren, about those who are asleep, so that you will not grieve as do the rest who have no hope... For the Lord Himself will descend from heaven with a

shout, with the voice of the archangel and with the trumpet of God, and the dead in Christ will rise first. Then we who are alive and remain will be caught up together with them in the clouds to meet the Lord in the air, and so we shall always be with the Lord. Therefore comfort one another with these words.

The priest read the account of the death and resurrection of Lazarus from John's Gospel:

Jesus said to her, "I am the resurrection and the life; he who believes in Me will live even if he dies, and everyone who lives and believes in Me will never die. Do you believe this?

At the conclusion of the Mass, the celebrant burned incense around the pall-draped casket, and I stood mesmerized as the sweet-smelling smoke drifted heavenward. I imagined my father's soul doing the same, perhaps smiling down at us from high above, amused at all the fuss we were making over him. I looked at my brother, who nodded as though he agreed with my thoughts.

"Hey, you're inside a church and lightning hasn't struck you," I whispered.

"Yeah, God must be slipping up, unless he's afraid he'll hit you, too, since you're sitting right next to me. In that case, thanks."

Then two black-suited men from the funeral home —we thought of them as "The Brightridge Boys"— wheeled the casket back out into the narthex of the church, where the white pall was removed and an American flag was draped over the coffin. And out to the waiting hearse they went.

"That hearse is a piece of work, you know," John said, as we walked to his car.

"You said it."

It was a brand new white Cadillac, with two little

American flags mounted on either side of the front bumper, as football fans do with their team's emblem. We looked at each other as the same thought struck us both.

"Who ya gonna call?"

"Ghostbusters!" I chimed in, and we both laughed.

Greenbriar Cemetery was only a few miles from the church, and the Honor Guard awaited us there. When we arrived, the Brightridge Boys set the flag-draped casket on the lowering device that straddled the open grave. We had a few moments to look at the box that contained all that was left of Dad on this green earth. I knew he was elsewhere. The priest said a few prayers, but by that time I wasn't hearing much anymore. I kept seeing Dad as the young and sexy fighter pilot, swaggering back to the Mess tent after another successful mission. Or the debonair dancer, before his knees betrayed him, romancing my mother on the dance floor. Or the devoted father bouncing my baby brother on his lap.

I was pulled from my reverie by the Commander of the Honor Guard, who approached the casket with another officer, removed the flag, and began the formal ceremony of folding it. There was something so special about the ritual that tucked our country's colors into a tight star-decked triangle. Then the Commander walked toward me with his precious gift, but I pointed to John, and he offered it to my grateful brother. I know I saw tears in John's eyes.

With a salute to John as he held the flag, the Commander barked the order, "Present arms!" Three veterans raised their rifles smartly, vertical with their bodies, trigger guards facing Dad's casket. It was the ultimate sign of respect. Then rifles to their shoulders, they unleashed a volley of fire that echoed across the cemetery, stilling every voice, frightening every bird into silence. In the eerie quiet that followed, the bugler began to play Taps. The sounds swirled up through the humid Florida air, as the incense smoke had done in the church, each note keening for the fallen hero. By the final bar, every heart was broken, every eye wet with tears. Grief at Dad's loss and joy at his homecoming to the Kingdom commingled in my mind as I reached for my brother and embraced him.

"Long live Dad," I whispered in his ear. "We'll see him again."

"At the Pearly Gates? Will you run interference for me like you did at the church?"

"I've got your back. You can count on it."

The End

Dear Reader,

I hope you have enjoyed this book. If you have, please tell your friends about it on Facebook and Twitter. Better still, write a review of it on Amazon. If you've never done that before, it's a very easy process. Simply navigate to the book's web page on Amazon.com, and then scroll down to the Write a Customer Review button. When you click on that, you will be prompted to give the book a certain number of stars and then write a comment. Your comment can be as brief as a single sentence or as long as several paragraphs. It will only take a few minutes of your time, but I would greatly appreciate it. We indie writers don't have big publishing companies supporting us, so word-of-mouth and reviews on Amazon are our best advertising.

If you'd like to look further into independent authors, please check out the Northwest Independent Writers Association at niwawriters.com.

Thank you for your support.

Bill Cook

About the Author

William J. Cook is a Connecticut native transplanted to Oregon in 1989. He is a graduate of the State University of New York at Albany, where he received a Master's Degree in Social Work. Years of study in two Catholic seminaries and a long career as a mental health therapist have shaped (or warped!) his world view. He is spending his retirement with his artist-wife Sharon, who paints in the dining room while he writes in the kitchen. He enjoys babysitting for his fifteen grandchildren and sneaking away to mid-week matinees at local movie theaters, a vice which he claims he contracted from his mother, an inveterate fan of action and sci-fi films. He is the author of the novel *Songs for the Journey Home*, *The Pieta in Ordinary Time and Other Stories*, and *Seal of Secrets: A Novel of Mystery and Suspense*.

Visit him at www.authorwilliamcook.com or at www.facebook.com/writerwilliamjcook/